HEROES
OF IRISH
MYTHOLOGY

HEROES
OF IRISH
MYTHOLOGY

JEREMIAH CURTIN

This edition published in 2024 by Arcturus Publishing Limited
26/27 Bickels Yard, 151–153 Bermondsey Street,
London SE1 3HA

AD012432UK

Printed in China

CONTENTS

INTRODUCTION

Jeremiah Curtin was born to farmers David Curtin and Ellen Furlong in 1835 in Detroit, Michigan. Both David and Ellen were farmers, and eventually relocated the family to a farm in Greenfield, Milwaukee, an Irish immigrant community in Wisconsin. Curtin's father died of pneumonia in 1856, but not before instilling a passion for learning in Jeremiah.

In 1858, Curtin enrolled at Carroll College and left home a year later to study at Phillips Exeter Academy in New Hampshire. Later, he gained admission to Harvard College where he would meet the likes of Francis James Child who shared his interest in folklore. After graduating in 1863, Curtin practised law in New York before moving to Russia to serve as a secretary to Cassius M. Clay. In 1868, Curtin returned to Milwaukee to study languages, and it was there that he married Alma Cardell who would serve as his travel partner and collaborator.

In 1883, the Curtins moved to Washington DC, where Jeremiah worked for the Bureau of American Ethnology. During this era of his life, he travelled to Ireland several times, fascinated with the connection between language and folklore. These voyages led him to write *Myths and Folklore of Ireland* in 1889 – a book that was extremely well-received, and led Curtin to sign a deal with Charles Dana, the editor of the *New York Sun*. This deal allowed Curtin to revisit Ireland and collect legends from native speakers. The result was Curtin's body of work including *Hero-Tales of Ireland* (1894) – published here in part – and *Tales of the Fairies and of the Ghost World Collected from Oral Tradition in South-West Munster* (1895).

Included here are Curtin's exquisite retellings of some of Ireland's most daring and courageous warriors. The tales recount the exploits of heroes such as the skilled swordsman Elin Gow, the great yet unassuming Conal, the grimly determined Miach Lay, the extraordinarily proportioned Coldfeet and the perspicacious Blaiman. These brave men embark on a number of dangerous quests that test their physical strength as much as their intellect and morals. Each of the gripping stories of adventure and peril are a testament to the rich and vibrant tradition of Irish mythology.

Curtin returned to Ireland a final time in 1899, and collected further stories that were published after his death in 1906. With a multifaceted legacy as a writer, adventurer, politician and language scholar, he leaves behind more than 40 publications. After his death, Theodore Roosevelt – an avid reader of Curtin's work – said of him that 'he travelled over the whole world calling all men his brothers and learning to speak to them in seventy languages.'

ELIN GOW, THE SWORDSMITH FROM ERIN, AND THE COW GLAS GAINACH

Once King Under the Wave went on a visit to the King of Spain, for the two were great friends. The King of Spain was complaining, and very sorry that he had not butter enough. He had a great herd of cows; but for all that, he had not what butter he wanted. He said that he'd be the richest man in the world if he had butter in plenty for himself and his people.

'Do not trouble your mind,' said King Under the Wave. 'I will give you Glas Gainach – a cow that is better than a thousand cows, and her milk is nearly all butter.'

The King of Spain thanked his guest for the promise, and was very glad. King Under the Wave kept his word; he sent Glas Gainach, and a messenger with instructions how to care for the cow, and said that if she was angered in any way she would not stay out at pasture. So the king took great care of her; and the report went through all nations that the King of Spain had the cow called Glas Gainach.

The King of Spain had an only daughter, and he was to give the cow with the daughter; and the cow was a great fortune, the best dower in the world at that time. The king said that the man who would do what he put on him would get the daughter and the cow.

Champions came from every part of the world, each man to try his fortune. In a short time hundreds and thousands of men lost their heads in combat. The king agreed then that any man who would serve seven years, and bring the cow safe and sound every day of that time to the castle, would have her.

In minding the cow, the man had to follow her always, never go before her, or stop her, or hold her. If he did, she would run home to the castle. The man must stop with her when she wanted to get a bite or a drink. She never travelled less than sixty miles a day, eating a good bite here and a good bite there, and going hither and over.

The King of Spain never told men how to mind the cow; he wanted them to lose their heads, for then he got their work without wages.

One man would mind her for a day; another would follow her to the castle for two days; a third might go with her for a week, and sometimes a man could not come home with her the first day. The man should be loose and swift to keep up with Glas Gainach. The day she walked least she walked sixty miles; some days she walked much more.

It was known in Erin that there was such a cow, and there was a smith in Cluainte above here, three miles north of Fintra, and his name was Elin Gow. He was the best man in Erin to make a sword or any weapon of combat. From all parts of Erin, and from other lands also, young princes who were going to seek their fortunes came to him to have him make swords for them. Now what should happen but this? It came to him in a dream three nights in succession that he was to go for Glas Gainach, the wonderful cow. At last he said, 'I will go and knock a trial out of her; I will go toward her.'

He went to Tramor, where there were some vessels. It was to the King of Munster that he went, and asked would he lend him a vessel. Elin Gow had made many swords for the king. The king said that he would lend the vessel with willingness, and that if he could do more for him he would do it. Elin Gow got the vessel, and put stores in it for a day and a year. He turned its prow then to sea and its stern to land, and was ploughing the main ocean till he steered into the kingdom of Spain as well as if he had had three pilots, and there was no one but himself in it. He let the wind guide the ship, and she came into the very harbour of the province where the king's castle was.

When Elin Gow came in, he cast two anchors at the ocean side and one at the shore side, and settled the ship in such a way that there was not a wave to strike her, nor a wind to rock her, nor a crow to drop on her; and he left her so that nothing would disturb her, and a fine, smooth strand before her: he left her fixed for a day and a year, though he might not be absent an hour.

He left the vessel about midday, and went his way walking, not knowing where was he or in what kingdom. He met no man or beast in the place. Late in the evening he saw, on a broad green field at a distance, a beautiful castle, the grandest he had ever set eyes on.

When he drew near the castle, the first house he found was a cottage at the wayside; and when he was passing, who should see him but a very old man inside in the cottage. The old man rose up, and putting his two hands on the jambs of the door, reached out his head and hailed him. Elin Gow turned on his heel; then the old man beckoned to him to enter.

There were four men in front of the castle, champions of valour, practising feats of arms. Flashes of light came from their swords. These men were so trained that they would not let a sword-stroke touch any part of their bodies.

'Come in,' said the old man; 'maybe you would like to have dinner. You have eaten nothing on the way.'

'That was a mistake of my own,' said Elin Gow; 'for in my ship are provisions of all kinds in plenty.'

'Never mind,' said the old man; 'you will not need them in this place'; and going to a chest, he took out a cloth which he spread on a table, and that moment there came on it food for a king or a champion. Elin Gow had never seen a better dinner in Erin.

'What is your name and from what place are you?' asked the old man of his guest.

'From Erin,' said he, 'and my name is Elin Gow. What country is this, and what castle is that out before us?'

'Have you ever heard talk of the kingdom of Spain?' asked the old man.

'I have, and 'tis to find it that I left home.'

'Well, this is the kingdom of Spain, and that building beyond is the castle of the king.'

'And is it here that Glas Gainach is?'

'It is,' said the old man. 'And is it for her that you left Erin?'

'It is then,' said Elin Gow.

'I pity you,' said the old man; 'it would be fitter for you to stop at home and mind something else than to come hither for that cow. 'Tis not hundreds but thousands of men that have lost their heads for her, and I am in dread that you'll meet the same luck.'

'Well, I will try my fortune,' said Elin Gow. ''Tis through dreams that I came.'

'I pity you,' said the old man, 'and moreover because you are from Erin. I am half of your country, for my mother was from Erin. Do you know now how this cow will be got?'

'I do not,' said Elin Gow; 'I know nothing in the world about it.'

'You will not be long,' said the old man, 'without knowledge. I'll tell you about her, and what conditions will be put on you by the king. He will bind you for the term of seven years to bring the cow home safe and sound to his castle every evening. If you fail to bring her, your head will be cut off that same evening. That is one way by which many kings' sons and champions that came from every part of the world were destroyed. There are spikes all around behind the castle, and a head on each spike of them. You will see for yourself tomorrow when you go to the castle, and a dreadful sight it is, for you will not be able to count the heads that are there on the spikes. I will give you now an advice that I have never given any man before this, but I have heard of you from my mother. You would be a loss to the country you came from. You are a great man to make swords and all kinds of weapons for champions.

'The king will not tell you what to do, but I'll tell you: you'll be as swift as you can when you go with the cow; keep up with her always. The day she moves least she will travel thirty miles going and thirty miles coming, and you will have rest only while she'll be feeding, and she will take only a few minutes here and a few minutes there; wherever she sees the best place she'll take a bite; and do not disturb her wherever she turns or walks, and do not go before her or drive her. If you do what I say, there will be no fear of you, if you can be so swift as to keep up with the cow.'

'I am not in dread of falling back,' said Elin Gow.

'Then there will be no fear of you at all,' said the old man.

Elin Gow remained in the cottage that night. In the morning the old man spread his cloth on the table; food and drink for a king or a champion were on it that moment. Elin Gow ate and drank heartily, left good health with the old man, and went to the castle. The king had a man called the Tongue-speaker, who met and announced every stranger. 'Who are you or why do you come to the castle?' asked this man of Elin Gow.

'I wish to speak to the king about Glas Gainach.'

'Oh,' said the speaker, 'you are badly wanted, for it is three days since the last man that was after her lost his head. Come, and I will show it to you on the spike, and I am in dread your own head will be in a like place.'

'Never mind,' said Elin Gow; 'misfortune cannot be avoided. We will do our best.'

The Tongue-speaker went to the king then, and said, 'There is a man outside who has come for Glas Gainach.'

The king went out, and asked Elin Gow what he wanted or what brought him. He told him, as he told the speaker, that it was for the cow he had come.

'And is it in combat or in peace that you want to get her?'

''Tis in peace,' said Elin Gow.

'You can try with swords or with herding, whichever you wish.'

'We will choose the herding,' said Elin Gow.

'Well,' said the king, 'this is how we will bind ourselves. You are to bring Glas Gainach here to me every evening safe and sound during seven years, and, if you fail, 'tis your head that you will lose. Do you see those heads on the spikes there behind? 'Tis on account of Glas Gainach they are there. If you come home with the cow every night, she will be yours when seven years are spent – I bind myself to that,' said the king.

'Well,' said Elin Gow, 'I am satisfied with the conditions.'

Next morning Glas Gainach was let out, and both went together all day, she and Elin Gow. She went so swiftly that he threw his cap from him; he could not carry it half the day. All the rest he had was while she was feeding in any place. He was after her then till she came home, and he brought her back as safe and sound as in the morning. The king came out and welcomed him, saying, 'You've taken good care of her; many a man went after her that did not bring her home the first day.'

'Life is sweet,' said Elin Gow; 'I did the best hand I could. I know what I have to get if I fail to bring her.'

The king gave Elin Gow good food and drink, so that he was more improving than failing in strength, and made his way and brought the cow every day till he had the seven years spent; then he said to the king, 'My time is up; will I get the cow?'

'Oh, why not?' said the king. 'You will: you have earned her well; you have done more than any man who walked the way before. See now how many have lost their heads; count them. You are better than any of them. I would not deny or break my word or agreement. You were bound to bring her, and I am bound to give her. Now she is yours and not mine, but if she comes back here again, don't have any eye after her; you'll not get her.'

'That will do,' said Elin Gow. 'I will take good care not to let her come to you. I minded her the last seven years.'

'Well,' said the king, 'I don't doubt you.'

They gave the cow food that morning inside; did not let her out at all. Elin Gow bound the cow in every way he wished, to bring her to the vessel. He used all his strength, raised the two anchors on the ocean side, pulled in the vessel to put the cow on board. When Elin Gow was on board, he turned the stem of the ship toward the sea, and the stern toward land. He was sailing across the wide ocean till he came to Tramor, the port in Erin from which he had started when going to Spain. Elin Gow brought Glas Gainach on shore, took her to Cluainte, and was minding her as carefully as when he was with the King of Spain.

Elin Gow was the best man in Erin to make swords and all weapons for champions; his name was in all lands. The King of Munster had four sons, and the third from the oldest was Cian. He was neither dreaming nor thinking of anything night or day but feats of valour; his grandfather, Art Mac Cuin, had been a great champion, and was very fond of Cian. He used to say, 'Kind father and grandfather for him; he is not like his three brothers.'

When twenty years old, Cian said, 'I will go to try my fortune. My father has heirs enough. I would try other kingdoms if I had a sword.'

'You may have my sword,' said the father. Cian gave the sword a trial, and at the first turn he broke it. 'No sword will please me,' said Cian, 'unless, while grasping the hilt with the blade pointed forward, I can bend the blade till its point touches my elbow on the upper side, then let it spring back and bend it again till the point touches my elbow on the under side.'

'There is not a man in Erin who could make a sword like that,' said the father, 'but Elin Gow, and I am full sure that he will not make it at this time, for he is minding Glas Gainach. He earned her well, and he will guard her; seven years did he travel bareheaded without hat or cap

– a thing which no man could do before him. It would be useless to go to him, for he has never worked a stroke in the forge since he brought Glas Gainach to Erin, and he would not let her go. He would make the sword but for that. It's many a sword he made for me.'

'Well, I will try him,' said Cian. 'I will ask him to make the sword.'

Cian started, and never stopped till he stood before Elin Gow at Cluainte, and told him who he was.

Elin Gow welcomed the son of the king, and said, 'Your father and I were good friends in our young years. It was often I made swords and other weapons for him. And what is it that brought you to-day?'

'It is a sword I want. I wish to go and seek my fortune in some foreign land. I want a good sword, and my father says you are the best man in Erin to make one.'

'I was,' said Elin Gow; 'and I am sorry that I cannot make you one now. I am engaged in minding Glas Gainach; and I would not trust any one after her but myself, and I have enough to do to mind her.'

Cian told how the sword was to be made.

'Oh,' said Elin Gow, 'I would make it in any way you like but for the cow, and I would not wish to let your father's son go away without a sword. I will direct you to five or six smiths that are making swords now, in place of me since I went for Glas Gainach.'

He gave the names, and the king's son went away.

None of them could make the sword in the way Cian wanted. He came back to Elin Gow.

'You have your round made?' said Elin Gow.

'I have,' said Cian, 'but in vain; for none of them would make the sword in the way asked of him.'

'Well, I do not wish to let you go. I will take the risk.'

'Very well,' said Cian; 'I will go after Glas Gainach tomorrow, while you are making the sword, and if I don't bring her, you may have my head in the evening.'

'Well,' said Elin Gow, 'I am afraid to trust you, for many a champion lost his head on account of her before; but I'll run the risk. I must make the sword for you.'

The king's son stopped that night with Elin Gow, who gave him the best food and drink he had, and let out Glas Gainach before him next morning, and told him not to come in front of her in any place where she might want to feed or drink. He advised him in every way how to take care of her. Away went Cian with the cow, and he was doing the right thing all day. She moved on always, and went as far as Caorha, southwest of Tralee, the best spot of land in Kerry for grass. When she had eaten enough, she turned toward home, and Cian was at her tail all the day. When he and Glas Gainach were five miles this side of Tralee, near the water at Derrymor, where she used to drink, Cian saw her going close to deep water; he came before her, and turned her back; and what did she do but jump through the air like a bird, and then she went out through the sea and left him. He walked home sad and mournful, and came to Elin Gow's house. The smith asked him had he the cow, and he said, 'I have not. I was doing well till I came to Derrymor, and she went so near deep water that I was afraid she would go from me. I stopped her, and what did she do but fly away like a bird, and go out through the sea.'

'God help us,' said Elin Gow, 'but the misfortune cannot be helped.'

'I am the cause,' said Cian; 'you may have my head.'

'What is done, is done. I would never take the head off you, but she is a great loss to me.'

'I am willing and satisfied to give you my head,' said Cian. 'Have you the sword made?'

'I have,' said Elin Gow.

Cian took the blade, tested it in every way, and found that he had the sword he wanted.

He swore an oath then to Elin Gow that he would not delay day or night, nor rest anywhere, till he had lost his head or brought back Glas Gainach.

'I am afraid your labour will be useless,' said Elin Gow, 'and that you will never be able to bring her back. I could not have brought her myself but for the advice of an old man that I met before I saw the King of Spain.'

Cian went home to his father's castle. The king saw him coming with the sword. 'I see that Elin Gow did not refuse you.'

'He did not,' said Cian. 'He made the sword, and it is a sore piece of work for him. He has parted with Glas Gainach. I promised to give my head if I did not bring her home to him in safety while he was making the sword. I minded her well all day till she came to a place where she used to drink water. I did not know that; but it was my duty to know it, for he directed me in every way needful how to mind her. I was bringing her home in safety till I brought her to Derrymor River; and I went before her to turn her back – and that was foolish, for he told me not to turn her while I was with her – and she did nothing but spring like a bird and out to sea and away. I promised Elin Gow in the morning if I did not bring the cow to give him my head; and I offered it when I came, as I had not the cow, but he said, 'I will never take the head off a son of your father, even for a greater loss.' And for this reason I will never rest nor delay till I go for Glas Gainach and bring her back to Elin Gow, or lose my head; so make ready your best ship.'

'The best ship,' said the king, 'is the one that Elin Gow took.'

The king's son put provisions for a day and a year in the vessel. He set sail alone and away with him through the main ocean, and he never stopped till he reached the same place to which Elin Gow had sailed before. He cast two anchors on the ocean side, and one next the shore, and left the ship where there was no wind to blow on her, no waves of the ocean to touch her, no crows of the air to drop on her. He went his way then, and was walking always till evening, when he saw at a distance the finest castle he had ever set eyes on. He went toward it; and when he was near, he saw four champions at exercise near the castle. He was going on the very same road that Elin Gow had taken, and was passing the same cottage, when the old man saw him and hailed him. He turned toward the cottage.

'Come to my house and rest,' said the old man. 'From what country are you, and what brought you?'

'I am a son of the King of Munster in Erin; and now will you tell me what place is this?'

'You are in Spain, and the building beyond there is the king's castle.'

'Very well and good. It was to see the king that I left Erin,' said Cian.

'It is for Glas Gainach that you are here, I suppose,' said the old man. 'It is useless for you to try; you never can bring her from the king. It was a hundred times easier when Elin Gow brought her; it is not that way now, but by force and bravery she is to be taken. It is a pity to have you lose your head, like so many kings and champions.'

'I must try,' said Cian; 'for it was through me that Elin Gow lost Glas Gainach. I wanted a sword to try my fortune, and there was not a smith in Erin who could make it as I wanted except Elin Gow; he refused. I told him that I would give my head if I did not bring the cow home to him in safety. I followed her well till, on the way home, she went to drink near the sea, and I went before her; that moment she sprang away like a bird, and went out through the water.'

'I am afraid,' said the old man, 'that to get her is more than you can do. You see those four men? You must fight and conquer them before you get Glas Gainach.'

The old man spread out the table-cloth, and they ate.

'I care not,' said the king's son, 'what comes. I am willing to lose my head unless I can bring back the cow.'

'Well,' said the old man, 'you can try.'

Next morning breakfast was ready for Cian; he rose, washed his hands and face, prayed for mercy and strength, ate, and going to the pole of combat gave the greatest blow ever given before on it.

'Run out,' said the king to the Tongue-speaker; 'see who is abroad.'

'What do you want?' asked the Tongue-speaker of Cian.

'The king's daughter and Glas Gainach,' said Cian.

The speaker hurried in and told the king. The king went out and asked, 'Are you the man who wants my daughter and Glas Gainach?'

'I am,' answered Cian.

'You will get them if you earn them,' said the king.

'If I do not earn them, I want neither the daughter nor the cow,' replied Cian.

The king ordered out then the four knights of valour to kill Cian. He was as well trained as they, for he had been practising from his twelfth year, and he was more active. They were at him all day, and he at them: he did not let one blow from them touch his body; and if a man were to go from the Eastern to the Western World to see champions, 'tis at them he would have to look. At last, when Cian was hungry, and late evening near, he sprang with the strength of his limbs out of the joints of his bones, and rose above them, and swept the heads off the four before he touched ground.

The young champion was tired after the day, and went to the old man. The old man asked, 'What have you done?'

'I have knocked the heads off the four champions of valour.'

The old man was delighted that the first day had thriven in that way with Cian. He looked at the sword. 'Oh, there is no danger,' cried he; 'you have the best sword I have ever seen, and you'll need it, for you'll have more forces against you tomorrow.'

The old man and Cian spent the night in three parts – the first part in eating and drinking, the second in telling tales and singing songs, the third in sound sleep.

The old man told how he had been the champion of Spain, and at last when he grew old the king gave him that house.

Next morning Cian washed his face and hands, prayed for help and mercy, ate breakfast with the old man, went to the pole of combat, and gave a greater blow still than before.

'What do you want this day?' asked the Tongue-speaker.

'I want three hundred men on my right hand, three hundred on my left, three hundred after my poll, three hundred out in front of me.' The king sent the men out four deep through four gates. Cian went at them, and as they came he struck the heads off them; and though they fought bravely, in the evening he had the heads off the twelve hundred. Cian then left the field, and went to the old man.

'What have you done after the day?' asked the old man.

'I have stretched the king's forces.'

'You'll do well,' said the old man.

The old champion put the cloth on the table, and there was food for a king or a champion. They made three parts of that night – the first for eating and drinking, the second for telling tales and singing songs, the third for sleep and sound rest.

Next morning, Cian gave such a blow on the pole of combat that the king in his chamber was frightened.

'What do you want this time?' asked the Tongue-speaker.

'I want the same number of men as yesterday.'

The king sent the men out; and the same fate befell them as the other twelve hundred, and Cian went home to the old man untouched. Next morning Cian made small bits of the king's pole of combat.

'Well, what do you want?' asked the Tongue-speaker.

'Whatever I want, I don't want to be losing time. Let out all your forces against me at once.'

The king sent out all the forces he wished that morning. The battle was more terrible than all the others put together; but Cian went through the king's forces, and at sunset not a man of them was living, and he let no one nearer than the point of his sword.

'How did the day thrive with you?' asked the old man when Cian came in.

'I have killed all the king's champions.'

'I think,' said the old man, 'that you have the last of his forces down now; but what you have done is nothing to what is before you. The king will come out and say tomorrow that you will not get the daughter with Glas Gainach till you eat on one biscuit what butter there is in his storehouses, and they are all full; you are to do this in the space of four hours. He will give you the biscuit. Take this biscuit from me, and do you hide the one that he will give you – never mind it; put as much as you will eat on this, and there'll be no tidings of what butter there is in the king's stores within one hour – it will vanish and disappear.'

Cian was very glad when the old man told him what to do. They spent that night as they had the nights before. Next morning Cian breakfasted, and went to the castle. The king saw him coming, and was out before him.

'What do you want this morning?' asked the king.

'I want your daughter and Glas Gainach,' said Cian.

'Well,' said the king, 'you will not get my daughter and Glas Gainach unless within four hours you eat on this biscuit what butter there is in all my storehouses in Spain; and if you do not eat the butter, your head will be on a spike this evening.'

The king gave him the biscuit. Cian went to the first storehouse, dropped the king's biscuit into his pocket, took out the one the old man had given him, buttered it, and began to eat. He went his way then, and in one hour there was neither sign nor trace of butter in any storehouse the king had.

That night Cian and the old man passed the time in three parts as usual. 'You will have hard work tomorrow,' said the old man, 'but I will tell you how to do it. The king will say that you cannot have his daughter and Glas Gainach unless within four hours you tan all the hides in Spain, dry and green, and tan them as well as a hand's breadth of leather that he will give you. Here is a piece of leather like the piece the king will give. Clap this on the first hide you come to; and all the hides in Spain will be tanned in one hour, and be as soft and smooth as the king's piece.'

Next morning the king saw Cian coming, and was out before him. 'What do you want now?' asked the king.

'Your daughter and Glas Gainach,' said Cian.

'You are not to get my daughter and Glas Gainach unless within four hours you tan all the dry and green hides in Spain to be as soft and smooth as this piece; and if you do not tan them, your head will be on one of the spikes there behind my castle this evening.'

Cian took the leather, dropped it into his pocket, and, taking the old man's piece, placed it on the first hide that he touched. In one hour all the hides in Spain were tanned, and they were as soft and fine as the piece which the king gave to Cian.

The old man and Cian spent this night as they had the others.

'You will have the hardest task of all tomorrow,' said the old man.

'What is that?' asked the young champion.

'The king's daughter will come to a window in the highest chamber of the castle with a ball in her hand: she will throw the ball through the window, and you must catch it on your hurley, and keep it up during two hours and a half; never let it touch the ground. There will be a hundred champions striving to take the ball from you, but follow my advice. The champions, not knowing where the ball will come down when the king's daughter throws it, will gather near the front of the castle; and if either of them should get the ball, he might keep it and spoil you. Do you stand far outside; you will have the best chance. I don't know, though, what you are to do, as you have no hurley, but wait. In my youth I was great to play at hurley, and I never met a man that could match me. The hurley I had then must be in this house somewhere.'

The old man searched the house through, and where did he find the hurley but up in the loft, and it full of dust; he brought it down. Cian swung it, knocked the dust from the hurley, and it was as clean as when made.

'It is glad I am to find this, for any other hurley in the kingdom would not do you, but only this very one. This hurley has the virtue in it, and only for that it would not do.'

Both were very glad, and made three parts of that night, as they had of the nights before. Next morning Cian rose, washed his hands and face, and begged mercy and help of God for that day.

After breakfast he went to the king's castle, and soon many champions came around him. The king was outside before him, and asked what he wanted that day.

'I want your daughter and Glas Gainach.'

'You will not get my daughter and Glas Gainach till you do the work I'll give, and I'll give you the toughest task ever put before you. At midday, my daughter will throw out a ball through the window, and you must keep that ball in the air for two hours and a half: it must never touch ground in that time, and when the two hours and a half are spent, you must drive it in through the same window through which it went out; if not, I will have your head on a spike this evening.'

'God help us!' said Cian.

All the champions were together to see which man would get the ball first; but Cian, thinking of the old man's advice, stood outside them all. At midday the king's daughter sent out the ball through the highest window; and to whom should it go but to Cian, and he had the luck of getting it first. He drove the ball with his hurley, and for two hours and a half he kept it in the air, and did not let another man touch it. Then he gave it a directing blow, and sent it in through the window to the king's daughter.

The king watched the ball closely; and when it went in, he ran to Cian, shook his hand warmly, and never stopped till he took him to his daughter's high chamber. She kissed him with joy and great gladness. He had done a thing that no other had ever done.

'I have won the daughter and Glas Gainach from you now,' said Cian.

'You have,' said the king; 'and they are both yours. I give them with all my heart. You have earned them well, and done what no other man could do. I will give you one-half of the kingdom till my death, and all of it from that out.'

Cian and the king's daughter were married. A great feast was made, and a command given out that all people of the kingdom must come to the wedding. Every one came; and the wedding lasted seven days and nights, to the pleasure of all, and the greatest delight of the king. Cian remained with the king; and after a time his wife had a son, the finest and fairest child ever born in Spain, and he was increasing so that what of him didn't grow in the day grew in the night, and what did not grow in the night grew in the day, and if the sun shone on any child, it shone on that one. The boy was called Cormac after Cian's father, Cormac Mac Art.

Cian remained with the King of Spain till Cormac's age was a year and a half. Then he remembered his promise to Elin Gow to bring back Glas Gainach.

Cian put stores in the vessel in which he had come, and placed Glas Gainach inside, firmly fettered. He gave then the stem of his ship to the ocean, the stern to land, raised the limber sails; and there was the work of a hundred men on each side, though Cian did the work all alone. He sailed through the main ocean with safety till he came to Tramor – the best landing-place in Erin at that time. Glas Gainach was brought to shore carefully, and Cian went on his way with her to go to Elin Gow's house at Cluainte.

There was no highway from Tramor but the one; and on that one were three brothers, three robbers, the worst at that time in Erin. These men knew all kinds of magic, and had a rod of enchantment. Cian had brought much gold with him on the way, coming as a present to his father.

The three brothers stopped Cian, saluted him, and asked would he play a game. He said that he would. They played, and toward evening the robbers had the gold won; then they said to Cian, 'Now bet the cow against the gold you have lost, and we will put twice as much with it.' He laid the cow as a wager, and lost her.

One of the three robber brothers struck Cian with the rod of enchantment, and made a stone pillar of him, and made an earth mound of Glas Gainach with another blow. The two remained there, the man and the cow, by the roadside.

Cian's son Cormac was growing to manhood in Spain, and heard his mother and grandfather talk of his father, and he thought to himself, 'There was no man on earth that could fight with my father; and I promise now to travel and be walking always till I find out the place where he is, living or dead.'

As Cormac had heard that his father was from Erin, to Erin he faced, first of all. The mother was grieved, and advised him not to go wandering. 'Your father must be dead, or on the promise he made me he'd be here long ago.'

'There is no use in talking; the world will not stop me till I know what has happened to my father,' said Cormac.

The mother could not stop him; she gave her consent. He turned then to his grandfather. 'Make ready for me the best vessel you have,' said he.

The vessel was soon ready with provisions for a day and a year, and gold two thousand pieces. He embarked, and went through the main ocean faster than his father had gone till he sailed into Tramor. He was on his way walking till he came to the robbers about midday.

They saluted him kindly, thinking he had gold, and asked, 'Will you play a game with us?'

'I will,' said Cormac; 'I have never refused.'

They played. The robbers gained, and let him gain; they were at him the best of the day, till they won the last piece of gold of his two thousand pieces.

When he had lost what he had, he was like a wild man, and knew not what to do for a while. At last Cormac said to himself, 'It is an old saying never contradicted that strength will get the upper hand of enchantment.' He jumped then, and caught two of the three robbers, one in each hand, and set them under his two knees. The third was coming to help the two; but Cormac caught that one with his hand and held the three, kept them there, and said, 'I will knock the heads off every man of you.'

'Do not do that,' begged the three. 'Who are you? We will do what you ask of us.'

'I am seeking my father, Cian Mac Cormac, who left Spain eighteen years ago with Glas Gainach.'

'Spare us,' said the three brothers; 'we will give back your gold and raise up your father with Glas Gainach.'

'How can ye do that,' asked Cormac, 'or where is my father?'

'He is that pillar there opposite.'

'And where is Glas Gainach?'

They showed him the earth mound.

'How can ye bring them back to their own shapes?' asked Cormac. 'We have a rod of enchantment,' said the brothers; and they told where the rod was. When Cormac had a true account of the rod, what he did was to draw out his sword and cut the heads off the three brothers, saying, 'Ye will never again rob any man who walks this way.' Cormac then found the rod of enchantment, went to the pillar, gave it a blow, and his father came forth as well and healthy as ever.

'Who are you?' asked Cian of Cormac.

'I am your son Cormac.'

'Oh, my dear son, how old are you?'

'I'm in my twentieth year,' said Cormac. 'I heard my mother and grandfather talk of your bravery, and I made up my mind to go in search of you, and be walking always till I found you. I said I'd face Erin first, for 'twas there you went with Glas Gainach. I landed this morning, met these three robbers; they won all my gold. I was like a wild man. I caught them, and swore I would kill them. They asked who was I; I told them. They said you were the stone pillar; that they had a rod that would raise you up with Glas Gainach. They told where the rod was. I took the heads off them, and raised you with the rod.'

Now Cormac struck the earth mound, and Glas Gainach rose up as well as before. Everything was now in its own place, and they were glad. Cian would not stop till he brought Glas Gainach to Elin Gow, so he was walking night and day till he came here behind to Cluainte, where Elin Gow was living. He screeched out Elin Gow's name, told him to come. He came out; and when he saw Cian and Glas Gainach he came near fainting from joy. Cian put Glas Gainach's horn in his hand, and said, 'I wished to keep the promise I made when you spared my head; and it was gentle of you to spare it, for great was the loss that I caused you'; and he told all that had happened – how he had won and lost Glas Gainach, and lost her through the robbers.

'Who is this brave youthful champion with you?' asked Elin Gow.

'This is my son, and but for him I'd be forever where the three robbers put me. I was eighteen years where they left me; but for that, the cow would have been with you long ago. What were you doing all this time?' asked Cian of Elin Gow.

'Making swords and weapons, but I could not have lived without the support of your father.'

'He promised me that,' said Cian, 'before I left Erin. I knew that he would help you.'

'Oh, he did!' said Elin Gow.

The father and son left good health with Elin Gow, and never stopped nor stayed till they reached the castle of Cian's father. The old king had thought that Cian was dead, as he had received no account of him for so many years. Great was his joy and gladness, and great was the feast that he made.

Cian remained for a month, and then went to the house of the robbers, took out all its treasures, locked up the place in the way that no man could open it; then he gave one-half his wealth to his father. He took the rest to Spain with his son, and lived there.

Elin Gow had grown old, and he was in dread that he had not the strength to follow Glas Gainach, and sent a message to Caol na Crua, the fleetest champion in Kerry. Caol came. Elin Gow agreed to pay him his price for minding the cow, and was glad to get him. He told Caol carefully how to herd the cow. She travelled as before, and was always at home before nightfall.

Glas Gainach had milk for all; and when any one came to milk her she would stop, and there never was a vessel that she did not fill. One woman heard this; and once when Glas Gainach was near a river, the woman brought a sieve and began to milk. She milked a long time. At last the cow saw the river white with milk; then she raised her leg, gave the woman a kick on the forehead, and killed her.

Caol na Crua was doing well, minding the cow all the time, till one evening Glas Gainach walked between the two pillars where she used to scratch herself; when she was full, her sides would touch both pillars. This evening she bellowed, and Elin Gow heard her. Instead of going home then, she went down to a place northwest of Cluainte, near a ruin; she used to drink there at times, but not often. Caol na Crua did not know this. He thought she was going into the sea, and caught her tail to hold her back. With that, instead of drinking, she went straight toward the water. Caol tried to hold her. She swept him along and went through the ocean, he keeping the grip he had, and she going with such swiftness that he was lying flat on the sea behind her; and she took him with her to Spain and went to the king, and very joyful was the king, for they were in great distress for butter while Glas Gainach was gone.

MOR'S SONS AND THE HERDER FROM UNDER THE SEA

In old times, there was a great woman in the southwest of Erin, and she was called Mor. This woman lived at Dun Quin; and when she came to that place the first time with her husband Lear, she was very poor. People say that it was by the water she came to Dun Quin. Whatever road she took, all she had came by the sea, and went the same way.

She built a small house, and their property was increasing little by little. After a while she had three sons, and these grew to be very fine boys and then strong young men.

The two elder sons set out to try their fortunes; they got a vessel, sailed away on the sea, and never stopped nor halted till they came to the kingdom of the White Strand, in the Eastern World. There they stayed for seven years, goaling and sporting with the people.

The king of that country wished to keep them forever, because they were strong men, and had risen to be great champions.

The youngest son remained at home all the time, growing to be as good a man as his brothers. One day he went out to look at a large field of wheat which his mother had, and found it much injured.

'Well, mother,' said he when he came in, 'all our field is destroyed by something. I don't know for the world what is it. Something comes in, tramples the grain and eats it.'

'Watch the field tonight, my son, and see what is devouring our grain.'

'Well, mother, boil something for me to eat to give me strength and good luck for the night.'

Mor baked a loaf, and boiled some meat for her son, and told him to watch well till the hour of night, when perhaps the cattle would be before him.

He was watching and looking there, till all at once, a little after midnight, he saw the field full of cattle of different colours – beautiful colours, blue, and red, and white. He was looking at them for a long time, they were so beautiful. The young man wanted to drive the beasts home with him, to show his mother the cattle that were spoiling the grain. He had them out of the field on the road when a herder stood before him, and said, 'Leave the cattle behind you.'

'I will not,' said Mor's son; 'I will drive them home to my mother.'

'I will not let them with you,' said the herder.

'I'll carry them in spite of you,' replied Mor's son.

He had a good strong green stick, and so had the herder; the two faced each other, and began to fight. The herder was too strong for Mor's son, and he drove off the cattle into the sea.

'Oh,' said the herder, as he was going, 'your mother did not boil your meat or bake your loaf rightly last night; she gave too much fire to the loaf and the meat, took the strength out of them. You might do something if your mother knew how to cook.'

When Mor's son went home, his mother asked, 'Did you see any cattle, my son?'

'I did, mother; the field was full of them. And when I was bringing the herd home with me to show you, a man stood there on the road to take the beasts from me; we fought, and when he beat me and was driving the cattle into the sea, what did he say but that you boiled the meat and baked the loaf too much last night. Tonight, when you boil my meat, do not give it half the fire; leave all the strength in the meat and the loaf.'

'I will,' said the mother.

When night came, the dinner was ready. The young man ate twice as much of the meat and the loaf as the evening before. About the same hour, just after midnight, he went to the field, for he knew now what time the cattle would be in it. The field was full of the same cattle of beautiful colours.

Mor's son drove the beasts out, and was going to drive them home, when the herder, who was not visible hitherto, came before him and said, 'I will not let the cattle with you.'

'I will take them in spite of you,' replied Mor's son.

The two began to fight, and Mor's son was stronger this time.

'Why do you not keep your cattle out of my wheat?' asked he of the herder.

'Because I know very well that you are not able to take them with you.'

'If I am not able to take the cattle, you may have them and the wheat as well,' said Mor's son.

The herder was driving the cattle one way, and Mor's son was driving them the opposite way; and after they had done that for a while, they faced each other and began to fight again.

Mor's son was doubly angry at the herder this night for the short answers that he gave. They fought two hours; then the herder got the upper hand. Mor's son was sorry; and the herder, as he drove the cattle to the sea, called out, 'Your mother gave too much fire to the meat and the loaf; still you are stronger tonight than you were last night.'

Mor's son went home.

'Well, my son,' asked the mother, 'have you any news of the cattle and the herder?'

'I have seen them, mother.'

'And what did the herder do?'

'He was too strong for me a second time, and drove the cattle into the sea.'

'What are we to do now?' asked the mother. 'If he keeps on in this way, we'll soon be poor, and must leave the country altogether.'

'The herder said, as he drove the cattle away, "Your mother gave too much fire to the meat and the loaf; still you are stronger tonight than you were last night." Well, mother, if you gave too much fire to my dinner last night, give but little tonight, and I will leave my life outside or have the cattle home with me this time. If I do not beat him, he may have the wheat as well as the cattle after tonight.'

Mor prepared the dinner; and this time she barely let the water on the meat begin to bubble, and to the bread she gave but one roast.

He ate and drank twice as much as the day before. The dinner gave him such strength that he said, 'I'll bring the cattle tonight.'

He went to the field, and soon after midnight it was full of cattle of the same beautiful colours; the grain was spoiled altogether. He drove the cattle to the road, and thought he had them. He got no sight of the herder till every beast was outside the field, and he ready to drive them home to his mother. Then the herder stood before him, and began to drive the cattle toward the sea.

'You'll not take them this time,' said Mor's son.

'I will,' said the herder.

They began to fight, caught each other, dragged, and struggled long, and in the heel of the battle Mor's son was getting the better of the herder.

'I think that you'll have the upper hand of me this time,' said the herder; 'and 'tis my own advice I blame for it. You'll take the cattle tonight in spite of me. Let me go now, and take them away with you.'

'I will,' said Mor's son. 'I will take them to the house, and please my mother.'

He drove the cattle home, and said to his mother, 'I have the cattle here now for you, and do whatever you wish with them.'

The herder followed Mor's son to the house.

'Why did you destroy all my grain with your cattle?' asked Mor.

'Let the cattle go with me now, and I promise that after tonight your field of wheat will be the best in the country.'

'What are we to do?' asked Mor of the son. 'Is it to let the cattle go with him for the promise he gives?'

'I will do what you say, mother.'

'We will give him the cattle,' said Mor.

'Well,' said the son to the herder, 'my mother is going to give you the cattle for the promise that our grain will be the best in the country when 'tis reaped. We ought to be friends after the fighting; and now take your cattle home with you, though you vexed and hurt me badly.'

'I am very grateful to you,' said the herder to Mor's son, 'and for your kindness you will have plenty of cattle and plenty of wheat before you die, and seeing that you are such a good man I will give you a chance before I leave you. The King of Mayo has an only daughter; the fairies will take her from him tomorrow. They will bring her through Daingean, on the shoulders of four men, to the fairy fort at Cnoc na Hown. Be at the cross-roads about two o'clock tomorrow night. Jump up quickly, put your shoulder under the coffin, the four men will disappear and leave the coffin on the road; do you bring what's in the coffin home with you.'

Mor's son followed the herder's directions. He went toward Daingean in the night, for he knew the road very well. After midnight, he was at the cross-roads, waiting and hidden. Soon he saw the coffin coming out against him, and the four men carrying it on their shoulders.

The young man put his shoulder under the coffin; the four dropped it that minute, and disappeared. Mor's son took the lid off the coffin; and what did he find lying inside but a beautiful woman, warm and ruddy, sleeping as if at home in her bed. He took out the young woman, knowing well that she was alive, and placing her on his back, left the coffin behind at the wayside.

The woman could neither walk nor speak, and he brought her home to his mother. Mor opened the door, and he put the young woman down in the corner.

'What's this you brought me? What do I want with the like of her in the house?'

'Never mind, mother; it may be our luck that will come with her.'

They gave her every kind of drink and nourishing food, for she was very weak; when daylight came, she was growing stronger, and could speak. The first words she said were, 'I am no good to you in the way that I am now; but if you are a brave man, you will meet with your luck tomorrow night. All the fairies will be gathered at a feast in the fort at Cnoc na Hown; there will be a horn of drink on the table. If you bring that horn, and I get three sips from it (if you have the heart of a brave man you will go to the fort, seize the horn, and bring it here), I shall be as well and strong as ever, and you will be as rich yourself as any king in Erin.'

'I have stood in great danger before from the like of them,' replied Mor's son. 'I will make a trial of this work, too.'

'Between one and two o'clock in the night you must go to the fort,' said the young woman, 'and you must carry a stick of green rowan wood in your hand.'

The young man went to the fairy fort, keeping the stick carefully and firmly in his hand. At parting, the young woman warned him, saying, 'They can do you no harm in the world while you have the stick, but without the stick there is no telling what they might do.'

When Mor's son came to Cnoc na Hown, and went in through the gate of the fairy fort, he saw a house and saw many lights flashing in different places. In the kitchen was a great table with all sorts of food and drink, and around it a crowd of small men. When he was making toward the table, he heard one of the men say –

'Very little good will the girl be to Mor's son. He may keep her in the corner by his mother. There will be neither health nor strength in her; but if she had three drinks out of this horn on the table here, she would be as well as ever.'

He faced them then, and, catching the horn, said, 'She will not be long without the drink!'

All the little men looked at one another as he hurried through the door and disappeared. He had the stick, and they could not help themselves; but all began to scold one another for not having the courage to seize him and take the horn from him.

Mor's son reached home with the horn. 'Well, mother,' said he, 'we have the cure now'; and he didn't put the horn down till the young woman had taken three drinks out of it, and then she said –

'You are the best champion ever born in Erin, and now take the horn back to Cnoc na Hown; I am as well and hearty as ever.'

He took the horn back to the fairy fort, placed it on the table, and hurried home. The fairies looked at one another, but not a thing could they do, for the stick was in his hand yet.

'The woman is as well as ever now,' said one of the fairies when Mor's son had gone, 'and we have lost her'; and they began to scold one another for letting the horn go with him. But that was all the good it did them; the young woman was cured.

Next day the young woman said to Mor's son, 'I am well now, and I will give you a token to take to my father and mother in Mayo.'

'I will not take the token,' said he; 'I will go and seek out your father, and bring back some token to you first.'

He went away, searched and enquired till he made out the king's castle; and when he was there, he went around all the cattle and went away home to his mother at Tivorye with every four-footed beast that belonged to the king.

'Well, mother,' said he, 'it is the luck we have now; and we'll have the whole parish under stock from this out.'

The young woman was not satisfied yet, and said, 'You must go and carry a token to my father and mother.'

'Wait a while, and be quiet,' answered Mor's son. 'Your father will send herders to hunt for the stock, and these men will have token enough when they come.'

Well, sure enough, the king's men hunted over hills and valleys, found that the cattle had been one day in such a place and another day in another place; and they followed on till at length and at last they came near Mor's house, and there they saw the cattle grazing above on the mountain.

There was no house in Dun Quin at that time but Mor's house, and there was not another in it for many a year after.

'We will send a man down to that house,' said the herders, 'to know can we get any account of what great champion it was that brought the cattle all this distance.'

What did the man see when he came near the house but his own king's daughter. He knew the young woman, and was struck dumb when he saw her, and she buried two months before at her father's castle in Mayo. He had no power to say a word, he forgot where he was, or why he was sent. At last he turned, ran up to the men above on the mountain, and said, 'The king's daughter is living below in that house.'

The herders would not believe a word he said, but at last three other men went down to see for themselves. They knew the king's daughter, and were frightened; but they had more courage, and after a while asked, 'Where is the man that brought the cattle?'

'He is sleeping,' said the king's daughter. 'He is tired after the long journey; if you wish, I will wake him.'

She woke Mor's son, and he came out.

'What brought you here?' asked he of the men.

'We came looking for our master's cattle; they are above on the mountain, driven to this place by you, as it seems. We have travelled hither and over till we found them.'

'Go and tell your master,' said Mor's son, 'that I brought the cattle; that Lear is my father, and Mor is my mother, and that I have his daughter here with me.'

'There is no use in sending them with that message,' said the young woman; 'my father would not believe them.'

'Tell your master,' said Mor's son, 'that it is I who brought the cattle, and that I have his daughter here in good health, and 'tis by my bravery that I saved her.'

'If they go to my father with that message, he will kill them. I will give them a token for him.'

'What token will you give?'

'I will give them this ring with my name and my father's name and my mother's name written inside on it. Do not give the ring,' said she to the men, 'till ye tell my father all ye have seen; if he will not believe you, then give the ring.'

Away went the men, and not a foot of the cattle did they take; and if all the men in Mayo had come, Mor's son would not have let the cattle go with them, for he had risen to be the best champion in Erin. The men went home by the straightest roads; and they were not half the time going to the king's castle that they were in finding the cattle.

On the way home, one man said to the others, 'It is a great story we have and good news to tell; the king will make rich men of us for the tidings we are taking him.'

When they reached the king's castle, there was a welcome before them.

'Have ye any news for me after the long journey?' asked the king.

'We found your daughter with a man in Tivorye in the southwest of Erin, and all your cattle are with the same man.'

'Ye may have found my cattle, but ye could not get a sight of my daughter.'

'If you do not believe us in this way, you will, in another. We may as well tell you all.'

'Ye may as well keep silent. I'll not believe a word of what ye say about my daughter.'

'I will give you a token from your daughter,' said one of the men, pulling out a purse. He had the purse rolled carefully in linen. (And he did well, for the fairies cannot touch linen, and it is the best guard in the world against them. Linen thread, too, is strong against the fairies. A man might travel all the fairy forts of the world if he had a skein of flax thread around his neck, and a steel knife with a black handle in his pocket.) He took out the ring, and gave it to the king. The king sent for the queen. She came. He put the ring in her hand and said, 'Look at this, and see do you know it.'

'I do indeed,' said she; 'and how did you come by this ring?'

The king told the whole story that the men had brought.

'This is our daughter's ring. It was on her finger when we buried her,' said the queen.

'It was,' said the king, 'and what the men say must be true.' He would have killed them but for the ring.

On the following morning, the king and queen set out with horses, and never stopped till they came to Tivorye (Mor's house). The king knew the cattle the moment he saw them above on the mountain, and then he was sure of the rest. They were sorry to find the daughter in such a small cabin, but glad that she was alive. The guide was sent to the house to say the king and queen were coming.

'Your father and mother are coming,' said he to the king's daughter.

She made ready, and was standing in the door before them. The father and mother felt weak and faint when they looked at her; but she ran out, took them by the hands, and said, 'Have courage; I am alive and well, no ghost, and ye ought to thank the man who brought me away from my enemies.'

'Bring him to us,' said they; 'we wish to see him.'

'He is asleep, but I will wake him.'

'Wake him,' said the father, 'for he is the man we wish to see now.'

The king's daughter roused Mor's son, and said, 'My father and mother are above in the kitchen. Go quickly, and welcome them.'

He welcomed them heartily, and he was ten times gladder to see them than they were to see him. They enquired then how he got the daughter, and she buried at home two months before. And he told the whole story from first to last: How the herder from the sea had told him, and how he had saved her at Cnoc na Hown. They had a joyful night in the cabin after the long journey, and anything that would be in any king's castle they had in Mor's house that night, for the king had plenty of everything with him from the castle. Next morning the king and queen were for taking the daughter home with them; but she refused firmly, and said –

'I will never leave the man who saved me from such straits. I'll never marry any man but him, for I'm sure that he is the best hero ever reared in Erin, after the courage that he has shown.'

'We will never carry you away, since you like him so well; and we will send him twice as many cattle, and money besides.'

They brought in the priest of whatever religion was in it at the time (to be sure, it was not Catholic priests were in Erin in those days), and Mor's son and the king's daughter were married. The father and mother left her behind in Tivorye, and enjoyed themselves on the way home, they were that glad after finding the daughter alive.

When Mor's son was strong and rich, he could not be satisfied till he found his two brothers, who had left home years before, and were in the kingdom of the White Strand, though he did not know it. He made up a fine ship then, and got provisions for a day and a year, went into it, set sail, and went on over the wide ocean till he came to the chief port of the King of the White Strand. He was seven days on the water; and when he came in on the strand, the king saw him, and thought that he must be a brave man to come alone on a ship to that kingdom.

'That must be a great hero,' said he to his men. 'Let some of the best of you go down and knock a trial out of him before he comes to the castle.'

The king was so in dread of the stranger that out of all the men he selected Mor's two elder sons. They were the best and strongest men he had, and he sent them to know what activity was in the new-comer. They took two hurleys for themselves and one for the stranger, and a ball.

The second brother challenged the stranger to play. When the day was closing, the stranger was getting the upper hand. They invited him to the king's castle for the night, and the elder brother challenged him to play a game on the following day.

'How did the trial turn out?' asked the king of the elder brother.

'I sent my brother to try him, and it was the strange champion that got the upper hand.'

Mor's son remained at the castle that night, and found good welcome and cheer. He ate breakfast next morning, and a good breakfast it was. They took three hurleys then and a ball, and went to the strand. Said the eldest brother to the second, 'Stop here and look at us, and see what the trial will be between us.'

They gave the stranger a choice of the hurleys, and the game began. It couldn't be told who was the better of the two brothers. The king was in dread that the stranger would injure himself and his men. In the middle of the day, when it could not be determined who was the better man, the elder brother said, 'We will try wrestling now, to know which of us can win that way.'

'I'm well satisfied,' said Mor's son.

They began to wrestle. The elder brother gave Mor's son several knocks, and he made several turns on the elder.

'Well, if I live,' said the elder, 'you are my brother; for when we used to wrestle at home, I had the knocks, and you had the turns. You are my younger brother, for no man was able to wrestle with me when I was at Tivorye but you.'

They knew each other then, and embraced. Each told his story.

'Come home with me now,' said the youngest brother, 'and see our mother. I am as rich as any king, and can give you good entertainment.'

The three went to the King of the White Strand, and told him everything. The eldest and second brother asked leave of him to go home to see their father and mother. The king gave them leave, and filled their vessel with every kind of good food, and the two promised to come back.

The three brothers set sail then, and after seven days came in on the strand near Tivorye. The two found their brother richer than any king in any country. They were enjoying themselves at home for a long time, having everything that their hearts could wish, when one day above another they saw a vessel passing Dun Quin, and it drew up at the quay in Daingean harbour. Next day people went to the ship; but if they did, not a man went on board, for no man was allowed to go.

There was a green cat on deck. The cat was master of the vessel, and would not let a soul come near it. A report went out through the town that the green cat would allow no one to go near the ship, and for three weeks this report was spreading. No one was seen on the vessel but the cat, and he the size of a big man.

Mor's sons heard of the ship and the green cat at Daingean, and they said, 'Let us have a day's pleasure, and go to the ship and see the cat.'

Mor bade them stay at home. 'Don't mind the ship or the cat,' said she, 'and follow my advice.' But the sons would not follow her advice, nor be said by her, and away they went, in spite of all she could do.

When the cat saw them coming, he knew very well who were in it. He jumped out on the shore, stood on two legs, and shook hands with the three brothers. He was as tall himself as the largest man, and as friendly as he could be. The three brothers were glad to receive an honour which no one else could get.

'Come down now to the cabin and have a trial of my cooking,' said the cat.

He brought them to the cabin, and the finest dinner was on the table before them – meat and drink as good as ever they tasted either in Tivorye or the kingdom of the White Strand.

When the cat had them below in the cabin, and they eating and drinking with great pleasure and delight, he went on deck, screwed down the hatches, raised the sails, and away went the vessel sailing out of the harbour; and before the three brothers knew where they were, the ship was miles out on the ocean, and they thought they were eating dinner at the side of the quay in Daingean.

'We'll go up now,' said they when their dinner was eaten, 'thank the cat, and go on shore for ourselves.'

When on deck, they saw water on all sides, and did not know in the world where they were. The cat never stopped till he sailed to his own kingdom, which was the kingdom of the White Strand, for who should the cat be but the King of the White Strand. He had come for the two brothers himself, for he knew that they would never come of their own will, and he could not trust another to go for them. The king needed them, for they were the best men he had. In getting back the two, he took the third, and Mor was left without any son.

Mor heard in the evening that the ship was gone, and her own three sons inside in it.

'This is my misfortune,' cried she. 'After rearing my three sons, they are gone from me in this way.' She began to cry and lament then, and to screech wonderfully.

Mor never knew who the cat was, or what became of her sons. The wife of Mor's youngest son went away to her father in Mayo, and everything she had went with her. Mor's husband, Lear, had died long before, and was buried at Dunmore Head. His grave is there to this day. Mor became half demented, and died soon after.

If women are scolding at the present time, it happens often that one says to another, 'May your children go from you as Mor's sons went with the enchanted cat!'

SAUDAN OG AND THE DAUGHTER OF THE KING OF SPAIN; YOUNG CONAL AND THE YELLOW KING'S DAUGHTER

Ri Na Durkach (the King of the Turks) lived many years in Erin, where he had one son, Saudan Og. When this son grew up to be twenty years old, he was a prince whose equal was hard to be found.

The old king was anxious to find a king's daughter as wife for his son, and began to enquire of all wayfarers, rich and poor, high and low, where was there a king's daughter fit for his son, but no one could tell him.

At last the king called his old druid. 'Do you know,' asked he, 'where to find a king's daughter for Saudan Og?'

'I do not,' said the druid; 'but do you order your guards to stop all people passing your castle, and enquire of them where such a woman may be.'

As the druid advised, the king commanded; but no man made him a bit the wiser.

A year later, an old ship captain walked the way, and the guards brought him to the king.

'Do you know where a fitting wife for my son might be found?' asked the king.

'I do,' said the captain; 'but my advice to you, and it may be a good one, is to seek a wife for your son in the land where he was born, and not go abroad for her. You can find plenty of good women in Erin.'

'Well,' said the king, 'tell me first who is the woman you have in mind.'

'If you must know,' said the old captain, 'the daughter of the King of Spain is the woman.'

Straightway the king had a notice put up on the high-road to bring no more tidings to the castle, as he had no need of them.

When Saudan Og saw this notice, he knew that his father had the tidings, but would not give them. Next morning he went to the father and begged him to tell. 'I know,' said he, 'that the old captain told you.'

The king would say nothing for he feared that his son might fall into trouble.

'I will start tomorrow,' said Saudan Og at last, 'in search of the woman; and if I do not find her, I will never come back to you, so it is better to tell me at once.'

'The daughter of the King of Spain is the woman,' said the father; 'but if you take my advice, you'll stay at home.'

On the following day, Saudan Og dressed himself splendidly, mounted a white steed, and rode away, overtaking the wind before him; but the wind behind could not overtake him. He travelled all that was dry of Erin, and came to the seashore; so he had nowhere else to travel on land, unless he went back to his father. He turned toward a wood then, and saw a great ash-tree: he grasped the tree, and tore it out with its roots; and, stripping the earth from the roots, he threw the great ash into the sea. Leaving the steed behind him, he sat on the tree, and never stopped nor stayed till he came to Spain. When he landed, he sent word to the king that Saudan Og wished to see him.

The answer that Saudan got was not to come till the king had his castle prepared to receive such a great champion.

When the castle was ready, the King of Spain sent a bellman to give notice that every man, woman, or child found asleep within seven days and nights would lose their heads, for all must sing, dance, and enjoy themselves in honour of the high guest.

The king feasted Saudan Og for seven days and nights, and never asked him where was he going or what was his business. On the evening of the seventh day, Saudan said to the king, 'You do not ask me what brought me this way, or what is my business.'

'Were you to stay twenty years I would not ask. I'm not surprised that a prince of your blood and in full youthful beauty should travel the world to see what is in it.'

'It was not to see the world that I came,' said Saudan Og, 'but hearing that you have a beautiful daughter, I wished her for wife; and if I do not get her with your consent, I will take her in spite of you.'

'You would get my daughter with a hundred thousand welcomes,' said the king; 'but as you have boasted, you must show action.'

The king then sent a messenger to three kings – to Ri Fohin, Ri Laian, and Conal Gulban – to help him. 'If you will not come,' said he, 'I am destroyed, for Saudan Og will take my daughter in spite of me.'

The kings made ready to sail for Spain. When Conal Gulban was going, he called up his three sons and said, 'Stay here and care for the kingdom while I am gone.'

'I will not stay,' said the eldest son. 'You are old and feeble: I am young and strong; let me go in place of you.'

The second son gave a like answer. The youngest had his father's name, Conal, and the king said to him, 'Stay here at home and care for the kingdom while I am gone, since your brothers will not obey me.'

'I will do what you bid me,' said Conal.

'Now I am going,' said the old king; 'and if I and your brothers never return, be not bribed by the rich to injure the poor. Do justice to all, so that rich and poor may love you as they loved your father before you.'

He left young Conal twelve advisers, and said, 'If we do not return in a day and a year, be sure that we are killed; you may then do as you like in the kingdom. If your twelve advisers tell you to marry a king's daughter of wealth and high rank, it will be of help to you in defending the kingdom. You will be two powers instead of one.'

The day and the year passed, and no tidings came of Conal's two brothers and father. At the end of the day and the year, the twelve told him they had chosen a king's daughter for him, a very beautiful maiden. When the twelve spoke of marriage, Conal let three screeches out of him, that drove stones from the walls of old buildings for miles around the castle.

Now an old druid that his father had twenty years before heard the three screeches, and said, 'Young Conal is in great trouble. I will go to him to know can I help him.'

The druid cleared a mountain at a leap, a valley at a hop, twelve miles at a running leap, so that he passed hills, dales, and valleys; and in the evening of the same day, he struck his back against the kitchen door of Conal's castle just as the sun was setting.

When the druid came to the castle, young Conal was out in the garden thinking to himself, 'My father and brothers are in Spain; perhaps they are killed.' The dew was beginning to fall, so he turned to go, and saw the old man at the door. The druid was the first to speak; but not knowing Conal, he said –

'Who are you coming here to trouble the child? It would be fitter for you to stay in your own place than to be trying to wake young Conal with your screeches.'

'Are you,' asked Conal, 'the druid that my father had here years ago?'

'I am that old druid; but are you little Conal?'

'I am,' said Conal, and he gave the druid a hundred thousand welcomes.

'I was in the north of Erin,' said the druid, 'when I heard the three screeches, and I knew that some one was troubling you, and your father in a foreign land. My heart was grieved, and I came hither in haste. I hear that your twelve advisers have chosen a princess, and that you are to marry tomorrow. Put out of your head the thought of that princess; she is not your equal in rank or power. Be advised by me, as your father was. The right wife for you is the daughter of the Yellow King, Haughty and Strong. If the king will not give her, take her by force, as your fathers before you took their queens.'

Conal was roused on the following morning by his advisers, who said, 'Make ready and go with us to the king's daughter we have chosen.'

He mounted his steed, and rode away with the twelve till they came to a cross-road. The twelve wished to turn to one side; and when Conal saw this, he put spurs to his horse, took the straight road, and never stopped till he put seven miles between himself and the twelve. Then he turned, hurried back to the cross-road, came up to the adviser whom he liked best, and, giving him the keys of the castle, said –

'Go back and rule till I or my father or brothers return. I give you the advice that I myself got: Never let the poor blame you for taking bribes from the rich; live justly, and do good to the poor, that the rich and the poor may like you. If you twelve had not advised me to marry, I might be going around with a ball and a hurley, as befits my age; but now I will go out in the world and seek my own fortune.'

He took farewell of them then, and set his face toward the Yellow King's castle. A long time before it was prophesied that young Conal, son of Gulban, would cut the head off the Yellow King, so seven great walls had been built around the castle, and a gate to each wall. At the first gate, there were seven hundred blind men to obstruct the entrance; at the second, seven hundred deaf men; at the third, seven hundred cripples; at the fourth, seven hundred sensible women; at the fifth, seven hundred idiots; at the sixth, seven hundred people of small account; at the seventh, the seven hundred best champions that the Yellow King had in his service.

All these walls and defenders were there to prevent any man from taking the Yellow King's daughter; for it had been predicted that the man who would marry the daughter would take the king's head, and that this man would be Conal, son of Conal Gulban.

The only sleep that the guards at the seven gates had was half an hour before sunrise and half an hour after sunset. During these two half hours, a plover stood on the top of each gate; and if any one came, the bird would scream, and wake all the people in one instant.

The Yellow King's daughter was in the highest storey of the castle, and twelve waiting-maids serving her. She was so closely confined that she looked on herself as a prisoner; so one morning early she said to the twelve maids, 'I am confined here as a criminal – I am never free even to walk in the garden; and I wish in my heart that some powerful young king's son would come the way to me. I would fly off with him, and no blood would be shed for me.'

It was about this time that young Conal came, and, seeing all asleep, put spurs to his steed, and cleared the walls at a bound. If the birds called out, he had the gates cleared and was in before the champions were roused; and when he was inside, they did not attack him.

He let his horse out to graze near the castle, where he saw three poles, and on each one of two of them a skull.

'These are the heads of two kings' sons who came to win the Yellow King's daughter,' thought Conal, 'and I suppose mine will be the third head; but if I die, I shall have company.'

At this time the twelve waiting-maids cast lots to know who was to walk in the yard, and see if a champion had come who was worthy of the princess. The maid on whom the lot fell came back in a hurry, saying, 'I have seen the finest man that I ever laid eyes on. He is beautiful, but slender and young yet. If there is a man born for you, it is that one.'

'Go again,' said the Yellow King's daughter, 'and face him. Do not speak to him for your life till he speaks to you; say then that I sent you, and that he is to come under my window.'

The maid went and crossed Conal's path three times, but he spoke not; she crossed a fourth time, and he said, 'I suppose it is not for good that you cross my path so early?'

(It is thought unlucky to meet a woman first in the morning.)

'My mistress wishes you to go under her window.'

Conal went under the window; and the king's daughter, looking down, fell deeply in love with him. 'I am too high, and you are too low,' said the Yellow King's daughter. 'If we speak, people will hear us all over the castle; but I'll take some golden cord, and try can I draw you up to me, that we may speak a few words to each other.'

'It would be a poor case for me,' said young Conal, 'to wait till you could tie strings together to raise me.' He stuck his sword in the earth then, and, making one bound, went in at the window. The princess embraced him and kissed him; she knew not what to give him to eat or to drink, or what would please him most.

'Have you seen the people at the seven gates?' asked the Yellow King's daughter.

'I have,' answered Conal.

'They are all awake now, and I will go down and walk through the gates with you; seeing me, the guards will not stop us.'

'I will not do that. It will never be said of young Conal of Erin that he stole his wife from her father. I will win you with strength, or not have you.'

'I'm afraid there is too much against you,' said the Yellow King's daughter.

These words enraged Conal, and, making one bound through the window, he went to the pole of combat, and struck a blow that roused the old hag in the Eastern World, and shook the castle with all the land around it. The Yellow King was sleeping at the time; the shake that he got threw him out of his bed. He fell to the floor with such force that a great lump came out on his forehead; he was so frightened that he said to the old druid who ran in to help him, 'Many a year have I lived without hearing the like of that blow. There must be a great champion outside the castle.'

The guard was sent to see if any one was left alive near the castle.

'For,' said the king, 'such a champion must have killed all the people at the gates.' The guard went, saw no one dead, but every one living, and a champion walking around, sword in hand.

The guard hurried back, and said to the king, 'There is a champion in front of the castle, handsome, but slender and young.'

'Go to him,' said the king, 'and ask how many men does he want for the combat.' The guard went out and asked.

'I want seven hundred at my right hand, seven hundred at my left, seven hundred behind me, and as many as all these out in front of me. Let them come four deep through the gates: do you take no part in this battle; if I am victorious, I will see you rewarded.'

The guard told the king how many men the champion demanded. Before the king opened the gates for his men, he said to the chief of them, 'This youth must be mad, or a very great champion. Before I let my men out, I must see him.'

The king walked out to young Conal, and saluted him. Conal returned the salute. 'Are you the champion who ordered out all these men of mine?' asked the king.

'I am,' said young Conal.

'There is not one among them who would not kill a dozen like you,' said the king. 'Your bones are soft and young. It is better for you to go out as you came in.'

'You need not mind what will happen to me,' answered Conal. 'Let out the men; the more the men, the quicker the work. If one man would kill me in a short time, many will do it in less time.'

The men were let out, and Conal went through them as a hawk goes through a flock of birds; and when one man fell before him, he knocked the next man, and had his head off. At sunset every head was cut from its body. Next he made a heap of the bodies, a heap of the heads, and a heap of the weapons. Young Conal then stretched himself on the grass, cut and bruised, his clothes in small pieces from the blows that had struck him.

'It is a hard thing,' said Conal, 'for me to have fought such a battle, and to lie here dying without one glimpse of the woman I love; could I see her even once, I would be satisfied.'

Crawling on his hands and knees, he dragged himself to the window to tell her it was for her he was dying. The princess saw him, and told him to lie there till she could draw him up to her and care for him.

'It is a hard thing if I have to wait here till strings and cords are fastened together to raise me,' said he, and, making one bound from where he was lying on the flat of his back, he went up to her window; she snatched at him, and pulled him into the chamber.

There was a magic well in the castle; the Yellow King's daughter bathed him in the water of it, and he was made whole and sound as before he went to battle. 'Now,' said she, 'you must fly with me from this castle.'

'I will not go while there is anything that may be cast on my honour in time to come,' answered Conal.

Next day he struck the pole of combat with double the force of the first time, so that the king got a staggering fit from the shock that it gave him.

The Yellow King had no forces now but the deaf, the blind, the cripples, the sensible women, the idiots, and the people of small account. So out went the king in his own person. He and young Conal made the hills, dales, and valleys tremble, and clear spring wells to rise out of hard, gravelly places. Thus they fought for three days and two nights. On the evening of the third day, the king asked Conal for a time to rest and take food and drink.

'I have never begun any work,' said Conal, 'without finishing it. Fight to the end, then you can rest as long as you like.'

So they went at it again, and fought seven days and seven nights without food, drink, or rest, and each trying to get the advantage of the other. On the seventh evening, Conal swept the head off the king with one blow.

"'Tis your own skull that will be on the pole in place of mine, and I'll have the daughter,' said Conal.

The Yellow King's daughter came down and asked, 'Will you go with me now, or will you take the kingdom?'

'I will go,' answered Conal.

'You did not go to the battle?' asked Conal of the guard.

'I did not.'

'Well for you that you did not. Now,' said Conal to the princess, 'whomever of the maids you like best, the guard may marry, and they will care for this kingdom till we return.'

The guard and maid were married, and put in charge of the kingdom. The following morning young Conal got his steed ready and set out for home with the princess. As they were riding along near the foot of a mountain, Conal grew very sleepy, and said to the princess, 'I'll go down now and take a sleep.'

The place was lonely – hardly two houses in twenty miles. The Yellow King's daughter advised Conal: 'Take me to some habitation and sleep there; this place is too wild.'

'I cannot wait – I'm too drowsy and weary after the long battle; but if I might sleep a little, I could fight for seven days and seven nights again.' He dismounted, and she sat on a green mossy bank. Putting his head on her lap, he fell asleep, and his steed went away on the mountain side grazing.

Conal had slept for three days and two nights with his head in the lap of the Yellow King's daughter, when on the evening of the third day the princess saw the largest man she had ever set eyes on, walking toward her through the sea and a basket on his back. The sea did not reach to his knees; a shield could not pass between his head and the sky. This was the High King of the World. This big man faced up to where Conal and his bride were; and, taking the tips of her fingers, he kissed her three times. 'Bad luck to me,' said the King of the World, 'if the young woman I am going for were beyond the ditch there I would not go to her. You are fairer and better than she.'

'Where were you going?' asked the princess. 'Don't mind me, but go on.'

'I was going for the Yellow King's daughter, but will not go a step further now that I see you.'

'Go your way to her, for she is the finest princess on earth; I am a simple woman, and another man's wife.'

'Well, pain and torments to me if I go beyond this without taking you with me!'

'If this man here were awake,' said the Yellow King's daughter, 'he would put a stop to you.' She was trying all this time to rouse Conal.

'It is better for him to be as he is,' said the High King; 'if he were awake, it's harm he'd get from me, and that would vex you.'

When she saw that he would take her surely, she bound him not to make her his wife for a day and a year.

'This is the worst promise that ever I have made,' said the High King, 'but I will keep it.'

'If this man here were awake, he would stop you,' said the princess.

The High King of the World thrust the tip of his forefinger under the sword-belt of Conal, and hurled him up five miles in the air. When Conal came down, he let out three waves of blood from his mouth.

'Do you think that is enough?' asked the king of the princess.

'Throw him a second time,' said the Yellow King's daughter.

He threw him still higher, and Conal put out three greater waves. 'Is that enough?'

'Try him a third time.' He threw him still higher this time. Conal put out three greater waves, but waked not.

While the High King was throwing up Conal, the princess was writing a letter telling all – that she knew not whither she was going, that she had bound the High King of the World not to make her his wife for a day and a year, 'and,' said she, 'I'm sure that you will find me in that time.'

The king took her in his arms, and away he went walking in the sea, throwing fish into his basket as he travelled through the water.

Conal slept a hero's sleep of seven days and nights, and woke four days after his bride had been stolen. He rubbed his eyes, and, glancing toward the mountain side, saw neither steed nor wife, and said, 'No wonder that I cannot see wife nor horse when I'm so sleepy; what am I to do?'

Not far away were some small boys, and they herding cows. The boys began to make sport of Conal for sleeping seven days and nights. 'I do not blame you for laughing,' said Conal (ever since, when there is a great sleeper, people say that he sleeps like Conal on the side of Beann Edain), 'but have you tidings of my wife and my steed; where are they, or has any man taken them?'

A boy older and wiser than the others said, 'Your horse is on the mountain side feeding; and every day he came hither and sniffed you, and you sleeping, and then went away grazing for himself. Four days ago the greatest giant ever seen by the eye of man walked in through the ocean; he tossed you three times in the air. Every time we thought you'd be broken to dust; and the lady you had, wrote something and put it under your belt.'

Conal read the letter, and knew that, in spite of her, the Yellow King's daughter had been carried away. He then preferred battle to peace, and asked the boys was there a ship that could take him to sea.

'There is no right ship in the place, but there is an old vessel wrecked in a cove there beyond,' said the oldest boy.

The boys went with Conal, and showed him the vessel.

'Put your backs to her now, and help me,' said Conal.

The boys laughed, thinking that two hundred men could not move such a vessel. Conal scowled, and then they were in dread of him, and with one shove they and Conal put the ship in the sea; but the water was going in and out through her. Conal knew not at first what to do, as there was no timber near by, but he killed seven cows, fastened the hides on the ship, and made it proof against water. When the boys saw the cows slaughtered, they began to cry, saying, 'How can we go home now, and our cows killed?'

'There is not a cow killed,' said Conal, 'but you will get two cows in place of her.' He gave two prices for each cow of the seven, and said to the boys, 'Go home now, and tell what has happened.'

Conal sailed away for himself; and when his ship was in the ocean, he let her go with the wind. On the third afternoon, he saw three islands, and on the middle island a fine open strand, with a great crowd of people. He threw out three anchors, two at the ocean side and one at the shore side, so that the ship would not stir, no matter what wind blew, and, planting his sword in the deck, he gave one bound and went out on the strand seven miles distant. He saluted a good-looking man, and asked, 'Why are so many people here? What is their business?'

'Where do you live? Of what nation are you that you ask such a question?'

'I am a stranger,' said Conal, 'just come to this island.'

The islander showed Conal a man sitting on the beach as large as twelve of the big men of the island. 'Do you see him?'

'I do,' said Conal.

'There are three brothers of us on these three islands; that man is our youngest brother, and he has grown so strong and terrible that we are in dread he will drive us from our share of the islands, and that is why we are here to-day. My eldest brother and I have come with what men we have to this middle island, which belongs to our youngest brother. We are to play ball against all his forces; if we beat them, we shall think ourselves safe. Now, which side will you take, young champion?'

'If I go on your side, some may say that I fear your men; and if I go with your younger brother, you and your elder brother may say that I fear your strong brother's forces. Bring all the men of the three islands. I will play against them.'

'Well,' asked the stranger, 'what wager will you lay?'

'I'll wager,' said Conal, 'those two islands out there on the ocean side.'

'They are ours already,' said the man.

'Bad luck to you! Why claim everything?' said Conal. 'Well, I'll lay another wager. If I lose, I'll stand in the middle of the strand, and every man of the three islands may give me a blow of the hurley; and if I win, I am to have a blow on every man who played against me. But first, I must have my choice of the hurleys; all must be thrown in a heap. I will take the one I like best.'

This was done, and Conal took the largest and strongest hurley he could find. The ball was struck about the middle of the strand; and there was a goal at each end of it, and these goals were fourteen miles apart. Conal took the ball with hurley, hand and foot, and never let it touch ground till he put it through the goal. 'Is that a fair inning?' asked he of the other side.

Some said it was foul, for he kept the ball in the air all the time.

'Well, I'll make a second trial; I will put it through the opposite goal.' He struck the ball in the middle of the strand, and sent it toward the other goal with such force that whoever tipped it never drew breath again, and every man whom it passed was driven sixty feet to one side or the other. Conal was always within a few yards of the ball, and he put it through the goal seven miles distant from the middle of the strand with two blows.

'Is that a fair inning?' asked Conal.

'It would be hard to say that it is not,' said one man, and no man gainsaid him.

'Let all stand now in ranks two deep, till I get my blow on each man of you.'

All the men were arranged two deep; and when Conal came up, the foremost man sprang behind the one in the rear of him, and that one behind the man at his side, and so on throughout. None would stand to receive Conal's blow.

Away rushed every man, woman, and child, and never stopped till they were inside in their houses. First of all, ran the brothers of the islands.

When they reached the castle, they began to lament because they had insulted the champion, and knew not who he was or whence he had come.

The three brothers had one sister; and when she saw them lamenting and grieving, she asked: 'What trouble is on you?'

'We fled from the champion, and the people followed us.'

'None of you invited the champion to the castle,' said the sister; 'now he will fall into such a rage on the strand that in one hour he will not leave a person alive on the islands. If I had some one to go with me, I would invite him, and the people would be spared.'

'I will go with you,' said her chief maid.

Away they went, walking toward the strand; and when they had come near, they threw themselves on their knees before Conal. He asked who they were and what brought them.

'My brothers sent me to beg pardon for them, and invite you to the castle.'

'I will go,' said Conal; 'and if you had not come, I would not have left a man alive on the three islands.' Conal went with the princess, and saw at the castle a very old and large man; and the old man rose up before him and said, 'A hundred thousand welcomes to you, young Conal from Erin.'

'Who are you who know me, and I never before on this island?' asked Conal.

'My name is Donach the Druid, from Erin. I was often in your father's house, and it was a good place for rich or poor to visit, for they were alike there; and now I hope you will take me home to be buried among my own people. It was God who drove you hither to this island to take me home.'

'And I will do that,' said Conal, 'if I go there myself. Tell me now how you came to this place.'

'I was taken,' said Donach, 'out on the wild arm of the wind, and was thrown in on this island. I am here ever since. I am old now, and I wish to be home in my own place in Erin.'

Now young Conal, the sister, and three brothers sat down to dinner. When dinner was over, and they had eaten and drunk, they were as happy as if they had lived a thousand years together. The three brothers asked Conal where was he going, and what was his business. Conal did not say that he was in search of his wife, but he said that he was going to his own castle and kingdom. The old druid, two of the brothers, and the sister said, 'We will go with you, and serve you till you come to your kingdom.'

They got a boat and took him to the ship. He weighed anchor, and sailed away. For two or three days they saw nothing wonderful. The fourth day they came to a great island; and as they neared it, they saw three champions inside, and the three fighting with swords and spears. Young Conal was surprised to see three fighting at the same time.

'Well,' said he, 'it is nothing to see two champions in combat, but 'tis strange to see three. I will go in and see why they are fighting.' He threw out his chains, and made his ship fast; then he made a rush from the stern of the vessel to the bow, and as he ran, he caught Donach the Druid and carried him, and with one leap was in on the strand, seven miles from the ship.

Young Conal faced the champions, and, saluting the one he thought best, asked the cause of their battle. The champion sat down, and began. 'I will tell you the reason,' said he. 'Seven miles from this place there stands a castle; in that castle is the most beautiful woman that the eye of man has ever seen, and the three of us are in love with her. She says she will take only the best man; and we are striving to know who is best, but no man of us three can get the upper hand of another. We can kill every man who comes to the island, but no man of us can kill another of the three.'

When Conal heard this he sprang up, and told the champions to face

him and he would see what they could do. The three faced him, and
went at him. Soon he swept the heads off two of them, but the third man
was pressing hard on Conal. His name was the Short Dun Champion;
but in the end Conal knocked him with a blow, and no sooner had he
knocked him than Donach the Druid had him tied with strong cords
and strings of enchantment. Then young Conal spoke to Donach the
Druid and said, 'Come to this champion's breastbone and split it, take
out his heart and his liver, and give them to my young hound to eat';
and turning to the Short Dun Champion, he asked, 'Have you ever been
so near a fearful death as you are at this moment?'

''Tis hard for me to answer you,' said he, 'for 'tis firmly I am bound
by your Druid, bad luck to him.'

'Unbind the champion,' said Conal, 'till he tells us at his ease was
he ever nearer a fearful death than he is at this moment.'

'I was,' said the champion to Conal. 'Sit down there on that stool.
I will sit here and tell you. I did not think much of your torture, for I
knew that when my heart and liver were taken, I should be gone in that
moment. Once I had a longer torture to suffer. Not many months ago,
I was sailing on my ship in mid-ocean when I saw the biggest man
ever seen on earth, and he with a beautiful woman in his hand. The
moment I saw that woman I was in love with her, and I sailed toward
the High King of the World, for it was he that was in it; but if I did, he
let my ship go out in full sail between his two legs, and travelled on in
another direction. I turned the ship again, and went after him. I climbed
to the topmast, and stood there. I came up to the King of the World,
for wind and wave were with me, and, being almost as high as the
woman in his hand, I made a grasp at her; he let my ship out between
his legs, but if he did, I took the woman with me and kissed her three
times. This enraged the High King. He came to my ship, bound and
tied me with strong hempen cords, then, putting a finger under me,
he tossed me out on the sea and let my ship drift with the wind. I had
some enchantment of my own, and the sea did not drown me. When

little fish came my way, I swallowed them, and thus I got food. I was in this state for many days, and the hempen cords began to rot and weaken. Through good luck or ill, I was thrown in on this island. I pulled the cords, and struggled with them till one hand was free; then I unbound myself. I came to shore where the island is wildest. A bird called Nails of Daring had a nest in a high, rugged cliff. This bird came down, and, seizing me, rose in the air. Then she dropped me. I fell like a ball, and struck the sea close to land. I feigned death well, and was up and down with the waves that she might not seize me a second time, but soon she swooped down and placed her ear near me to know was I living. I held my breath, and she, thinking me dead, flew away. I rose up, and ran with all speed to the first house I found. Now, was I not nearer a worse death than the one to which you condemned me? Nails of Daring would have given me a frightful and slow death, and you wished to give me a quick one.'

'Short Dun Champion,' said Conal, 'the woman you saw with the High King was my wife. It was luck that brought me in your way, and it was luck that Donach the Druid tied you in such a fashion. Now you must guide me to the castle of the High King.'

'Come, now, druid, bind my hands and feet, take my heart and liver and give them to young Conal's hound whelp, rather than take me to that king. I got dread enough before from him.'

'Believe me, all I want of you now is to guide my ship; you will come back in safety and health,' said young Conal.

'I will go with you and guide you, if you put me beneath your ship's ballast when you see him nearing us, for fear he will get a glimpse of me.'

'I will do that,' said Conal.

Now they went out to the ship, and steered away, with the Short Dun Champion as pilot. They were the fifth day at sea when he steered the ship toward the castle of the High King. 'That,' said the Short Dun Champion, pointing to a great building on an island, 'is the castle of the High King of the World; but as good a champion as you are, you cannot free your wife from it. That castle revolves; and as it goes around it throws out poison, and if one drop of that poison were to fall on you the flesh would melt from your bones. But the King of the World is not at home now, for tomorrow the day and the year will be up since he stole the wife from you. I have some power of enchantment and I will bring the woman to you in the ship.'

The Short Dun Champion went with one leap from the deck of the ship to the strand, and, caring for no man, walked straight to the castle where the Yellow King's daughter was held. The castle had an opening underneath, and the Short Dun Champion, keeping the poison away by his power, passed in, found the princess, and wrapping her in the skirt of an enchanted cloak that he had, took her out, and running to the strand was in on the deck of the ship with one bound.

The moment the princess set eyes on Conal, she gave such a scream that the High King heard her, and he off in the Western World inviting all the great people to his wedding. He started that minute for the castle, and did not wait to throw fish in his basket as he went through the sea. When he came home, the princess was not there before him. 'Where has my bride gone, or has some one stolen her?' asked he.

'A man who has a ship in the harbour came and stole the lady.'

'A thousand deaths! What shall I do, and all the high people on the way to the wedding?'

He seized a great club and killed half his servants, then rushed to the strand, and seeing the ship still at anchor, shouted for battle.

When the Short Dun Champion heard the king's voice, he screamed to be put under the ballast. He was put there and hidden from sight. 'If I whistle with my fingers,' asked young Conal, 'will you come to me?'

'I will, if I were to die the next moment,' said the Short Dun Champion.

Conal told Donach the Druid to stand at the bows of the ship, then, walking to the stern, he was so glad at having his wife on the vessel, and he going to fight with the High King, that he made a run, seized the druid, and carried him with one leap to the strand, eleven miles distant.

The High King demanded his wife.

'She is not your wife, but mine,' said young Conal. 'I won her with my sword, and you stole her away like a thief, and I sleeping. Though she is mine, I did not flee when I took her away from you.'

'It is time for battle,' said the king, and the two closed in combat. The king, being so tall, had the advantage. 'I might as well make him shorter,' thought Conal, and with one blow he cut the two legs off the king at the knee joints. The king fell. No sooner was he down than the druid had him tied with hard cords of enchantment. Conal whistled through his finger. The Short Dun Champion, hearing the whistle, screamed to be freed from the ballast. The men took him out. He went in on the strand with one bound, and when he came up to where the High King was lying, Conal said, 'Cut this man at the breastbone, take out his heart with his liver, and give them as food to my hound whelp.'

'He is well bound by your druid; but firmly as he is bound, I am in dread to go near him to do this.'

Conal then drew his own sword, and with a blow swept the head off the High King. Then Conal, Donach the Druid, and the Short Dun Champion went to the ship and sailed homeward. On their way, where should they sail but along the coast of Spain? While they were sailing, Conal espied three great castles, and not far from them a herd of cattle grazing.

'Will one of you go and enquire why these three castles are built near together?' asked Conal of the two island brothers.

'I will go,' said the elder.

He went on shore to the herdsman and asked, 'Why are those three castles so near one another?'

'I will tell you,' said the herdsman; 'but you must come first and touch my finger tips.'

No sooner had the champion done this, than the man drew a rod of enchantment, struck him a blow, and turned him to stone.

Conal saw this from the ship, and asked, 'Who will go in now?'

'I will go,' said the second brother. 'I have the best right.' He went and met the same fate as his brother.

'I will go this time,' said Conal.

The Yellow King's daughter, Donach the Druid, and the Short Dun Champion seized Conal to keep him from going.

'If I do not live but a moment, I must go and knock satisfaction out of the herdsman for what he has done to my men,' cried out Conal. So he went, and walking up to the herdsman, asked the same questions as the two brothers.

'Come here and touch my finger tips.'

Conal walked up to the herdsman, caught his fingers, then ran under the rod and seized the herdsman; but if he did, the herdsman had him that moment on the flat of his back. But Conal was up, and had the herdsman down, and, drawing his sword, said, 'I'll have your head now unless you tell me why these three castles are here close together.'

'I will tell you, but do you remember, young Conal, when in our father's castle how I used to get the first blow on you?'

'Are you my brother?' asked Conal.

'I am,' said the herdsman.

'Why did you kill my men?'

'If I killed them, I can raise them'; and going to the two brothers, he struck each a blow, and they rose up as well and strong as ever.

'Well,' said the brother to Conal, 'Saudan Og arrived in Spain the day before we did, and he had one-third of the kingdom taken before us. We went against him the following day, and kept him inside that third, and we have neither gained nor lost since. The King of Spain had a castle here; my father and the King of Leinster built a second castle near that; Saudan Og built the third near the two, for himself and his men, and that is why the three castles are here. We are ever since in battle; Saudan has the one-third, and we the rest of Spain.'

Conal arrayed himself as a champion next morning, and went to Saudan's castle. He struck a blow on the pole of combat that shook the whole kingdom, and that day he killed Saudan and every man of his forces.

Conal's eldest brother married the daughter of the King of Spain. He took the second brother with him, married him to the sister of the two island brothers, and gave him the three islands. He went home then, gave the kingdom of the Yellow King to the Short Dun Champion, and had the two island brothers well married to king's daughters in Erin. All lived happily and well; if they did not, may we!

THE BLACK THIEF AND KING CONAL'S THREE HORSES

There was a king once in Erin who had a beautiful queen, and the queen's heart was as good as her looks. Every one loved her, but, above all, the poor people. There wasn't a needy man or woman within a day's journey of the castle who was not blessing the beautiful queen. On a time this queen fell ill suddenly, and said to the king, 'If I die and you marry a second wife, leave not my three sons to a strange woman's rule. Send them away to be reared till they come to age and maturity.'

The queen died soon after. The king mourned for her one year and a second; then his chief men and counsellors urged him to seek out a new queen.

The king built a castle in a distant part of his kingdom, and put his three sons there with teachers and servants to care for them. He married a second wife then; and the two lived on happily till the new wife had a son. The young queen never knew that the king had other children than her son, or that there was a queen in the kingdom before her.

On a day when the king was out hunting in the mountains, the queen went to walk near the castle, and as she was passing the cottage of a greedy old henwife, she stumbled and fell.

'May the like of that meet you always!' said the henwife.

'Why do you say that?' asked the queen, who overheard her.

'It is all one to you what I say. It is little you care for me or the like of me. It wasn't the same with the queen that was here before you. There wasn't a week that she did not give support to poor people, and she showed kindness to every one always.'

'Had the king a wife before me?' asked the queen.

'He had, indeed; and I could tell enough to keep you thinking for a day and a year, if you would pay me.'

'I will pay you well if you tell all about the queen that was in it before me.'

'If you give me one hundred speckled goats, one hundred sheep, and one hundred cows I will tell you.'

'I will give you all those,' said the queen, 'if you tell everything.'

'The queen that was here at first had three sons; and before the king married you, he prepared a great castle, and the sons are in that castle now with teachers and men taking care of them. When the three are of age, your son will be without a place for his head.'

'What am I to do to keep my son in the kingdom?' asked the queen.

'Persuade the king to bring his three sons to the castle, then play chess with them. I will give you a board with which you can win. When you have won of the three young men, put them under bonds to go for the three steeds of King Conal for you to ride three times around all the boundaries of the kingdom. Many and many is the champion and hero who went for King Conal's horses; but not a man of them was seen again, and so it will be with these three. Your son will be safe at home, and will be king himself when his time comes.'

The queen went home to the castle, and if ever she had a head full of plans it was that time. She began the same night with the king.

'Isn't it a shame for you to keep your children away from me, and I waiting this long time for you to bring them home to us?'

'How am I keeping my children from you?' asked the king. 'Haven't you your own son and mine with you always?'

'You have three sons of your own. You were married before you saw me. Bring your children home. I will be as fond of them as you are.'

No matter what the king said, the queen kept up her complaining with sweet words and promises, and never stopped till the king brought his sons to the castle.

The king gave a great feast in honour of the young men. After the feast the queen played chess for a sentence with the eldest. She played twice; won a game and lost one. Next day she played one game with the second son. On the third day, she played with the youngest; won one game and lost one.

On the fourth day, the three were in the queen's company.

'What sentence do you put on me and my brothers?' asked the eldest.

'I put you and your brothers under sentence not to sleep two nights in the same house, nor to eat twice off the same table, till you bring me the three steeds of King Conal, so that I may ride three times around the kingdom.'

'Will you tell me,' asked the eldest son, 'where to find King Conal?'

'There are four quarters in the world; I am sure it is in one of these that he lives,' said the queen.

'I might as well give you sentence now,' said the eldest brother. 'I put you under bonds of enchantment to stand on the top of the castle and stay there without coming down, and watch for us till we come back with the horses.'

'Remove from me your sentence; I will remove mine,' said the queen.

'If a young man is relieved of the first sentence put on him, he will never do anything good,' said the king's son. 'We will go for the horses.'

Next day the three brothers set out for the castle of King Conal. They travelled one day after another, stopping one night in one place and the next in another, and they were that way walking till one evening, when whom should they meet but a limping man in a black cap. The man saluted them, and they returned the salute.

'What brought you this road, and where are you going?' asked the stranger.

'We are going to the castle of King Conal to know can we bring his three horses home with us.'

'Well,' said the man, 'my house is nearby, and the dark night is coming; stay with me till morning, and perhaps I can help you.'

The young men went with the stranger, and soon came to his house. After supper the man said, 'It is the most difficult feat in the world to steal King Conal's three horses. Many a good man went for them, and never came back. Why do you go for those horses?'

'Our father is a king in Erin, and he married a second time. Our stepmother bound us to bring the three horses, so she may ride three times around our father's kingdom.'

'I will go with you,' said the man. 'Without me, you would lose your lives; together, we may bring the horses.'

Next morning the four set out, and went their way, walking one day after another, till at long last they reached the castle of King Conal at nightfall.

On that night, whatever the reason was, the guards fell asleep at the stables. The stranger and the three young men made their way to the horses; but if they did, the moment they touched them the horses let three screeches out of them that shook the whole castle and woke every man in the country around it.

The guards seized the young men with the stranger, and took the four to King Conal.

The king was in a great room on the ground-floor of his castle. In front of him was an awfully big pot full of oil, and it boiling.

'Well,' said the king when he saw the stranger before him, 'only that the Black Thief is dead, I'd say you were that man.'

'I am the Black Thief,' said the stranger.

'We will know that in time,' said the king; 'and who are these three young men?'

'Three sons of a king in Erin.'

'We'll begin with the youngest. But stir up the fire there, one of you,' said King Conal to the attendants; 'the oil is not hot enough.' And turning to the Black Thief, he asked, 'Isn't that young man very near his death at this moment?'

'I was nearer death than he is, and I escaped,' said the Black Thief.

'Tell me the story,' said the king. 'If you were nearer death than he is, I will give his life to that young man.'

'When I was young,' said the Black Thief, 'I lived on my land with ease and plenty, till three witches came the way, and destroyed all my property. I took to the roads and deep forests then, and became the most famous thief that ever lived in Erin. This is the story of the witches who robbed and tried to kill me: –

'There was a king not long ago in Erin, and he had three beautiful daughters. When they grew up to be old enough for marriage, they were enchanted in the way that the three became brazen-faced, old-looking, venomous hags every night, and were three beautiful, harmless young women every day, as before.

'I was living for myself on my land, and had laid in turf enough for seven years, and I thought it the size of a mountain. I went out at midnight, and what did I see but the hags at my reek; and they never stopped till they put every sod of the turf into three creels on their backs, and made off with it.

'The following season I brought turf for another seven years, and the next midnight the witches stole it all from me; but this time I followed them. They went about five miles, and disappeared in a broad hole twenty fathoms deep. I waited, then looked down, and saw a great fire under a pot with a whole bullock in it. There was a round stone at the mouth of the hole. I used all my strength, rolled it down, broke the pot, and spoiled the broth on the witches.

'Away I ran then, but was not long on the road when I saw the three racing after me. I climbed a tree to escape from them. The witches came in a rage, stopped under the tree, and looked up at me. The eldest rested a while, then made a sharp axe of the second, and a venomous hound of the third, to destroy me. She took the axe herself then, gave one blow of it, and cut one-third of the tree; she gave a second blow, and cut another third; she had the axe raised a third time when a cock crowed, and there before my eyes the axe turned into a beautiful woman, the hag who had raised it into a second, and the venomous hound into a third. The three walked away then, harmless and innocent as any young women in Erin. Wasn't I nearer death that time than this young man?'

'Oh, you were,' said the king; 'I give him his life, and it's his brother that's near death now. He has but ten minutes to live.'

'Well, I was nearer death than that young man,' said the Black Thief.

'Tell how it was. If you convince me, I'll give him his life, too.'

'After I broke their pot, the witches destroyed my property night after night, and I had to leave that place and find my support on the roads and in forests. I was faring well enough till a year of hunger and want came. I went out once into a great wood, walked up and down to know could I find any food to take home to my wife and my children.

'I found an old white horse and a cow without horns. I tied the tails of the two to each other, and was driving them home for myself with great labour; for when the white horse pulled backward, the cow would pull forward, and when the horse tried to go on, the cow wouldn't go with him. They were that way in disagreement till they drew the night on themselves and on me. I had a bit of flint in my pocket, and put down a fire. I could not make my way out of the wood in the night-time, and sat down by the fire. I was not long sitting when thirteen cats, wild and enormous, stood out before me. Of these, twelve were each the bulk of a man; the thirteenth, a red one, the master of the twelve, was much larger. They began to purr on the opposite side of the fire, and make a noise like the rumbling of thunder. At last the big red cat lifted his head, opened his wide eyes, and said to me, "I'll be this way no longer; give me something to eat."'

'I have nothing to give you,' said I, 'unless you take that white horse below there and kill him.'

'He went down then, and made two halves of the horse, left half to the twelve, and ate the other half himself. They picked every bone, and were not long at it.

'The thirteen came up again, sat opposite me at the fire, and were purring. The big red cat soon spoke a second time, "I'll not be long this way. Give me more food to satisfy my hunger."

'"I have nothing to give unless you take the cow without horns," replied I.

'He made two halves of the cow, ate one-half himself, and left the other to the twelve. While they were eating the cow, I took off my coat, for I knew what was coming, wrapped it around a block which I made like myself, and then climbed a tree quickly. The red cat came up to the fire a third time, opened his great eyes, looked toward my coat, and said, "I'll not be long this way; give me more food."

'My coat gave no answer. The big cat sprang at it, struck the block with his tail, and found it was wood.

'"Ah," said he, "you are gone; but whether above ground or under ground, we will find you."

'He put six cats above and six under ground to find me. The twelve cats were gone in a breath. The big red cat sat there waiting; and when the other twelve had run through all Erin, above ground and under ground, and come back to the fire, he looked up, saw me, and cried, "Ah, there you are, you deceiver. You thought to escape, but you will not. Come, now," said he to the cats, "and gnaw down this tree."

'The twelve sprang at the tree under me, and they were not long cutting it through. Before it fell, I escaped to another tree near by, and they attacked that, gnawing it down. I sprang to a third. We were that way, I escaping and they cutting, till near daybreak, when I was on the last tree next the open country. When the tree was half cut, what should come the way but thirteen terrible wolves – twelve, and a thirteenth above them, their master. They fell upon the cats, and fought desperately a good while. At length the twelve on each side were stretched, but the two chiefs were fighting each other yet. At last the wolf nearly took the head off the cat with one snap; the cat whirled in falling, struck the wolf with the sharp hook in his tail, made two halves of his skull, and the two fell dead, side by side.

'I slipped down then, but the tree shook in the way that I was in dread it would tumble beneath me, but it didn't. Now, wasn't I nearer death that time than this young man?'

'Oh, you were,' said King Conal. 'He's not near death at all, for I give his life to him; but if the two have escaped, we'll put the third man in the pot; and have you ever seen any one nearer death than he is?'

'I was nearer myself,' said the Black Thief.

'If you were, I will give his life to this young man as well as his brothers.'

'I had apprentices in my time,' said the Black Thief. 'Among them was one, a young man of great wit, and he pleased me. I gave no real learning to any but this one; and in the heel of the story he was a greater man than myself – in his own mind. There was a giant in the other end of the kingdom; he lived in a mountain den, and had great wealth gathered in there. I made up my mind to go with the apprentice, and take that giant's treasures. We travelled many days till we reached the mountain den. We hid, and watched the ways of the giant. He went out every day, brought back many things, but often men's bodies. At last we went to the place in his absence. There was only one entrance, from the top. I was lowering the young man with a rope, but when half-way to the bottom he called out as if in pain. I drew him up. "I am in dread," said he, "to go down in that place. Go yourself. I will do the work here for you."

'I went down, found gold and precious things in plenty, and sent up what one man could carry. :I will go out of this now," thought I, "before the giant comes on me." I called to the apprentice; no answer. I called again; not a word from him. At last he looked down and said –

'"You gave me good learning, and I am grateful; I will gain my own living from this out. I hope you'll spend a pleasant night with the giant."

'With that, he made off with himself, and carried the treasure. Oh, but I was in trouble then! How was I to bring my life home with me?

How was I to escape from the giant? I looked, but found no way of escape. In one corner of the giant's kitchen were bodies brought in from time to time. I lay down with these, and seemed dead. I was watching. After a while I heard a great noise at the entrance, and soon the giant came in carrying three bodies; these he threw aside with the others. He put down a great fire then, and placed a pot on it: he brought a basket to the bodies, and began to fill it; me he threw in first, and put six bodies on the top of me. He turned the basket bottom upward over the pot, and six bodies fell in. I held firmly to my place. The giant put the basket aside in a corner bottom upward – I was saved that time. When the supper was ready, the giant ate the six bodies, and then lay down and slept soundly. I crept from under the basket, went to the entrance; a tree trunk, standing upright in the wall at one end of it, was turned around. There were steps in its side from bottom to top; this was the giant's ladder. Whenever the giant wished to go up, he turned the tree till the steps came outside; and when on top, he turned it till the smooth side was out in the way no one could go down in his absence. When he wished to go down, he turned the steps out; and when at the bottom, he turned them in again in the way no one could follow him. This time he forgot to turn the tree, and that gave me the ladder. I went up without trouble; and, by my hand, I was glad, for I was much nearer death at the giant's pot than this man at yours.'

'You were, indeed, very near death,' said King Conal, 'and I give his life to the third man. The turn is on you now; the three young men are safe, and it's you that will go into the pot.'

'Must I die?' asked the Black Thief.

'You must, indeed,' said King Conal, 'and you are very near death.'

'Near as I am,' said the Black Thief, 'I was nearer.'

'Tell me the story; and if you were ever nearer death than you are at this minute, I will give your life to you.'

'I set out another day,' said the Black Thief, 'and travelled far. I came at last to a house, and went into it. Inside was a woman with a child on her knee, a knife in her hand, and she crying. Twice she made an offer of the knife at the child to kill it. The beautiful child laughed, and held out its hands to her.

"'Why do you raise the knife on the child," asked I, "and why are you crying?"

"'I was at a fair,' said the woman, "last year with my father and mother; and while the people were busy each with his own work, three giants came in on a sudden. The man who had a bite of bread in his hand did not put the bread to his mouth, and the man who had a bite in his mouth did not swallow it. The giants robbed this one and that, took me from my father and mother, and brought me to this place. I bound them, and they promised that none of the three would marry me before I was eighteen years of age. I'll be that in a few days, and there is no escape for me now unless I raise hands on myself.

"'Yesterday the giants brought this child; they said it was the son of some king, and told me to have it cooked and prepared in a pie for their supper this evening."

"'Spare the child," said I. "I have a young pig that I brought to roast for myself on the road; take that, and prepare it instead of the child."

"'The giants would know the pig, and kill me," said the woman.

"'They would not," said I; "there is only a small difference between the flesh of a young pig and a child. We will cut off the first joint of the left little finger. If they make a remark, show them that."

'She cooked the pie, and I watched outside for the giants. At last I saw the three coming. She hid the child in a safe place aside; and I went to the cellar, where I found many dead bodies. I lay down among them, and waited. When the giants came home, the eldest ate the pie, and called to the woman, "That would be very good if we had enough of it." Then he turned to his second brother, and sent him down to the cellar to bring a slice from one of the bodies. The brother came down, took hold of one body, then another, and, catching me, cut a slice from the end of my back, and went up with it. He was not long gone when he came down again, raised me on his back, and turned to take me with him. He had not gone many steps when I sent my knife to his heart, and there he fell on his face under me. I went back, and lay in my old place.

'The chief giant, who had tasted my flesh and was anxious for more of it, now sent the youngest brother. He came, saw the middle brother lying there, and cried out –

'"Oh, but you are the lazy messenger, to be sleeping when sent on an errand!"

'With that, he raised me on his back, and was going, when I stabbed him and stretched him on the ground not far from his brother.

'The big giant waited and waited, grew angry, took his great iron club with nine lumps and nine hooks on it. He hurried down to the cellar, saw his two brothers, shook them, found them dead. I had no chance of life but to fight for it; I rose and stood a fair distance in front of the giant. He ran toward me, raised the club, and brought it down with what strength there was in him. I stepped aside quickly; the club sank in the earth to the depth of a common man's knee. While the giant was drawing the club with both hands, I stabbed him three times in the stomach, and sprang away to some distance. He ran forward a second time, and came very near hitting me; again the club sank in the ground, and I stabbed him four times, for he was weaker from blood loss, and was a longer time freeing the club. The third time the club grazed me, and tore my whole side with a sharp iron hook. The giant fell to his knees, but could neither rise nor make a cast of the club at me; soon he was on his elbow, gnashing his teeth and raging. I was growing weaker, and knew that I was lost unless some one assisted me. The young woman had come down, and was present at the struggle. "Run now," said I to her, "for the giant's sword, and take the head off him." She ran quickly, brought the sword, and as brave as a man took the head off the giant.

'"Death is not far from me now," said I.

'"I will carry you quickly to the giant's cauldron of cure, and give you life," said the woman.

'With that, she raised me on her back, and hurried out of the cellar. When she had me on the edge of the cauldron, the death faint was on me, I was dying; but I was not long in the pot when I revived, and soon was as well as ever.

'We searched the whole house of the giants, found all their treasures. I gave some to the woman, kept some myself, and hid the remainder. I took the woman home to her father and mother. She kept the child, which was well but for the tip of its little finger. Now wasn't I nearer death that time than I was when I began this story?'

'You were, indeed,' said King Conal; 'and even if you were not, I would not put you in the pot, for if you had not been in the house of the three giants that day there would be no sign of me now in this castle. I was that child. Look here at my left little finger. My father searched for you, and so did I when I grew up, but we could not find you. We made out only one thing, that it was the Black Thief who saved me. Men told me that the Black Thief was dead, and I never hoped to see you. A hundred thousand welcomes! Now we'll have a feast. The three young men will get the three horses for your sake, and take them home after we have feasted together. You will stay with me now for the rest of your life.'

'I must go with the young men as far as my own house,' said the Black Thief; 'then I'll come back to you.'

King Conal made a feast the like of which had never been in his kingdom. When the feast was over, he gave the three horses to the young men, and said at parting, 'When you have done the work with the horses, let them go, and they will run home to me; no man could stop them.'

'We will do that,' said the brothers.

They set out then with them, stopped one night with the Black Thief at his house, and after that travelled home to their father, and stood in front of the castle. The stepmother was above, watching for them. She was glad when she saw them, and said, 'Ye brought the horses, and I am to have them.'

'If we were bound to bring the horses,' said the elder brother, 'we were not bound to give them to you.'

With that, he turned the horses' heads from the castle, and let them go. They ran home to King Conal.

'I will go down now,' said the queen, 'and it is time for me.'

'You will not go yet,' said the youngest; 'I have a sentence which I had no time to give when we were going. I put you under sentence to stay where you are till you find three sons of a king to go again to King Conal for the horses.'

When she heard that sentence, she dropped dead from the castle.

THE KING'S SON FROM ERIN, THE SPRISAWN, AND THE DARK KING

There was a king in Erin long ago who was called King of Lochlinn, and his wife died. He had two sons. The elder of the two was Miach Lay; the second was Manus. Miach Lay was a fine champion, and trained in every art that befitted a king's son.

One day the father called Miach Lay to his presence, and said, 'It is time for you to marry, and I have chosen for you a maiden of great beauty and high birth.'

'I am willing to marry,' said Miach Lay.

The king and his son then left the castle, and went to the house of the young woman's father, and there they spent seven days and seven nights. On their way home, the king said to his son, 'How do you like the young lady?'

'I like her well, but I'll not marry her.'

'Oh, my shame!' said the father. 'How can I ever face those people a second time?'

'I cannot help that,' said Miach Lay.

The king was greatly confused. After another while he said to his son, 'I have another maiden chosen for you, and it is well for us to go to her father's, and settle the match.'

'I am willing,' said Miach Lay.

They went away together, and never stopped nor stayed till they reached the house of the young lady's father. They were welcomed there warmly, and spent seven days and seven nights, and were better attended each day than the day before.

'Well, my son,' asked the father, 'how do you like this match?'

'Well, and very well,' said Miach Lay; 'but I will not marry this lady either. She is ten times better than the first; and if I had married the first, I could not marry this one, and so I will not marry the second any more than the first lady.'

'Oh, my shame!' said the father. 'I can never show my face to these people again.'

After another while the king told Miach Lay that he had a better lady than ever selected, and asked him to go with him to arrange the marriage.

'I am willing,' answered the son.

The two went to the father of the maiden; they spent seven days and seven nights at his house, and were fully satisfied with everything. They were on the way home a third time. 'Well,' said the king, 'you have no reason to refuse this time.'

'Well, and very well, do I like the match,' said Miach Lay; 'but I will not marry this lady. If I had married the first lady, I should have had no chance of getting the second, and the second is ten times better than the first; if I had married the second lady, I should have had no chance of this one, and she is twenty times better than the second.'

'I have lost all patience with you,' said the king, 'and I turn the back of my hand to you from this out.'

'I'm fully satisfied,' said Miach Lay, so they came home, and passed that night without conversation. The following morning, when Miach Lay rose, he said to his father, 'I am for leaving the house now; will you prepare for me the best ship that you have, and put in it a good store of provisions for a long voyage?'

The vessel was prepared, and fully provisioned for a day and a year. The king's son went on board, sailed out of the harbour, and off to sea. He never stopped sailing till he entered a harbour in the kingdom of

Greece. There was a guard there on watch at the harbour with a keen eye on all ships that were passing or coming. The King of Greece was at war in that time with the King of Spain, and knew not what moment his kingdom would be invaded.

The guard saw the vessel coming when she was so small to the eye that he could not tell was it a bird or a vessel that he was looking at. He took quick tidings to the castle; and the king ordered him to go a second time and bring tidings. When he reached the sea, the ship was inside, in the harbour.

'Oh,' said the king, when the guard ran to him a second time, 'that is a wonderful vessel that was so far away a few minutes ago as not to be told from a bird, and is now sailing into harbour.'

'There is but one man to be seen on board,' said the guard.

In front of the king's castle was the landing-place, the only one of the harbour; and even there no one went beyond the shore without passing through a gate where every man had to give an account of himself. There was a chosen champion guarding the gate, who spoke to Miach Lay, and asked, 'Who are you, and from what country?'

'It is not the custom for a man of my people to answer a question like that till he is told first what country he is in, and who asks the question.'

'It was I asked the question,' said the champion; 'and you must tell me who you are, first of all.'

'I will not tell you,' said Miach Lay. With that, he drew his ship nearer land till it grounded; then, taking an oar, he put the blade end in the sand, and sprang to shore. He asked then the champion at the gate to let him pass, but the champion refused. Miach Lay raised his hand, gave him a blow on the ear, and sent him backward spinning like a top, till he struck the pillar of the gate and broke his skull. As Miach Lay had no thought to kill the man, he was grieved, and, delaying a short time, went to the castle of the king, not knowing what country he was in or what city.

When he came to the castle, he knelt down in front of it. The people in the castle saw a young champion with bared head outside; the king came out, and asked what trouble was on him. Miach Lay told of all that had happened at the harbour, and how he had killed the champion at the gate without wishing it.

'Never mind that,' said the king.

'I did not intend to kill or harm him at all,' said Miach Lay; 'he wanted to know who I was, and from what country. By the custom of my land, I cannot tell that till I know where I am, and who are the people among whom I am travelling.'

'Do you know now where you are?'

'I do not,' answered Miach Lay.

'You are in front of the castle of the King of Greece, and I am that king.'

'I am the son of the King of Lochlinn from Erin,' said Miach Lay, 'and have come this way to seek my fortune.'

The King of Greece welcomed him then, took the young champion by the hand, and did not stop till he brought him to where all the princes and nobles were assembled; he was rejoiced at his coming, for, being at war, he expected aid from this champion.

'Will you remain with me for a day and a year,' asked the king, 'and perform what service I ask of you?'

'I will,' said Miach Lay.

Manus, the second son of the King of Lochlinn, stopped going to school when Miach Lay, his elder brother, left home, and, after a time, the father wished him to marry. As the elder son had acted, so did the second; he refused to marry each of the three maidens whom the king had chosen, and left his father at last.

Manus was watching when his brother sailed away, and noticed the course of the vessel, so now he sailed the same way.

Miach Lay was gaining favour continually; and just as the day and the year of his service were out to a month, the king's guard saw a vessel sailing in swiftly. He ran with tidings to the king, and added, 'There is only one man on board.'

The king and the nobles said it was best not to let him land till he gave an account of himself. Miach Lay was sent to the landing-place to get account of him.

He was not long at the landing-place when the vessel came within hailing, and Miach Lay asked the one man on board who was he and from what land he came. The man would not tell, as it was not the custom in his country.

'But,' said he, 'I want something to eat.'

'There is plenty here,' said Miach Lay; 'but if there is, you will get none of it – you would better be sailing away.'

'I have enough of the sea; I'll come in.'

He put down the blade of his oar, and sprang ashore. No sooner had he touched land than he was grappled by Miach Lay. As neither man knew the other, they were in hand grips all day. They were nearly equal in strength, but at last Miach Lay was getting the worst of it. He asked Manus for a truce.

'I will grant you that,' said Manus; 'but you do not deserve it, for you began the battle.'

They sat apart then, and Miach Lay asked, 'How long can you hold out?'

'It is getting stronger and braver I am,' replied Manus.

'Not so with me. I could not hold out five minutes longer,' said Miach Lay. 'My bones were all falling asunder, and I thought the earth was trembling beneath me. Till this day I thought to myself, "There is no champion I cannot conquer." Now tell me your name and your country.'

'I am from Erin and a son of the King of Lochlinn,' said Manus.

'Oh,' said Miach Lay, 'you are my brother.'

'Are you Miach Lay?' enquired Manus.

'I am.'

They embraced each other, and sat down then to eat. Miach Lay was so tired that he could taste nothing, but Manus ate his fill. Then they went arm in arm to the castle. The king and all the nobles of Greece had seen the combat from the castle, and were surprised to see the men coming toward them in such friendliness, and all went out to know the reason. The king asked Miach Lay, 'How is all this?'

'This man is my brother,' said Miach Lay. 'I left him at home in Erin, and did not know him at the harbour till after the combat.'

The king was well pleased that he had another champion. The following day Manus saw the king's daughter, and fell in love with her and she with him. Then the daughter told the king if she did not get Manus as husband, the life would leave her.

The king called Miach Lay to his presence, and asked, 'Will you let your brother marry my daughter?'

'If Manus wishes to marry her, I am willing and satisfied,' answered Miach Lay. He asked his brother, and Manus said he would marry the king's daughter.

The marriage was celebrated without delay, and there was a wedding feast for three days and three nights; and the third night, when they were going to their own chamber, the king said, 'This is the third husband married to my daughter, and after the first night no tidings could be had of the other two, and from that time to this no one knows where they are.'

Miach Lay was greatly enraged that the king had permitted the marriage without mentioning this matter first.

'I will do tonight,' said the king, 'what has never been done hitherto; I will place sentries all around the grounds, and my daughter and Manus will not lodge in the castle at all, but in one of the houses apart from it.'

'I'll watch myself,' said Miach Lay; 'and if it is the devil that is taking the husbands, I'll not let him take my brother.'

Sentries were stationed in all parts; a house was prepared in the courtyard. Miach Lay stood on guard at the entrance all the time. Soon after midnight a gust of wind blew through the yard; it blew Miach Lay to the ground, and he fainted. When he recovered, he rushed to search for his brother, but he was not in his chamber. He then roused the king's daughter, and asked, 'Where is my brother?'

'I cannot tell where he is,' said she: 'it is you who were on guard; it is you who should know where to find him.'

'I will have your head, wicked woman, unless you give tidings of my brother.'

'Do not take my head; it would not serve you. I have no account of what happened to your brother.'

Miach Lay then refrained from touching her, and waited till morning. The king came in the morning to see was Manus well; and when Miach Lay saw him, he ran at him to destroy him, but the king fled away. After a while, when the household was roused, the king's daughter was brought in and asked where was her husband, or could she give any account of him.

'I cannot tell,' replied she; 'but one day before I was married the first time, something came to my chamber window in the form of a black bee, and asked would I let it in. I said that I would not. The bee remained outside all the day, watching to see could it enter my chamber. I did not let it come in; before going away in the evening, the black bee said, "Well, I will worry the heart in you yet."'

The king's old druid, who was present, slapped his knee with his hand, and said, 'I know the story now; that was Ri Doracha (the Dark King). He is a mighty magician, and it is he who has taken the husbands.'

'I will travel the world till I find my lost brother,' said Miach Lay.

'I will go with you, and take all my forces,' said Red Bow, the son of the King of Greece.

'I need no assistance,' said Miach Lay. 'If I myself cannot find him, I think that no man can; but if you wish to come, you are welcome.'

Miach Lay went to his vessel; and Red Bow chose the best ship from all that his father had, and went on board of it. The two ships sailed away together. In time they neared land; and on reaching the mouth of the harbour, they saw a third ship sailing toward them as swiftly as the wind blew, and it was not long till it came alongside. There was only one man on board; he hailed Miach Lay, and asked, 'Where are you going?'

'It would not be the custom of my country for me to tell you what you ask till you tell me who you are yourself, and where your own journey lies.'

'I know myself,' said the warrior, 'where you are going; you are in search of the Dark King, and I myself would like to see him.'

With that, he took a bundle of branches he had on deck, and blew them overboard. Then every rod and twig of the bundle became an enormous log of wood, so that the harbour was covered with one raft of timber, and then he sailed away without waiting.

After much struggling with the logs, shoving them hither and over, Miach Lay was able by pushing with oars to make room for his vessel, and at last came to land. Red Bow and his men were cast into deep sleep by the man on the vessel that had sailed away.

After Miach Lay landed, he passed through a great stretch of wild country, and, drawing near a large forest, saw rising up a small, slender smoke far in among trees. He made for the place where the smoke was, and there he discovered a large, splendid castle in the depth of the forest, but could find no sign of an entrance.

When Miach Lay had stood outside some time, a young woman looked through the window, hailed him, and said, 'You are a stranger, and will find no lodgings in these parts; but if I could at all, I would let you come in here.'

'Open the window if you are able,' said Miach Lay.

The window had hinges, and she opened it in the middle; he stepped backward nine yards, and went in at one bound to the chamber.

'You are welcome,' said she, and soon she had dinner prepared for him. When he had eaten, she enquired who was he, from what place had he come, and what brought him that way.

He told her all that had happened to him from the first; and when he had finished, he said, 'I know not where to find my brother.'

'You are not far from him now,' said she; ''tis in this country he is living, and the land he is in bounds our land.'

When they had talked long, she said, 'You are tired and need rest, so sleep in this chamber.' She went then to her own place. The following morning his breakfast was ready before him; and after he had eaten, the young woman said, 'I suppose you will be thankful if I tell you where to find the castle of the Dark King.'

'I shall, indeed,' said he. Then she gave him full directions how to go. He took his sword then, and sprang out as he had sprung in, in the evening, and went in the direction which she told him to take. About midday he met a man, who hailed him, and asked, 'Who are you, and from what country?'

''Tis not the custom for a man of my country to answer that question till told where he is, and to whom he is speaking.'

'I know who you are and whither you are going. You are going to the castle of the Dark King, and here he is before you; now show your daring.'

They made at each other; and if they did, they made soft ground hard and hard ground soft, they made high places low and low places high, they brought cold spring water through dry, gravelly places, and if any one were to come from the Eastern to the Western World, it is to look at these two he should come.

They were this way till evening, and neither had the better of the other. Miach Lay was equal to the Dark King; but the Dark King, having magic, blew a gust of wind at Miach Lay which knocked him flat on the earth, and left him half dead. Then the Dark King took Miach Lay's sword, and went away. When he recovered, Miach Lay regretted his sword more than all else, and went back to the castle where he had spent the night before. He was barely able to go in at the window.

'How have you fared this day?' asked the young woman.

He told her of all that had happened.

'Be not grieved; you will meet him another time,' said the young woman.

'What is the use? I have no sword now.'

'If 'tis a sword you need, I will bring you a blade far better than the one which the Dark King took from you.'

After breakfast next morning she brought him her father's sword, which he grasped in his hand, and shook. Miach Lay bade farewell to the young woman, and sprang out through the window. Knowing the way better this time, he hastened forward, and met the Dark King just where he met him before.

'Did not yesterday tire you?' asked the king.

'No,' said Miach Lay.

'Your journey is useless,' said the king.

'We shall see,' answered Miach Lay, and they made at each other; and terrible as the battle was on the first day, it was more terrible on the second; but when the Dark King thought it time to go home, he blew a gust of wind which threw Miach Lay to the earth, and left him senseless. The Dark King did not take the sword this time.

After the Dark King had gone, another man came the way, who was called Sprisawn Wooden Leg.

'Well, my good man, you are nearly dead,' said the Sprisawn.

'I am,' said Miach Lay, rousing up.

'You are his equal but for the magic. I watched the combat these two days, and you would have overcome him but for his magic; he will finish you tonight if he finds you. He has three magic tricksters who are leaving his house at this moment. They have a spear which the rear man of the three hurls forward, the trickster in front catches the spear in the heel of his foot, and in turn hurls it with all his force forward; those behind rush ahead of the front man, and in turn catch the spear in their heels. No matter how far nor how often the spear is thrown forward, there is always a man there before it to catch it. They are rushing hither a long distance apart.'

The Sprisawn saw the tricksters approach, and told Miach Lay that they were coming. When they came within a spear-cast, one of them hurled the spear at Miach Lay; it went through his heart, passed out through his body, and killed him.

When the Sprisawn saw Miach Lay lying dead, he fell to weeping and wailing; and so loud was his wail that every one heard it throughout the whole kingdom. Red Bow was sleeping yet in the harbour; but so loud was the wail of the mourning Sprisawn that it roused him from the slumber which the Dark King had put on him. He landed at once with his forces, and made on toward the wailing. When they came to the place, and saw Miach Lay lying dead, they themselves began to wail; they asked the Sprisawn then, 'Are there any means by which we might raise him to life?'

'There are,' replied the Sprisawn. 'The Dark King is rejoicing now in his castle with the King of Mangling, and the Gruagach of Shields. They are drinking each other's health from a horn, and the Dark King is telling the other two that Miach Lay was the best man that ever stood in front of him; and if he could drink from that horn, he would rise up as well as he ever was.'

'I with my men will go for that horn,' said Red Bow.

'Not you nor all the men like you living on earth could bring that horn from the castle of the Dark King,' replied the Sprisawn. 'That castle is surrounded by three walls. Each wall is four feet in thickness and twenty feet high. Each wall has a gate as high and as thick as the wall is itself. How could you pass through those walls? Remain here and watch over this body; I will bring the horn hither myself.'

Off went the Sprisawn, and he had more control over magic than even the Dark King. When he arrived at the castle, he struck the gate with the heel of his wooden foot and it opened before him; the second and third gate opened too, in like manner, when he struck them. In he went to the room where the king and his two friends were drinking. There he found them raising toasts to each other. He was himself invisible. As soon as they rested the horn on the table, he snatched it and made off for the place where Miach Lay was lying dead. Then Red Bow and his men raised up the dead man, and poured down his throat some of the wine or whatever liquor was held in the horn.

After a time Miach Lay opened his eyes, and yawned. They were all so delighted that they raised three shouts of joy.

'Come on with me now,' said the Sprisawn, 'to the castle of the Dark King. We will have a trial of strength with him. I will take the Dark King in hand myself. Do you, Miach Lay, take the King of Mangling, and you, Red Bow, take the Gruagach of Shields.'

'This will be very good for us to keep,' said Red Bow, when he saw the virtue of the horn.

'No,' said the Sprisawn; 'it is good for the man who owns it, and I will return it.'

The Sprisawn, who could travel as swiftly as his own thought, vanished with the horn, placed it on the table from which he had snatched it, and came back to the others. No one had missed the horn; when they turned to use it, it was there on the table before them, in the chamber of the Dark King. Miach Lay and his friends went on together, and never stopped till they stood in the chamber where the Dark King was sitting with his friends. The gates had remained open since the Sprisawn opened them. When the Dark King saw the dead man alive, standing in his chamber before him, he said, 'Never a welcome to you, you miserable creature with the wooden foot. What brought you hither, or how did you come?'

'I have come to you with combat,' said the Sprisawn; 'and now do you choose the manner of fighting.'

In the castle were three chambers, in each chamber a cross-beam as high from the floor as a man's throat; in the middle of each cross-beam was a hole, through this hole passed a chain, at each end of the chain was an iron loop; above the hole and lengthwise with the beam was a sword with a keen edge on it. Each pair of champions was to take one room of the three, and each man of them was to place a loop on his own neck; each then was to pull the other to the hole if he could, and then pull till the sword cut his head off.

The Sprisawn and the Dark King took one room, Miach Lay and the King of Mangling another, Red Bow and the Gruagach of Shields took the third.

The first pair were not long at each other, as the Sprisawn was greatly anxious for the other two, and with the second pull that he gave he had the head off the Dark King. He ran then to see how it fared with Miach Lay. Miach Lay was tired and nearly beaten.

'Come out of that for me,' said the Sprisawn. 'What playing is it you have with him?'

'Fully satisfied am I to give this place to you,' said Miach Lay, raising the loop; and the Sprisawn put it quickly on his own neck.

With the first pull the Sprisawn gave he had the head off the King of Mangling. They ran then to Red Bow, whose head was within two feet of the sword.

'Go on out of this,' said the Sprisawn, putting the loop on his own neck. The Gruagach, by reason of having Red Bow so near the beam, was himself at a distance, but at the first pull which the Sprisawn gave he drew the Gruagach within a foot of the beam. Fearing that if he killed the third man there would be no one to give an account of those carried off by the Dark King, the Sprisawn offered the Gruagach his life if he told him where Manus and the other two husbands of the king's daughter were.

'If I tell you that,' said the Gruagach, 'the Dark King will knock the head off me.'

'If you saw the head of the Dark King would you tell me?'

'I would.'

The Sprisawn sent Miach Lay for the head of the Dark King; he brought it.

'Is that his head?' asked the Sprisawn.

'It is,' said the Gruagach.

'Well, tell me now.'

'Were I to tell you,' said the Gruagach, 'the King of Mangling would knock the head off me.'

'If you saw his head would you tell me?'

'I would.'

The head of the King of Mangling was brought.

'Is this the head?'

'It is.'

'Well, tell me, or you'll lose your own head.'

'Near this castle is a lake,' said the Gruagach, 'and under its water is an enchanted steel tower, with high walls three feet in thickness; around that tower on the outside a long serpent has wound herself closely from the bottom to the top. This serpent is called the Worm of Nine Eyes. Inside in the tower are the three men.'

'And how can we come at them?' asked the Sprisawn.

'Whoever wants to free them,' said the Gruagach, 'must stand on the shore of the lake and shout to the serpent, calling her the Worm of Nine Eyes. Hearing this, the serpent will unwind, and with lashing will drive all the water of the lake in showers through the country and flood the whole land. The basin of the lake will be dry then, and the serpent will rush at the man who uttered the insult and try to devour him. The serpent must be killed, and the champion must run to the tower; if he can break in, he will rescue the three men.'

'Is that all?' asked the Sprisawn.

'It is,' said the Gruagach. 'I have no further account of the matter; that is all I know.'

'Then you'll lose your head, too,' said the Sprisawn; and with one pull of the chain he swept the head off the Gruagach. The three champions went to the lake then. Miach Lay and Red Bow wished to help the Sprisawn, but he forced them to remain behind, saying that they would be swept away by the waters if they went.

The Sprisawn, coming to the bank of the lake, shouted: 'Worm of Nine Eyes!' No sooner did the serpent hear the name than she uncoiled from the tower, lashed the lake, and sent the water over the country. When the lake bed was dry the serpent rushed toward the Sprisawn with open mouth. When the Sprisawn saw the serpent he took his sword in both hands and held it crosswise in front of his face, and when the serpent was coming to swallow him so great was the force with which she rushed forward and sucked the air to draw him in, that the Sprisawn split her in two from the mouth to the tail, dividing the back from the belly, and the two pieces fell apart like the two halves of a split log of timber.

Miach Lay and Red Bow came then to the Sprisawn and went to the tower, but if they did, they could not go in.

'Oh,' said the Sprisawn, 'if you had all the arms in the world you could not break through that tower.' He went himself to the door then, and striking it slightly with his wooden foot, for fear of killing the men inside by too hard a blow, he burst in the door. The three men inside came out, and Miach Lay embraced his own brother. All were glad, and all started for home, but had not gone far when the other two men began to dispute whose would the king's daughter be. The first husband said his claim was strongest; the second said his was. The Sprisawn tried to settle the quarrel, but could not. 'I would advise you,' said he, 'to leave the matter to the first man you meet.'

All agreed to do this.

The Sprisawn now left them and vanished as if he had never been with them. They had not gone far when they met a man. 'Well met,' said they; 'we are glad to see you.'

'What is the trouble that is on you?' asked the man.

'So and so,' said they, telling him the whole story; 'and now you are to be our judge.'

'I will do my best,' said the man, 'if each one will be satisfied with my decision.'

'We will,' said they.

'Now let each man tell his story.'

Each man told his story to the end.

'Who rescued you?' asked he.

'Miach Lay and his forces,' said they.

'Had not this man and his forces come, you would have been there till this time?'

'We should,' said the three.

'If so,' said the man, 'my decision is that the first and second husband should each be thankful, go to his own people, and get another wife for himself; and that the daughter of the King of Greece belongs to the brother of the man who rescued all three.'

The two princes went away toward their own homes, and the man remained, and who was he when he took his own form again but the Sprisawn. They went then to the castle where the young lady had entertained Miach Lay, and whose castle was it but the Sprisawn's; the young woman was his daughter. After resting there for some days, the Sprisawn asked Miach Lay would he marry his daughter. Miach Lay was willing and glad, and remained there.

Manus and Red Bow returned to the King of Greece. Manus lived in Greece happily, and so did his children.

The two brothers did well not to marry any woman their father found for them, for they would not have had the grand ladies that they had in the end, and Miach Lay had the dominions of the Dark King, as well as those of the Sprisawn, and they were very rich kingdoms.

THE AMADAN MOR AND THE GRUAGACH OF THE CASTLE OF GOLD

On a time in Erin the King of Leinster resolved to make war on the King of Munster, and sent him a message to be ready for battle on a day mentioned. They raised flags for combat when the day came, and stood face to face. The forces closed in battle, and were at one another then till the King of Leinster and his men killed all the warriors of the King of Munster and the king himself.

After the King of Munster and all his champions were slain, the King of Leinster thought it better to live in Munster than in his own kingdom, so he took possession of Munster and went to live in the king's castle.

The wife of the King of Munster fled in haste to a forest, a thing easily done, for all Erin was under forests in that time. The queen had a son in the forest, and after a time she had no clothes for herself or the child. Hair came out on them as on wild beasts of the wilderness. The child was thriving and growing; what of him did not grow in the day grew threefold at night, till at last there was no knowing what size was he.

The queen was seven years without leaving the place around her hut in the forest. In the eighth year she went forth from the forest and saw her husband's castle and open kingdom, and began to weep and lament. There was a great crowd of people around the castle where she had herself lived in past years. She went to see what was happening. It was a summer of great want, and the king was giving out doles of meal to people daily, and the man who was giving the meal gave her a dole also. He was greatly surprised when he saw her, and in the evening he was telling the king that he had never seen such a sight in his life; she was all covered with hair like a beast of the forest.

'She will come again tomorrow,' said the king; 'then do you enquire what sort is she, and where is her place of abode.'

She went next day to the castle; the man in charge gave her meal. After she had gone he followed her, and when he was coming near she sat down at the roadside from shame.

'Fear me not,' said the man. 'I wish to know if you are of the dead or the living, and what sort are you.'

'I am a living person, though I may seem like one from the dead.'

'Where do you live?'

'I have no house or home save a small hut in the forest, and I have the look of a beast because I eat fruits and leaves of trees and grass of the earth.'

The man told the king, and the king said, 'Tell the woman tomorrow that I will give her a house of some kind to live in.'

The king gave the strange woman a house, and she went to live with her son in it. The son was seven years old at that time, and not able to walk or speak, although he was larger than any giant. His mother had called him Micky, and soon he was known as Micky Mor (Big Micky).

She was there for a while in the house with her son, and she taking doles of food like any poor person. One fine summer day she was sitting at the doorstep, and she began to weep and lament.

'What is the cause of your crying?' asked the boy, who had never spoken before till that moment.

'God's help be with us,' said the mother. 'It is time for you to get speech. Thank God you are able to talk now.'

'It is never too late, mother.'

'That is right, my child,' said she, 'it is better late than never.'

'Tell me, mother, why do you cry in this way and lament?'

'It is no use for me to tell you, my child; three men have just gone back to the strand, and once I was able to give the like of them a good warm dinner.'

'Well, mother, you must go and invite them to dinner this time.'

'What have I to give them to eat, my poor child?'

'If you have nothing to give them but only to be talking till morning, you will have to go and invite them.'

When she was ready he said: 'Mother, before you go tie my two hands to the beam that is here in the house above the hearth, that I may not fall in the fire while you are absent.'

Before the mother went out she passed a rope under his arms, tied him to the cross-beam, and put a stool under his feet. He kicked the stool away; he had to pull and drag himself to swing, the fire was catching his feet, the beam was cracking from his weight and the swinging. The sinews of his legs stretched, he got his footing then, and walked to the door.

'Thanks be to God,' said the mother, when she came back. 'It is curious how your talk and your walk came to you on the one day.'

'It is nearly always the case that 'tis together talk and walk come to a child; but now it is time for us to be providing something for the friends that are coming tonight.'

He went away then and asked the man who brought turf out of the reeks to the king's castle to give him as much as would make fire for himself and his mother for the night.

'Go away,' said the man; 'I will not give you a sod of turf. Go to the king and get an order; then I will give you turf in plenty.'

'I would not be tiring myself going for an order, but I will have plenty in spite of you.'

Micky took away then a great basket of turf and no thanks to the man.

'Well, mother,' said he, 'here is turf enough for you, and make down a good fire.'

He went to the mill and said to the miller: 'My mother sent me for flour. There will be three at the house tonight, and what will not be used will be brought to you in the morning.'

'You stump of a fool, why should I give you flour? Go to my master, the king; if he gives an order, I will give you flour in plenty.'

Micky caught the miller. 'I will put you,' said he, 'in one of the hoppers of the mill unless you make away with yourself out of this.'

The miller ran away in dread that Micky would kill him. Micky laid hold of a strong, weighty chain, and tied a great sack of flour and put it on his back. When the sack was across his back he could not pass through the doorway, and knew not what to do.

'It would be a shame for me to say of the first load I put on my back that I left that same after me.' He stepped backward some paces and made such a rush that he carried out the frame of the door with him.

'Well, mother,' said he, 'we have fire and flour enough now, and let you be making loaves for the visitors.'

He went next to the woman in charge of the milk-house. 'It is hither my mother sent me for a firkin of butter. There are three strangers above in our house. What will be left of the butter I will bring back in the morning, and all my own help and assistance to you for a week to come.'

'Be out of my milk-house, you stump of a fool,' said the woman. 'What assistance can you give to pay for my milk and butter?'

'Let you be out of this, my good woman,' said Micky, 'or I will not leave much life in you from this day out.'

She went away in a hurry, and he carried a firkin of butter home on his shoulder.

'Now, mother,' said he, 'you have bread, fire, butter, and all things you need. If we had a bit of meat, that would be all that we care for.'

He went away then and never stopped nor stayed till he reached the place where all the king's fine fat sheep were. He caught up one and brought it home on his shoulder.

Next day the turf-keeper, the miller, the dairywoman, and the shepherd went to complain to the king of what Micky had done.

'It is not luck we asked for the first day we drew him on us,' said the king.

The king started and never stopped nor stayed till he went to his old druid. 'Such a man as we have brought on us,' said the king. 'Tell me now how to put an end to him.'

'There is,' said the druid, 'a black mad hound in a wood beyond the mountain. Tell Micky that you lost that hound one day in the hunt, and to bring her and he will be well paid for his trouble.'

The king sent for Micky, and told him all as the druid advised.

'Will you send any man with me to show me the road?'

'I will,' said the king.

Micky and the man were soon travelling along the road toward the mountain. When Micky thought it too slow the man was walking, he asked, 'Have you any walk better than that?'

'Why, then, I have not,' said the man, 'and I am tired, and it is because I have such a good walk that I was sent with you.'

Micky took up his guide, put him under his arm, with the man's head near his own breast, and they began to talk as Micky moved forward. When they came near the wood, the man said, 'Put me down, and beware of the hound. Be not rash with her, or she may harm you.'

'If she is a hound belonging to a king or a man of high degree, it must be that she has training and will come with me quietly. If she will not come gently, I will make her come in spite of her.'

When he went into the wood the hound smelt him and rushed at his throat to tear him to pieces. He hurled her off quickly, and then she made a second drive at him, and a fierce one.

'Indeed,' said Micky, 'you are an impudent hound to belong to a king'; and, taking a long, strong tree branch, he gave her a blow on the flank that raised her high in the air.

After that blow the hound ran away as fast as her legs could carry her, and Micky made after her with all the speed of his own legs to catch her. On account of the blow she was losing breath fast, and he was coming nearer and nearer, till at length he ran before her and drove her in against the ditch. When she tried to go one way he shook the branch before her, and when she tried to rush off in another direction, he shook it there too, till he forced her into the road, and then she was mild and quiet and came with him as gently as any dog.

When he was near home some one saw Micky and the mad hound with him. A messenger ran and told the king he was coming and the mad hound walking with him. The king gave orders to close every door in the castle. He was in dread that the hound would devour every one living.

When the hound was brought before the closed door of the castle the king put his head out the window and said, 'That hound has been so long astray that she is of no use to me now; take her to your mother, and she will mind the house for her.'

Micky took the hound home, and she was that tame and watchful that not a hen, nor a duck, nor a goose belonging to the king's castle could come near the house.

The king went to the druid a second time, and asked, 'What can I do to kill Micky Mor?'

'There is a raging wild boar in the woods there beyond that will tear him to pieces,' said the druid. 'Tell Micky Mor that one of the servants, when coming from the town, lost a young pig, that the pig is in that wood, and to bring him.'

The king sent for the boy, and said, 'One of my men lost a young pig while coming from the town; it is in that wood there beyond. If you'll go to the wood and bring the pig hither, I'll pay you well when you come.'

'I will go,' said the boy, 'if you will send some one to show me the wood where the pig is.'

The king sent a man, but not the man who went the first time with

Micky Mor, for that man said, 'I am tired, and haven't the strength to go.' They went on then, walking toward the wood. This guide grew tired like the first man, for the wood was far distant from the castle of the king. When he was tired, the boy put him under his arm, and the two began to chat away as they journeyed. When near the wood, the man begged and said, 'Micky Mor, put me down now: it is a mad boar that is in the wood; and if you are not careful, he will tear you to pieces.'

'God help you!' said Micky; ''tis the innocent man you are to let such a small thing put dread on you.'

'I will leave you,' said the guide. 'I cannot help you; you are able to fight the battle yourself.'

Away went the man; and when Micky Mor entered the wood, the wild boar was facing him, and the beast foaming from both sides of the mouth. As the guide had warned him to be on his guard, Micky gave one spring out of his body, and came to the boar with such a kick that his leg went right into the mouth of the beast, and split his jaw back to the breast. The wild boar dropped lifeless, and the boy was going home, leaving the great beast behind him. He stopped then, and said to himself, 'If I go back without the boar, the king will not believe that I met him at all.' He turned back, caught the wild boar by the hind legs, and threw him across his shoulders.

The king thought, 'As he brought the mad hound the first day, he may bring the wild boar to me this time.' He placed guards on all roads leading to the castle.

The guards saw Micky coming with the boar on his back. Thinking the boar alive, they ran hither and over, closed every door, window, hole, or place that a mouse might pass through, for fear the wild boar would tear them to pieces.

The youth went up to the castle, and struck the door; the king put his head out the window, and asked, 'Can it be that you have the wild boar?'

'I have him; but if I have, he is dead.'

'As he is dead, you might take him home to your mother; and, believe me, he will keep you in meat for a long while.'

The king went to the druid again.

'I have no advice for you this time,' said the druid, 'but one: he is of as good blood as yourself; and the best thing you can do is to give him your daughter to marry.'

This daughter was the king's only child, and her name was Eilin Og. The king sent for the youth then, and said, 'I will give you my daughter to marry.'

'It is well,' said Micky Mor; 'if you give her in friendship, I will take her.'

Micky Mor made himself ready; they gave him fine clothes, and he seemed fit to marry any king's daughter. After the marriage he was a full week without going to see his own mother.

When he went to her at the end of the week, she cried out, 'What is keeping you away from me a whole week?'

'Dear mother,' said he, 'it is I that have met with the luck. I got the king's daughter to marry.'

'Go away out of my sight, and never come near me again!'

'Why so, mother, what ails you? Could I get a better wife than a king's daughter?'

'My dear son, if she is a king's daughter, you are a king's son, so you are as high as she.'

'If I am a king's son, why have you and I been so poor?'

She told him then that the king had killed his father and all his forces, and that the whole castle and kingdom had belonged to his father.

'Why did you not tell me that long ago?'

'I would never have told you,' said she, 'but that you have married the murderer's daughter.'

Away went the son when he heard what his mother said, and the eyes going out of his head with wild rage, and he saying that he would kill every one living about the king's castle. The people in the castle saw him coming, and thought from his looks that his mother had said some strong words to him, and they closed every door and window against him. The young man put his shoulder to the door of the castle, and it flew in before him. He never stopped nor stayed till he went to the highest chamber of the castle to the king and queen, killing every one that came in his way. 'Pardon me! Spare me!' cried the king.

'I will never kill you between my own two hands; but I'll give you the chance that you gave my own father while the spear was going from the hand to his breast.' With that, he caught the king, and threw him out through the window. When he had all killed who did not flee before him, he could find no sight of his own wife, though he looked for her everywhere.

'Well, mother,' said he when he went home, 'I have all killed before me, but I cannot find my own wife.'

The mother went with him to search for the wife, and they found her in a box. When they opened the box, she screamed wildly.

'Sure, you know well that I did not marry you to kill you; have no fear.'

She was glad to have her life. Micky Mor then moved into the castle, and had his father's kingdom and property back again. After a while he went to walk one day with his wife, Eilin Og. While he was walking for himself, the sky grew so dark that it seemed like night, and he knew not where to go; but he went on till he came at last to a roomy dark glen. When he was inside in the glen, the greatest drowsiness that ever came over a man came over him.

'Eilin Og,' said he, 'come quickly under my head, for sleep is coming on me.'

'It is not sleep that is troubling you, but something in this great gloomy glen, where you were never before in your life.'

'Oh, Eilin Og, come quickly under my head.'

She came under his head, and he got a short nap of sleep. When he woke, hunger and thirst came on him greater than ever came upon any man ever born. Then a vessel came to him filled with food, and one with drink.

'Taste not the drink, take not a bite of the food, in this dark glen, till you know what kind of a place is it.'

'Eilin Og, I must take one drink. I'll drink it whomsoever it vexes.'

He took a draught hard and strong from the vessel; and that moment the two legs dropped off Micky Mor from the knees down.

When Eilin Og saw this, she fell to wailing and weeping.

'Hold, hold, Eilin Og! silence your grief; a head or a leg will not be in the country unless I get my two legs again.'

The fog now dispersed, and the sky became clear. When he saw the sky clear, he knew where to go; and he put his knife and spear and wife on the point of his shoulder. Then his strength and activity were greater, and he was swifter on his two knees than nine times nine other men that had the use of their whole legs.

While he was going on, he saw huntsmen coming toward him. A deer passed him. He threw the spear that he had in his hand; it went through the deer, in one side and out through the other. A white dog rushed straightway after the deer. Micky Mor caught the deer and the dog, and kept them.

Now a young Gruagach, light and loose, was the first of the huntsmen to follow the white dog. 'Micky Mor,' said he, 'give me the white dog and the deer.'

'I will not,' said Micky. 'For it is myself that did the slaughter, strong and fierce, that threw the spear out of my right hand and put it through the two sides of the deer; and whoever it be, you or I, who has the strongest hand, let him have the white dog and the deer.'

'Micky Mor,' said Eilin Og, 'yield up the white dog and the deer.'

'I will,' said he, 'and more if you ask; for had I obeyed you in the glen, the two legs from the knees down would not have gone from me.'

The hunter, who was the Gruagach of Dun an Oir, was so glad to get his white dog and deer that he said, 'Come with me, Micky Mor, to my castle to dinner.'

The three were then passing along by the strand of Ard na Conye to the Gruagach's castle, when whom should they meet but a champion who began to talk with the men; but, seeing Eilin Og, he stopped on a sudden and asked Micky Mor, 'Who is this woman with you? I think there is not another of such beauty in all the great world.'

'That is my wife, Eilin Og,' said Micky Mor.

'It is to find her that I am here, and to take her in spite of herself or her father,' said the champion.

'If you take her, you will take her in spite of me,' said Micky Mor; 'but what champion are you with such words?'

'I am Maragach of the Green Gloves from Great Island. I have travelled the world twice, and have met no man to match me. No weapons have hurt my skin yet or my body. Where are your arms of defence in this great world, Micky Mor?'

'I have never wished for a weapon but my own two fists that were born with me.'

'I name you now and forever,' said Maragach, 'the Big Fool (Amadan Mor).'

'Not talk of the mouth performs deeds of valour, but active, strong bones. Let us draw back now, and close with each other. We shall know then who is the best man; and if there is valour in you, as you say, you dirty little Maragach, I will give you a blow with strength that will open your mouth to the bone.'

They went toward each other then threateningly, and closed like two striking Balors or two wild boars in the days of the Fenians, or two hawks of Cold Cliff, or two otters of Blue Pool. They met in close, mighty struggle, with more screeching than comes from a thousand. They made high places low, and low places high. The clods that were shot away by them, as they wrestled, struck out the eye of the hag in the Eastern World, and she spinning thread at her wheel.

Now Maragach drew his sword strong, keen-edged, and flawless; this sword always took with the second blow what it did not cut with the first; but there was no blow of it that time which the Big Fool did not dodge, and when the sun was yellow at setting, the sword was in small bits, save what remained in the hand of the champion. That moment the Fool struck the champion a blow 'twixt neck and skull, and took the head off his body.

The three went on then to the castle of Dun an Oir (Castle of Gold), and had a fine dinner. During the dinner they were discoursing and telling tales; and the Gruagach's wife took greatly to heart the looks that her husband was giving Eilin Og, and asked, 'Which is it that you will have, Negil Og's daughter or the wife of the Big Fool?'

Said Eilin Og to the Gruagach's wife, 'This man's name is not the Big Fool in truth or in justice, for he is a hero strong and active; he is master of all alive and of every place. All the world is under his command, and I with the rest.'

'If he is all this, why did he let the legs go from him?' asked the Gruagach's wife.

Eilin Og answered, 'I have said that he has high virtues and powers; and only for the drink that was brought him in the dark lonely glen, he would not have let the legs go from him.'

The Gruagach was in dread that the Big Fool might grow angry over their talks, and that enchantment would not get the upper hand of strength, and said, 'Give no heed to woman's talk, Micky Mor, but guard my castle, my property, and my wife, while I go to the Dun of the Hunt and return.'

'If any man comes in in spite of me,' said Micky Mor, 'while you are absent, believe me, he will not go out in spite of me till you return.'

The Gruagach went off then, and with the power of his enchantment put a heavy sleep on Micky Mor.

'Eilin Og,' said he, 'come quickly under my head, for over-strong sleep has come on me.'

Eilin Og came under his head, and he got a short nap of sleep. The Gruagach returned soon in a different form altogether, and he took a kiss from his own wife.

'Oh,' said Eilin Og to her husband, 'you are in your sleep, and it is to my grief that you are in it, and not at the right time.'

Micky Mor heard her, and he, between sleeping and waking, gave one leap from his body when he heard Eilin Og's words, and stopped at the door. It would have been a greater task to break any anvil or block made by blacksmith or wood-worker, than to force the Big Fool from the door.

'Micky Mor,' said the Gruagach, disguised, 'let me out.'

'I will not let you out till the Gruagach of Dun an Oir comes home, and then you will pay for the kiss that you took from his wife.'

'I will give you a leg swift and strong as your own was; it is a leg I took from the Knight of the Cross when he was entering his ship.'

'If you give me one of my legs swift and strong as ever, perhaps I may let you go out.'

That moment the Fool got the leg. He jumped up then, and said, 'This is my own leg, as strong and as active as ever.

'The other leg now, or your head!' said Micky Mor.

The Gruagach gave him the other leg, blew it under him with power of enchantment. Micky Mor jumped up. 'These are my own legs in strength and activity. You'll not go out of this now till the Gruagach comes, and you pay for the kiss you took from his wife.'

'I have no wish to knock a trial out of you,' said the Gruagach, and he changed himself into his own form again. 'You see who I am; and I am the huntsman who took your legs with the drink that you got from the cup, and I am your own brother born and bred.'

'Where were you,' asked the Big Fool, 'when my father was killed with all his men?'

'I was in the Eastern World at that time, learning enchantment and magic.'

'If you are my brother,' said the Big Fool, 'we will go with each other forevermore. Come with me now to such a wood. We will fight there four giants who are doing great harm to our people these many years.'

'Dear brother,' said the Gruagach, 'there is no use for us to go against the four giants; they are too powerful and strong for us, they will kill us.'

'Let me fight with three of them,' said Micky Mor, 'and I'll not leave a foot or a hand of them living on earth; you can settle one.'

The Gruagach had his great stallion of the road brought from the stable for himself and his brother to ride. When they led him out, the stallion gave three neighs – a neigh of lamentation, a neigh of loyalty, and a neigh of gladness.

This stallion had the three qualities of Fin MacCool's slim bay steed – a keen rush against a hill, a swift run on the level, a high running leap; three qualities of the fox – the gait of a fox gay and proud, a look straight ahead taking in both sides and turning to no side, neat in his tread on the road; three qualities of a bull – a full eye, a thick neck, a bold forehead.

They rode to the forest of the giants; and the moment they entered, the giants sniffed them, and one of them cried out, 'I find the smell of men from Erin, their livers and lights for my supper of nights, their blood for my morning dram, their jawbones for stepping-stones, and their shins for hurleys. We think you are too big for one bite and too small for two bites, and sooner or later we'll have you out of the way.'

The Big Fool and three of the giants made at one another then; and he didn't leave a hand nor a foot of the three alive. He stood looking then at his brother and the other giant. The young Gruagach was getting too much from the giant; and he called out, 'Dear born brother, give me some aid, or the giant will put me out of the world.'

'I will give him,' said the Big Fool, 'a blow of my fist that will drive his head through the air.'

He ran to him then, gave the giant one blow under the jawbone, and sent his head through the air. It is not known to man, woman, or child to this day where the head stopped, or did it stop in any place.

THE KING'S SON AND THE WHITE-BEARDED SCOLOG

Not in our time, nor the time of our fathers, but long ago, there lived an old king in Erin. This king had but the one son, and the son had risen up to be a fine strong hero; no man in the kingdom could stand before him in combat.

The queen was dead, and the king was gloomy and bitter in himself because old age was on him. The strength had gone from his limbs, and gladness from his heart. No matter what people said, they could not drive sorrow from him.

One day the king called up his son, and this is what he said to him, 'You are of age to marry. We cannot tell how long I'll be here, and it would cheer and delight me to see your wife; she might be a daughter to me in my last days.'

'I am willing to obey you,' said the son; 'but I know no woman that I care for. I have never seen any one that I would marry.'

With that, the old king sent for a druid, and said, 'You must tell where my son can find the right bride for himself. You must tell us what woman he should marry.'

'There is but one woman,' said the druid, 'who can be the right wife for your son, and she is the youngest daughter of the white-bearded scolog; she is the wisest young woman in the world, and has the most power.'

'Where does her father live, and how are we to settle it?' asked the king of the druid.

'I have no knowledge of the place where that scolog lives,' said the druid, 'and there is no one here who knows. Your son must go himself, and walk the world till he finds the young woman. If he finds her and gets her, he'll have the best bride that ever came to a king's son.'

'I am willing to go in search of the scolog's daughter,' said the young man, 'and I'll never stop till I find her.'

With that, he left his father and the druid, and never stopped till he went to his foster-mother and told her the whole story – told her the wish of his father, and the advice the old druid had given him.

'My three brothers live on the road you must travel,' said the foster-mother; 'and the eldest one knows how to find that scolog, but without the friendship of all of them, you'll not be able to make the journey. I'll give you something that will gain their good-will for you.'

With that, she went to an inner room, and made three cakes of flour and baked them. When the three were ready, she brought them out, and gave them to the young man.

'When you come to my youngest brother's castle,' said she, 'he will rush at you to kill you, but do you strike him on the breast with one of the cakes; that minute he'll be friendly, and give you good entertainment. The second brother and the eldest will meet you like the youngest.'

On the following morning, the king's son left a blessing with his foster-mother, took one for the road from her, and went away carrying the three cakes with him. He travelled that day with great swiftness over hills and through valleys, past great towns and small villages, and never stopped nor stayed till he came in the evening to a very large castle. In he went, and inside was a woman before him.

'God save you!' said he to the woman.

'God save yourself!' said she; 'and will you tell me what brought you the way, and where are you going?'

'I came here,' said the king's son, 'to see the giant of this castle, and to speak with him.'

'Be said by me,' replied the woman, 'and go away out of this without waiting for the giant.'

'I will not go without seeing him,' said the king's son. 'I have never set eyes on a giant, and I'll see this one.'

'I pity you,' said the woman; 'your time is short in this life. You'll not be long without seeing the giant, and it's not much you'll see in this world after setting eyes on him; and it would be better for you to take a drink of wine to give you strength before he comes.'

The king's son had barely swallowed the wine when he heard a great noise beyond the castle.

'Fee, faw, foh!' roared some one, in a thundering voice. The king's son looked out; and what should he see but the giant with a shaggy goat going out in front of him and another coming on behind, a dead hag above on his shoulder, a great hog of a wild boar under his left arm, and a yellow flea on the club which he held in his right hand before him.

'I don't know will I blow you into the air or put my foot on you,' said the giant, when he set eyes on the king's son. With that, he threw his load to the ground, and was making at his visitor to kill him when the young man struck the giant on the breast with one of the three cakes which he had from the foster-mother.

That minute the giant knew who was before him, and called out, 'Isn't it the fine welcome I was giving my sister's son from Erin?'

With that, he changed entirely, and was so glad to see the king's son that he didn't know what to do for him or where to put him. He made a great feast that evening; the two ate and drank with contentment and delight. The giant was so pleased with the king's son that he took him to his own bed. He wasn't three minutes in the bed when he was sound asleep and snoring. With every breath that the giant took in, he drew the king's son into his mouth and as far as the butt of his tongue; with every breath that he sent out, he drove him to the rafters of the castle, and the king's son was that way going up and down between the bed and the roof until daybreak, when the giant let a breath out of him, and closed his mouth; next moment the king's son was down on his lips.

'What are you doing to me?' cried the giant.

'Nothing,' said the king's son; 'but you didn't let me close an eye all the night. With every breath you let out of you, you drove me up to the rafters; and with every breath you took in, you drew me into your mouth and as far as the butt of your tongue.'

'Why didn't you wake me?'

'How could I wake you when time failed me to do it?'

'Oh, then, sister's son from Erin,' said the giant, 'it's the poor night's rest I gave you; but if you had a bad bed, you must have a good breakfast.'

With that, the giant rose, and the two ate the best breakfast that could be had out of Erin.

After breakfast, the king's son took the giant's blessing with him, and left his own behind. He travelled all that day with great speed and without halt or rest, till he came in the evening to the castle of the second giant. In front of the door was a pavement of sharp razors, edges upward, a pavement which no man could walk on. Long, poisonous needles, set as thickly as bristles in a brush, were fixed, points downward, under the lintel of the door, and the door was low.

The king's son went in with one start over the razors and under the needles, without grazing his head or cutting his feet. When inside, he saw a woman before him.

'God save you!' said the king's son.

'God save yourself!' said the woman.

The same conversation passed between them then as passed between himself and the woman in the first castle.

'God help you!' said the woman, when she heard his story. ''Tis not long you'll be alive after the giant comes. Here's a drink of wine to strengthen you.'

Barely had he the wine swallowed when there was a great noise behind the castle, and the next moment the giant came in with a thundering and rattling.

'Who is this that I see?' asked he, and with that, he sprang at the stranger to put the life out of him; but the king's son struck him on the breast with the second cake which he got from his foster-mother. That moment the giant knew him, and called out, 'A strange welcome I had for you, sister's son from Erin, but you'll get good treatment from me now.'

The giant and the king's son made three parts of that night. One part they spent in telling tales, the second in eating and drinking, and the third in sound, sweet slumber.

Next morning the young man went away after breakfast, and never stopped till he came to the castle of the third giant; and a beautiful castle it was, thatched with the down of cotton grass, the roof was as white as milk, beautiful to look at from afar or near by. The third giant was as angry at meeting him as the other two; but when he was struck in the breast with the third cake, he was as kind as the best man could be.

When they had taken supper together, the giant said to his sister's son, 'Will you tell me what journey you are on?'

'I will, indeed,' said the king's son; and he told his whole story from beginning to end.

'It is well that you told me,' said the giant, 'for I can help you; and if you do what I tell, you'll finish your journey in safety. At midday tomorrow you'll come to a lake; hide in the rushes that are growing at one side of the water. You'll not be long there when twelve swans will alight near the rushes and take the crests from their heads; with that, the swan skins will fall from them, and they will rise up the most beautiful women that you have ever set eyes on. When they go in to bathe, take the crest of the youngest, put it in your bosom next the skin, take the eleven others and hold them in your hand. When the young women come out, give the eleven crests to their owners; but when the twelfth comes, you'll not give her the crest unless she carries you to her father's castle in Ardilawn Dreeachta (High Island of Enchantment). She will refuse, and say that strength fails her to carry you, and she will beg for the crest. Be firm, and keep it in your bosom; never give it up till she promises to take you. She will do that when she sees there is no help for it.'

Next morning the king's son set out after breakfast, and at midday he was hidden in the rushes. He was barely there when the swans came. Everything happened as the giant had said, and the king's son followed his counsels.

When the twelve swans came out of the lake, he gave the eleven crests to the older ones, but kept the twelfth, the crest of the youngest, and gave it only when she promised to carry him to her father's. The moment she put the crest on her head, she was in love with the king's son. When she came in sight of the island, however much she loved him when they started from the lakeside, she loved him twice as much now. She came to the ground at some distance from the castle, and said to the young man at parting –

'Thousands of kings' sons and champions have come to give greeting to my father at the door of his castle, but every man of them perished. You will be saved if you obey me. Stand with your right foot inside the threshold and your left foot outside; put your head under the lintel. If your head is inside, my father will cut it from your shoulders; if it is outside, he will cut it off also. If it is under the lintel when you cry 'God save you!' he'll let you go in safety.'

They parted there; she went to her own place and he went to the scolog's castle, put his right foot inside the threshold, his left foot outside, and his head under the lintel. 'God save you!' called he to the scolog.

'A blessing on you!' cried the scolog, 'but my curse on your teacher. I'll give you lodgings tonight, and I'll come to you myself in the morning'; and with that he sent a servant with the king's son to a building outside. The servant took a bundle of straw with some turf and potatoes, and, putting these down inside the door, said, 'Here are bed, supper, and fire for you.'

The king's son made no use of food or bed, and he had no need of them, for the scolog's daughter came soon after, spread a cloth, took a small bundle from her pocket, and opened it. That moment the finest food and drink were there before them.

The king's son ate and drank with relish, and good reason he had after the long journey. When supper was over, the young woman whittled a small shaving from a staff which she brought with her; and that moment the finest bed that any man could have was there in the room.

'I will leave you now,' said she; 'my father will come early in the morning to give you a task. Before he comes, turn the bed over; 'twill be a shaving again, and then you can throw it into the fire. I will make you a new bed tomorrow.'

With that, she went away, and the young man slept till daybreak. Up he sprang, then turned the bed over, made a shaving of it, and burned it. It was not long till the scolog came, and this is what he said to the king's son, 'I have a task for you to-day, and I hope you will be able to do it. There is a lake on my land not far from this, and a swamp at one side of it. You are to drain that lake and dry the swamp for me, and have the work finished this evening; if not, I will take the head from you at sunset. To drain the lake, you are to dig through a neck of land two miles in width; here is a good spade, and I'll show you the place where you're to use it.'

The king's son went with the scolog, who showed the ground, and then left him.

'What am I to do?' said the king's son. 'Sure, a thousand men couldn't dig that land out in ten years, and they working night and day; how am I to do it between this and sunset?'

However it was, he began to dig; but if he did, for every sod he threw out, seven sods came in, and soon he saw that, in place of mending his trouble, 'twas making it worse he was. He cast aside the spade then, sat down on the sod heap, and began to lament. He wasn't long there when the scolog's daughter came with a cloth in her hand and the small bundle in her pocket.

'Why are you lamenting there like a child?' asked she of the king's son.

'Why shouldn't I lament when the head will be taken from me at sunset?'

''Tis a long time from this to sunset. Eat your breakfast first of all; see what will happen then,' said she. Taking out the little bundle, she put down before him the best breakfast a man could have. While he was eating, she took the spade, cut out one sod, and threw it away. When she did that, every spadeful of earth in the neck of land followed the first spadeful; the whole neck of land was gone, and before midday there wasn't a spoonful of water in the lake or the swamp – the whole place was dry.

'You have your head saved to-day, whatever you'll do tomorrow,' said she, and she left him.

Toward evening the scolog came, and, meeting the king's son, cried out, 'You are the best man that ever came the way, or that ever I expected to look at.'

The king's son went to his lodging. In the evening the scolog's daughter came with supper, and made a bed for him as good as the first one. Next morning the king's son rose at daybreak, destroyed his bed, and waited to see what would happen.

The scolog came early, and said, 'I have a field outside, a mile long and a mile wide, with a very tall tree in the middle of it. Here are two wedges, a sharp axe, and a fine new drawing knife. You are to cut down the tree, and make from it barrels to cover the whole field. You are to make the barrels and fill them with water before sunset, or the head will be taken from you.'

The king's son went to the field, faced the tree, and gave it a blow with his axe; but if he did, the axe bounded back from the trunk, struck him on the forehead, stretched him on the flat of his back, and raised a lump on the place where it hit him. He gave three blows, was served each time in the same way, and had three lumps on his forehead. He was rising from the third blow, the life almost gone from him, and he crying bitterly, when the scolog's daughter came with his breakfast. While he was eating the breakfast, she struck one little chip from the tree; that chip became a barrel, and then the whole tree turned into barrels, which took their places in rows, and covered the field. Between the rows there was just room for a man to walk. Not a barrel but was filled with water. From a chip she had in her hand, the young woman made a wooden dipper, from another chip she made a pail, and said to the king's son –

'You'll have these in your two hands, and be walking up and down between the rows of barrels, putting a little water into this and a little into that barrel. When my father comes, he will see you at the work and invite you to the castle tonight, but you are not to go with him. You will say that you are content to lodge tonight where you lodged the other nights.' With that, she went away, and the king's son was going around among the barrels pouring a little water into one and another of them, when the scolog came.

'You have the work done,' said he, 'and you must come to the castle for the night.'

'I am well satisfied to lodge where I am, and to sleep as I slept since I came here,' said the young man, and the scolog left him.

The young woman brought the supper, and gave a fresh bed. Next morning the scolog came the third time, and said, 'Come with me now; I have a third task for you.' With that, the two went to a quarry.

'Here are tools,' said the scolog, pointing to a crowbar, a pickaxe, a trowel, and every implement used in quarrying and building. 'You are to quarry stones to-day, and build between this and sunset the finest and largest castle in the world, with outhouses and stables, with cellars and kitchens. There must be cooks, with men and women to serve; there must be dishes and utensils of every kind and furniture of every description; not a thing is to be lacking, or the head will go from you this evening at sunset.'

The scolog went home; and the king's son began to quarry with crowbar and pickaxe, and though he worked hard, the morning was far gone when he had three small pieces of stone quarried. He sat down to lament.

'Why are you lamenting this morning?' asked the scolog's daughter, who came now with his breakfast.

'Why shouldn't I lament when the head will be gone from me this evening? I am to quarry stones, and build the finest castle in the world before sunset. Ten thousand men couldn't do the work in ten years.'

'Take your breakfast,' said the young woman; 'you'll see what to do after that.'

While he was eating, she quarried one stone; and the next moment every stone in the quarry that was needed took its place in the finest and largest castle ever built, with outhouses and cellars and kitchens. A moment later, all the people were there, men and women, with utensils of all kinds. Everything was finished but a small spot at the principal fireplace.

'The castle is ready,' said the scolog's daughter; 'your head will stay with you to-day, and there are no more tasks before you at present. Here is a trowel and mortar; you will be finishing this small spot at the fire when my father comes. He will invite you to his castle tonight, and you are to go with him this time. After dinner, he will seat you at a table, and throw red wheat on it from his pocket. I have two sisters older than I am; they and I will fly in and alight on the table in the form of three pigeons, and we'll be eating the wheat; my father will tell you to choose one of his three daughters to marry. You'll know me by this: there will be a black quill in one of my wings. I'll show it; choose me.'

All happened as the scolog's daughter said; and when the king's son was told to make his choice in the evening, he chose the pigeon that he wanted. The three sprang from the table, and when they touched the floor, they were three beautiful women. A dish priest and a wooden clerk were brought to the castle, and the two were married that evening.

A month passed in peace and enjoyment; but the king's son wished to go back now to Erin to his father. He told the wife what he wanted; and this is what she said to him, 'My father will refuse you nothing. He will tell you to go, though he doesn't wish to part with you. He will give you his blessing; but this is all pretence, for he will follow us to kill us. You must have a horse for the journey, and the right horse. He will send a man with you to three fields. In the first field are the finest horses that you have ever laid eyes on; take none of them. In the second field are splendid horses, but not so fine as in the first field; take none of these either. In the third field, in the farthest corner, near the river, is a long-haired, shaggy, poor little old mare; take that one. The old mare is my mother. She has great power, but not so much as my father, who made her what she is, because she opposed him. I will meet you beyond the hill, and we shall not be seen from the castle.'

The king's son brought the mare; and when they mounted her, wings came from her sides, and she was the grandest steed ever seen. Away she flew over mountains, hills, and valleys, till they came to the seashore, and then they flew over the sea.

When the servant man went home, and the scolog knew what horse they had chosen, he turned himself and his two daughters into red fire, and shot after the couple. No matter how swiftly the mare moved, the scolog travelled faster, and was coming up. When the three reached the opposite shore of the sea, the daughter saw her father coming, and turned the mare into a small boat, the king's son into a fisherman, and made a fishing-rod of herself. Soon the scolog came, and his two daughters with him.

'Have you seen a man and a woman passing the way riding on a mare?' asked he of the fisherman.

'I have,' said the fisherman. 'You'll soon overtake them.'

On went the scolog; and he never stopped till he raced around the whole world, and came back to his own castle.

'Oh, then, we were the fools,' said the scolog to his daughters. 'Sure, they were the fisherman, the boat, and the rod.'

Off they went a second time in three balls of red fire; and they were coming near again when the scolog's youngest daughter made a spinning-wheel of her mother, a bundle of flax of herself, and an old woman of her husband. Up rushed the scolog, and spoke to the spinner, 'Have you seen a mare pass the way and two on her back?' asked he.

'I have, indeed,' said the old woman; 'and she is not far ahead of you.'

Away rushed the scolog; and he never stopped till he raced around the whole world, and came back to his own castle a second time.

'Oh, but we were the fools!' said the scolog. 'Sure, they were the old woman with the spinning-wheel and the flax, and they are gone from us now; for they are in Erin, and we cannot take our power over the border, nor work against them unless they are outside of Erin. There is no use in our following them; we might as well stay where we are.'

The scolog and his daughters remained in the castle at Ardilawn of Enchantment; but the king's son rode home on the winged mare, with his wife on a pillion behind him.

When near the castle of the old king in Erin, the couple dismounted, and the mare took her own form of a woman. She could do that in Erin. The three never stopped till they went to the old king. Great was the welcome before them; and if ever there was joy in a castle, there was joy then in that one.

DYEERMUD ULTA AND THE KING IN SOUTH ERIN

There was a king in South Erin once, and he had an only daughter of great beauty. The daughter said that she would marry no man but the man who would sail to her father's castle in a three-masted ship, and the castle was twenty miles from deep water. The father said that even if the daughter was willing, he'd never give her to any man but the man who would come in a ship.

Dyeermud Ulta was the grandson of a great man from Spain who had settled in Erin, and he lived near Kilcar. Dyeermud heard of the daughter of the king in South Erin, and fixed in his mind to provide such a ship and go to the castle of the king.

Dyeermud left home one day, and was walking toward Killybegs, thinking how to find such a ship, or the man who would make it. When he had gone as far as Buttermilk Cliff, he saw a red champion coming against him in a ship that was sailing along over the country like any ship on the sea.

'What journey are you on?' asked the red champion of Dyeermud; 'and where are you going?'

'I am going,' answered Dyeermud, 'to the castle of a king in South Erin to know will he give me his daughter in marriage, and to know if the daughter herself is willing to marry me. The daughter will have no husband unless a man who brings a ship to her father's castle, and the king will give her to no other.'

'Come with me,' said the red man. 'Take me as comrade, and what will you give me.'

'I will give you what is right,' said Dyeermud.

'What will you give me?'

'I will give you the worth of your trouble.'

Dyeermud went in the ship, and they sailed on till they came to Conlun, a mile above Killybegs. There they saw twelve men cutting sods, and a thirteenth eating every sod that they cut.

'You must be a strange man to eat what sods twelve others can cut for you,' said Dyeermud; 'what is your name?'

'Sod-eater.'

'We are going,' said the red man, 'to the castle of a king in South Erin. Will you come with us?'

'What wages will you give me?'

'Five gold-pieces,' said the red man.

'I will go with you.'

The three sailed on till they came to the river Kinvara, one mile below Killybegs, and saw a man with one foot on each bank, with his back toward the sea and his face to the current. The man did not let one drop of water in the river pass him, but drank every drop of it.

'Oh,' said the red man, 'what a thirst there is on you to drink a whole river! How are you so thirsty?'

'When I was a boy, my mother used to send me to school, and I did not wish to go there. She flogged and beat me every day, and I cried and lamented so much that a black spot rose on my heart from the beating; that is why there is such thirst on me now.'

'What is your name, and will you go with us?'

'My name is Gulping-a-River. I will go with you if you give me wages.'

'I will give you five gold-pieces,' said the red man.

'I will go with you,' said Gulping-a-River.

They sailed on then to Howling River, within one mile of Dun Kinealy. There they saw a man blowing up stream with one nostril, and the other stopped with a plug.

'Why blow with one nostril?' asked the red man.

'If I were to blow with the two,' replied the stranger, 'I would send you with your ship and all that are in it up into the sky and so far away that you would never come back again.'

'Who are you, and will you take service with me?'

'My name is Greedy-of-Blowing, and I will go with you for wages.'

'You will have five gold-pieces.'

'I am your man,' said Greedy-of-Blowing.

They sailed away after that to Bunlaky, a place one mile beyond Dun Kinealy; and there they found a man crushing stones with the end of his back, by sitting down on them suddenly.

'What are you doing there?' asked the red man.

'My name is Ironback,' answered the stranger. 'I am breaking stones with the end of my back to make a mill, a bridge, and a road.'

'Will you come with us?' asked the red man.

'I will for just wages,' said Ironback.

'You will get five gold-pieces.'

'I will go in your company,' said Ironback.

They went on sailing, and were a half a mile below Mount Charles when they saw a man running up against them faster than any wind, and one leg tied to his shoulder.

'Where are you going, and what is your hurry? Why are you travelling on one leg?' asked the red man.

'I am running to find a master,' said the other. 'If I were to go on my two legs, no man could see me or set eyes on me.'

'What can you do? I may take you in service.'

'I am a very good messenger. My name is Foot-on-Shoulder.'

'I will give you five gold-pieces.'

'I will go with you,' said the other.

The ship moved on now, and never stopped till within one mile of Donegal they saw, at a place called Kilemard, a man lying in a grass field with his cheek to the earth.

'What are you doing there?' asked the red man.

'Holding my ear to the ground, and hearing the grass grow.'

'You must have good ears. What is your name; and will you take service with me?'

'My name is Hearing Ear. I will go with you for good wages.'

'You will have five gold-pieces.'

'I am your man,' said Hearing Ear.

They went next to Laihy, where they found a man named Fis Wacfis (Wise man, Son of Knowledge), and he sitting at the roadside chewing his thumb.

'What are you doing there?' asked the red man.

'I am learning whatever I wish to know by chewing my thumb.'

'Take service with me, and come on the ship.'

He went on the same terms as the others, and they never stopped nor halted till they came to the castle of the king. They were outside the walls three days and three nights before any man spoke a word to them. At last the king sent a messenger to ask who were they and what brought them.

'I have come in a ship for your daughter, and my name is Dyeermud Ulta,' was the answer the king got.

The king was frightened at the answer, though he knew himself well enough that it was for the daughter Dyeermud had come in the ship, and was greatly in dread that she would be taken from him. He went then to an old henwife that lived near the castle to know could he save the daughter, and how could he save her.

'If you'll be said by me,' said the henwife, 'you'll bid them all come to a feast in the castle. Before they come, let your men put sharp poisoned spikes under the cushions of the seats set apart for the company. They will sit on the spikes, swell up to the size of a horse, and die before the day is out, every man of them.'

Hearing Ear was listening, heard all the talk between the king and the henwife, and told it.

'Now,' said Fis Wacfis to Dyeermud, 'the king will invite us all to a feast tomorrow, and you will go there and take us. It is better to send Ironback to try our seats, and sit on them, for under the cushion of each one will be poisoned spikes to kill us.'

That day the king sent a message to Dyeermud. 'Will you come,' said he, 'with your men, to a feast in my castle tomorrow? I am glad to have such guests, and you are welcome.'

'Very thankful am I,' said Dyeermud. 'We will come to the feast.'

Before the company came, Ironback went into the hall of feasting, looked at everything, sat down on each place, and made splinters of the seats.

'Those seats are of no use,' said Ironback; 'they are no better than so many cabbage stalks.'

The king had iron seats brought in, strong ones. There was no harm to Dyeermud and his company from that feast.

Away went the king to the henwife, and told how the seats had been broken. 'What am I to do now?' asked he.

'Say that to get your daughter they must eat what food is in your castle at one meal.'

Next day Dyeermud went to the castle, and asked, 'Am I to have your daughter now?'

'You are not,' said the king, 'unless your company will eat what food is in my castle at one meal.'

'Very well,' said Dyeermud; 'have the meal ready.'

The king gave command to bring out the hundred and fifty tons of provisions in the castle all prepared and ready for eating.

Dyeermud came with his men, and Sod-eater began; and it was as much as all the king's servants could do to bring food as fast as he ate it, and he never stopped till there wasn't a pound of the hundred and fifty tons left.

'Is this all you have to give me?' asked Sod-eater. 'I could eat three times as much.'

'Oh, we have no more,' said the servants.

'Where is our dinner?' asked Dyeermud.

The king had nothing for the others, and he had nothing for himself. All had to go away hungry, and there was great dissatisfaction in the castle, and complaining.

The king had nothing to do now but to go to the henwife a third time for advice in his trouble.

'You have,' said she, 'three hundred and fifty pipes of wine. If his company cannot drink every drop of the wine, don't give him the daughter.'

Next day Dyeermud went to the castle. 'Am I to have the daughter now?' asked he of the king.

'I will not give my daughter,' said the king, 'unless you and your company will drink the three hundred and fifty pipes of wine that are in my castle.'

'Bring out the wine,' said Dyeermud; 'we'll come tomorrow, and do the best we can to drink it.'

Dyeermud and his men went next day to where the wine was. Gulping-a-River was the man for drinking, and they let him at it. After he got a taste, he was that anxious that he broke in the head of one pipe after another, and drank till there wasn't a drop left in the three hundred and fifty pipes. All the wine did was to put thirst on Gulping-a-River; and he was that mad with thirst that he drank up the spring well at the castle, and all the springs in the neighbourhood, and a loch three miles distant, so that in the evening there wasn't a drop of water for man or beast in the whole place.

What did the king do but go to the henwife the fourth time.

'Oh,' said she, 'there is no use in trying to get rid of him this way; you can make no hand of Dyeermud by eating or drinking. Do you send him now to the Eastern World to get the bottle of cure from the three sons of Sean [pronounced Shawn – John] Mac Glinn, and to have it at the castle before noon tomorrow.'

'Am I to get the daughter now?' asked Dyeermud of the king.

'You'll not get my daughter,' said the king, 'unless you have for me here tomorrow the bottle of cure which the three sons of Sean Mac Glinn have in the Eastern World.'

Dyeermud went to his ship with the king's answer.

'Let me go,' said Foot-on-Shoulder. 'I will bring you the bottle in season.'

'You may go,' said Dyeermud.

Away went Foot-on-Shoulder, and was at the sea in a minute. He made a ship of his cap, a mast of his stick, a sail of his shirt, and away with him sailing over the sea, never stopping nor halting till he reached the Eastern World.

In five hours, he came to a castle where the walls of defence were sixty-six feet high and fifty-five feet thick. Sean Mac Glinn's three sons were playing football on the top of the wall.

'Send down the bottle of cure to me,' said Foot-on-Shoulder, 'or I'll have your lives.'

'We will not give you the bottle of cure; and if you come up, it will be as hard to find your brains five minutes after as to find the clay of a cabin broken down a hundred years ago.'

Foot-on-Shoulder made one spring, and rose six feet above the wall. They were so frightened at the sight of what he did, and were so in dread of him that they cried, 'You'll get what you want, only spare us – leave us our lives. You are the best man that we have ever seen coming from any part; you have done what no man could ever do before this. You'll get the bottle of cure; but will you send it back again?'

'I will not promise that,' said Foot-on-Shoulder; 'I may send it, and I may not.'

They gave him the bottle, he went his way to his ship, and sailed home to Erin. Next morning the henwife dressed herself up as a piper, and, taking a rod of enchantment with her, went away, piping on a hill which Foot-on-Shoulder had to cross in coming to the castle. She thought he would stop to listen to the music she was making, and then she would strike him with the rod, and make a stone of him. She was piping away for herself on the hill like any poor piper making his living. Hearing Ear heard the music, and told Dyeermud. Fis Wacfis chewed his thumb at Dyeermud's command, and found out that the piper was the king's henwife, and discovered her plans.

'Oh,' said Fis Wacfis to Dyeermud, 'unless you take her out of that, she will make trouble for us.'

'Greedy-of-Blowing, can you make away with that old woman on the hill?' asked Dyeermud.

'I can indeed,' said Greedy-of-Blowing.

With that, he ran to the foot of the hill; and with one blast from both nostrils, he sent the old hag up into the sky, and away she went sailing so that neither tale nor word of her ever came back.

Foot-on-Shoulder was at the ship outside the castle walls half an hour before noon, and gave the bottle of cure to Dyeermud. Dyeermud went that minute to the castle, and stood before the king.

'Here is the bottle of cure which I got from the three sons of Sean Mac Glinn in the Eastern World. Am I to get the daughter now?'

'I'll send you my answer to the ship,' said the king.

Where should the king go now in his trouble but to find the henwife.

She was not at home. He sent men to look for the old woman; no tidings of her that day. They waited till the next day; not a sight of her. The following morning the king sent servants and messengers to look for the henwife. They searched the whole neighbourhood; could not find her. He sent all his warriors and forces. They looked up and down, searched the whole kingdom, searched for nine days and nights, but found no trace of the henwife.

The king consented at last to give the daughter to Dyeermud, and he had to consent, and no thanks to him, for he couldn't help himself. The daughter was glad and willing; she loved Dyeermud from the first, but the father would not part with her.

The wedding lasted a day and a year, and when that time was over, Dyeermud went home on the ship to Kilcar, and there he paid all his men their wages, and they went each to his own place.

The red man stayed sometime in the neighbourhood, and what should he do one day but seize Dyeermud's wife, put her in the ship, and sail away with her. When going, she put him under injunction not to marry her for a day and a year.

Now Dyeermud, who was hunting when the red man stole his wife, was in great grief and misery, for he knew not where the red man lived nor where he should travel to find him. At last he sent a message of enquiry to the King of Spain; and the king's answer was, 'Only two persons in the whole world know where that man lives, Great Limper, King of Light, and Black Thorn of Darkness. I have written to these two, and told them to go to you.'

The two men came in their own ship through the air to Kilcar, to Dyeermud, and talked and took counsel.

'I do not know where the red man can be,' said Black Thorn, 'unless in Kilchroti; let us go to that place.'

They sailed away in their ship, and it went straight to the place they wanted. They had more power than the red man, and could send their ship anywhere.

In five days and nights they were at Kilchroti. They went straight to the house, and no one in the world could see the red man's house there but these two. Black Thorn struck the door, and it flew open. The red man, who was inside, took their hands, welcomed them heartily, and said, 'I hope it is not to do me harm that ye are here.'

'It is not to harm you or any one that we are here,' replied they. 'We are here only to get what is right and just, but without that, we will not go from this.'

'What is the right and just that ye are here for?' asked the red man.

'Dyeermud's wife,' replied Black Thorn, 'and it was wrong in you to take her; you must give her up.'

'I will fight rather than give her,' said the red man.

'Fighting will not serve you,' said Black Thorn, 'it is better for you to give her to us.'

'Ye will not get her without seven tons of gold,' said the red man. 'If ye bring me the gold, I will give her to you. If ye come without it, ye'll get fight from me.'

'We will give you the gold,' said Great Limper, 'within seven days.'

'Agreed,' said the red man.

'Come to the ship,' said Great Limper to Black Thorn.

They went on board, and sailed away.

'I was once on a ship which was wrecked on the coast of Spain with forty-five tons of gold. I know where that gold is; we will get it,' said Great Limper.

The two sailed to where the gold was, took seven tons of it, and on the sixth day they had it in Kilchroti, in front of the red man's house. They weighed out the gold to him. They went then to find Dyeermud's wife. She was behind nine doors; each door was nine planks in thickness, and bolted with nine bars of iron. The red man opened the doors; all went in, and looked at the chamber. The woman went out first, next the red man; and, seizing the door, he thought to close it on Great Limper and Black Thorn, but Black Thorn was too quick for him, and before the red man could close the door he shot him, first with a gold and then with a silver bullet.

The red man fell dead on the threshold.

'I knew he was preparing some treachery,' said Black Thorn. 'When we weighed the gold to him, he let such a loud laugh of delight out of him.'

They took the woman and the gold to Dyeermud; they stayed nine days and nights with him in Kilcar, eating, drinking, and making merry. They drank to the King of Spain, to all Erin, to themselves, and to their well-wishers. You see, I had great work to keep up with them these nine days and nights. I hope they will do well hereafter.

CUD, CAD, AND MICAD, THREE SONS OF THE KING OF URHU

There was a king once in Urhu, and he had three sons. The eldest was three, the second two, the youngest one year old. Their names were Cud, Cad, and Micad. The three brothers were playing one day near the castle, which was hard by the seashore; and Cud ran in to his father, and said, 'I hope you will give me what I ask.'

'Anything you ask that I can give you will get,' said the father.

''Tis all I ask,' said Cud, 'that you will give me and my brothers one of your ships to sail in till evening.'

'I will give you that and welcome, but I think you and they are too weak to go on a ship.'

'Let us be as we are; we'll never go younger,' said Cud.

The king gave the ship. Cud hurried out, and, catching Cad and Micad, one under each of his arms, went with one spring to the best ship in the roadstead. They raised the sails then, and the three brothers did as good work as the best and largest crew. They left the harbour with the fairest wind a ship ever had. The wind blew in a way that not a cable was left without stretching, an oar without breaking, nor a helm without cracking with all the speed the ship had. The water rose in three terrible ridges, so that the rough gravel of the bottom was brought to the top, and the froth of the top was driven down to the bottom of the sea. The sight of the kingdom of the world soon sank from the eyes of the brothers; and when they saw nothing but blue sea around them, a calm fell on the water.

Cud was going back and forth on the deck, sorry for what was done; and a good right he had to be sorry, but he was not sorry long. He saw a small currachan (boat) a mile away, and went with one spring from his ship to the currachan. The finest woman in the world was sleeping in the bottom of the boat. He put a finger under her girdle, and went back with a spring to the ship. When he touched his own deck, she woke.

'I put you under bonds and the misfortune of the world,' cried she, 'to leave me where you saw me first, and to be going ever and always till you find me again.'

'What name am I to call you when I go in search of you?'

'The Cat of Fermalye, or the Swan of Endless Tales,' said the woman.

He took her with one spring to the little boat, and with another spring went back to his own ship. Whatever good wind they had coming, they had it twice better going home. In the evening the ship was anchored among the others again. The brothers went ashore in a boat. When Cud came in, his father put out a chair for him, and gave him great welcome. Cud sat down; but as he did, he broke three rungs in the chair, two ribs in himself, and a rafter in the roof of the castle.

'You were put under bonds to-day,' said the father.

'I was,' said Cud.

'What bonds?'

'To be going ever and always till I find the Cat of Fermalye, or the Swan of Endless Tales.'

Himself and his father spent that night together, and they were very sad and downhearted. As early as the dawn came, Cud rose and ate his breakfast.

'Stay with me; I'll give you half my kingdom now, and all when I die,' said the father.

'I cannot stay under bonds; I must go,' replied Cud.

Cud took the ship he liked best, and put supplies for a day and seven years in her.

'Now,' said the father, 'ask for something else; anything in the world I can give, I will give you.'

'I want nothing but my two brothers to go with me.'

'I care not where they go if yourself leaves me,' said the king.

The three brothers went aboard the ship; and if the wind was good the first day, it was better this time. They never stopped nor rested till they sailed to Fermalye. The three went on shore, and were walking the kingdom. They had walked only a short piece of it when they saw a grand castle. They went to the gate; Cud was just opening it when a cat came out. The cat looked at Cud, bowed to him, and went her way. They saw neither beast nor man in the castle, or near it; only a woman at the highest window, and she sewing.

'We'll not stop till we go as far as the woman,' said Cud.

The woman welcomed them when they came to her, put out a gold chair to Cud and a wooden chair to each of his brothers.

''Tis strange,' said Micad, 'to show so much greater respect to one than the other two.'

'No cause for wonder in that,' said the woman. 'I show respect to this one, for he is my brother-in-law.'

'We do not wonder now, but where is his wife?'

'She went out a cat when ye came in.'

'Oh, was that she?' cried Cud.

They spent the night with good cheer and plenty of food, the taste of honey in every bit they ate, and no bit dry. As early as the day dawned, the three rose, and the sister-in-law had their breakfast before them.

'Grief and sorrow, I'm in dread 'tis bad cooking ye have on the ship. Take me with you; you'll have better food.'

'Welcome,' said Cud. 'Come with us.'

Each of the others welcomed her more than Cud. The four went on board; the brothers raised sails, and were five days going when they saw a ship shining like gold and coming from Western waters.

'That ship has no good appearance,' said Cud. 'We must keep out of danger'; and he took another course. Whatever course he took, the other ship was before him always, and crossing him.

'Isn't it narrow the ocean is, that you must be crossing me always?' shouted Cud.

'Do not wonder,' cried a man from the other ship; 'we heard that the three sons of the King of Urhu were sailing on the sea, and if we find them, it's not long they'll be before us.'

The three strangers were the three sons of the King of Hadone.

'If it is for these you are looking,' said Cud, 'you need go no farther.'

'It is to find you that we are here,' said the man on the shining ship, 'to take you on a visit to our own kingdom for a day and seven years. After that, we will go for the same length of time to your kingdom.'

'You will get that and welcome,' said Cud.

'Come on board my ship,' said the eldest son of the King of Hadone: 'we'll make one company; your ship is not much to look at.'

'Of the food that our father gave us,' said Cud, 'there is no bit dry, and we have plenty on board. If it is dry food that you have in that big ship, leave it and come to us.'

The sons of the King of Hadone went to the small ship, and let the big one go with the wind. When Cud saw that they let their own ship go, he made great friends of them.

'Have you been on sea ever before?' asked he of the eldest of the strangers.

'I am on sea since I was of an age to walk by myself,' replied he.

'This is my first voyage,' said Cud. 'Now as we are brothers and friends, and as you are taking us to visit your kingdom, I'll give you command of my ship.'

The king's son took this from Cud willingly, and steered home in a straight course.

When the sons of the King of Hadone were leaving home, they commanded all in the kingdom, big and little, small and great, weak and strong, to be at the port before them when they came back with the sons of the King of Urhu. 'These,' said they, 'must never be let out alive on the shore.'

In the first harbour the ship entered, the shore was black and white with people.

'Why are all those people assembled?' asked Cud.

'I have no knowledge of that,' said the king's son; 'but if you'll let your two brothers go with me and my brothers, we'll find out the reason.'

They anchored the ship, put down a long-boat, and Cad and Micad went into it with the three sons of the King of Hadone. Cud and his sister-in-law stayed behind on the ship. Cud never took his eyes off his brothers as they sat in the boat. He watched them when near the shore, and saw them both killed. With one bound he sprang from the bowsprit to land, and went through all there as a hawk through small birds. Two hours had not passed when the head was off every man in the kingdom. Whatever trouble he had in taking the heads, he had twice as much in finding his brothers. When he had the brothers found, it failed him to know how to bury them. At last he saw on the beach an old ship with three masts. He pulled out the masts, drew the ship further on land, and said to himself, 'I will have my brothers under this ship turned bottom upward, and come back to take them whenever I can.'

He put the bodies on the ground, turned the ship over them, and went his way.

The woman saw all the slaughter. 'Never am I to see Cud alive,' thought she, and fell dead from sorrow.

Cud took the woman to shore, and put her under the ship with his brothers. He went to his ship then, sailed away alone, and never stopped till he came to the kingdom where lived Mucan Mor Mac Ri na Sorach. Cud went ashore, and while walking and looking for himself, he came to a castle. He was wondering at the pole of combat, such a terribly big one, and he gave a small blow to it. The messenger came out, and looked up and down to know could he find the man who gave the blow.

Not a soul could he see but a white-haired young child standing near the pole. He went into the castle again.

'Who struck the pole?' asked Mucan Mor.

'I saw no one but a small child with white hair; there is no danger from him.'

Cud gave a harder blow.

'That blow is harder,' said Mucan Mor, 'than any child can give. Go and see who is in it.'

The man searched high and low, and it failed him to find any one but the child.

'It would be a wonder if you are the one, you little child, that struck the blow.'

'What harm,' said the little child, 'if I gave the pole a touch?'

'Mucan Mor is going to dinner soon,' said the messenger; 'and if you vex him again, 'tis yourself that he'll eat in place of the dinner.'

'Is dinner ready?' asked Cud.

'It is going to be left down,' was the answer he got.

When the man went in, Cud gave the pole a hard blow, and didn't leave calf, foal, lamb, kid, or child awaiting its birth, or a bag of poor oats or rye, that didn't turn five times to the left, and five to the right with the fright that it got. He made such a noise and crash that dishes were broken, knives hurled around, and the castle shaken to its bottom stone. Mucan Mor himself was turned five times to the left and five to the right before he could put the soles of his feet under him. When he went out, and saw the small child, he asked, 'Was it you that struck the pole?'

'I gave it a little tip,' said Cud.

'You are a child of no sense to be lying so, and it is yourself that I'll eat for my supper.'

He thought he had only to take Cud into the castle, and roast him on the spit. He went to catch the child; but if he did, the child faced him, and soon they were fighting like two bulls in high grass. When it was very late in the day, Mucan Mor rose up in a lump of fog, and Cud didn't know where he had gone.

All Cud had to do was to go to the forest, and gather twigs for a fire to keep himself warm until morning. It wasn't many twigs he had gathered when twelve swans came near him.

'Love me!' said he. 'I believe ye are the blessed birds that came from my father's kingdom to be food to relieve me in need.'

'Sorry am I that I have ever looked on you or you on me,' said one of the swans; and the twelve rose and flew away.

Cud gathered the twigs for the fire, and dried the blood in his wounds. In the morning, Mucan Mor struck his own pole of combat. He and Cud faced each other, and fought till late in the day, when Mucan Mor rose as a lump of fog in the air. Cud went to the forest as before to gather twigs. It was few he had gathered when the twelve swans came again.

'Are ye the blessed birds from my own kingdom?' asked he.

'No,' said one of the swans; 'but I put you under bonds not to turn me away as you did last night.'

'As you put me under bonds,' said Cud, 'I will not turn you away.'

The twelve began to gather twigs, and it wasn't long till they had a great fire made. One of the twelve sat at the fire then with Cud, and said, 'There is nothing in the world to kill Mucan Mor but a certain apple. For the last three days I have been looking for that apple. I found it to-day, and have it here for you. Tomorrow you'll be getting the upper hand of Mucan Mor earlier than other days. He has no power to rise as a fog until a given hour. When the time comes, he'll raise his two hands and be striving to go in the air. If you strike him then in the right side in the ribs with the apple, you'll make a green stone of him. If you do not, he'll come down and make a green stone of you.'

Cud took the apple, and had great thanks for the swan. She left down the best food then before him. She had the food with her always.

Glad was he, for he was greatly in want of it after the fast of two days. She put her own wing and head over his head and sheltered him till day break. There wasn't a wound on him next morning that wasn't cured. As early as the day dawned she roused him.

'Be up now,' said she, 'and have the soles of your feet under you.' He went first to the pole and struck a blow that took three turns out of the stomach of Mucan Mor and three more out of his brain, before he could stand on the soles of his feet, so great was the dread that came on him.

They fought the third day, and it wasn't very late when Cud was getting the upper hand. Mucan Mor raised his two arms toward the sky, striving to escape in a fog from his enemy. Cud struck him then with the apple, and made a green stone of him. Hardly had he Mucan Mor killed when he saw an old hag racing up; she took one hill at a step and two at a leap.

'Your face and your health to you,' said the hag, when she stood before Cud. 'I am looking at you for three days, fighting without food or drink. I hope that you'll come with me now.'

'It's long that you were thinking of asking me,' said he.

'I hope you'll not refuse me,' said the hag.

'I will not,' replied Cud.

'Give me your hand,' said the hag, 'and I'll help you to walk.'

He took the hag's hand. There wasn't a jump that she gave while she had a grip of his hand but he thought she was dragging the arm from him.

'Curses on you for an old hag! Is it little I have gone through that you treat me in this way?'

'I have a cloth about my shoulders. Go into that, and I will carry you,' said the hag.

There wasn't a joint in the hag's back that wasn't three inches long. When she had him on her back there wasn't a leap that she gave that the joints of her backbone were not going into Cud's body.

'Hard luck to you for a hag, after all I have gone through to have me killed at last.'

'You have not far to go now,' said she; and after a few leaps she was at the end of her journey. She took him into a grand castle. The best table of food that he had ever set eyes on was left down there before him.

'Sit there, now, son of the King of Urhu; eat and drink.'

'I have never taken food without company,' said Cud, 'and I will not take it this time.'

'Will you eat with me?'

'Bad luck to you for a hag, I will not.'

She opened a door and let in twelve pigs, and one pig, the thirteenth, without a head.

'Will you take food with these, son of the King of Urhu?'

'Indeed, then, old hag, bad as you are yourself, I'd rather eat with you than with these, and I'll not eat with you.'

She put them back, opened another door and let out twelve of the rustiest, foulest, ugliest old hags that man could set eyes on.

'Will you take food with these?' asked she.

'Indeed, then, I will not.'

She hurried them back, opened a door, and brought out twelve beautiful young women.

'Will you take food with these?'

'These are fit to take food with any one,' said Cud.

They sat down and ate with good-will and pleasure. When they had the dinner eaten the hag opened the door, and the twelve went back to their own chamber.

'I'll get great blame,' said the old hag, 'for all the delay I've had. I'll be going now.'

'What trouble is on you that you'll be blamed for your delay?'

'Those twelve pigs that you saw,' said the hag, 'are twelve sons of mine, and the pig without a head is my husband. Those twelve foul, yellow hags that you saw are my twelve daughters. The twelve beautiful women who ate with you are my daughters' attendants.'

'Why are your twelve sons and your husband pigs, and your twelve daughters yellow old hags?'

'The Awus in that house there beyond has them enchanted and held in subjection. There isn't a night but I must go with a gold apple to him.'

'I will go with you tonight,' said Cud.

'There is no use in going,' said the hag.

They were talking a long time before she would let him go. She went first, and he followed. She knocked, and they opened the door. Cud was in with her that instant. One Awus rose and put seven bolts and seven locks on the door. Cud rose and put on seven locks and seven bolts more. All began to laugh when they saw Cud doing this. The old chief, who was standing at the hearth, let such a roar out of him that Cud saw the heart inside in his body.

'Why are you laughing?' asked Cud.

'We think you a nice bit of meat to roast on the spit. Rise up,' said he to a small attendant, 'and tie that fellow.'

The attendant rose and tried to tie Cud, but soon Cud had him down and tied.

'Bad luck to you, 'tis sorry I am that I ever lost food on the like of you,' said the old chief to the small attendant. 'Rise up,' said he to a big attendant, 'and tie him.'

The big one rose up, and whatever time the small one lasted, the big one didn't last half that length. Cud drew strings from his pocket and began tying the Awuses. He caught the old Awus by the shins, dragged him down, and put his knee on him.

'You are the best champion ever I have seen,' said the old Awus. 'Give me quarter for my soul; there is never a place where you need it but my help will attend you with bravery. I'll give you also my sword of light that shines in the dark, my pot of cure that makes the dead alive, and the rod of enchantment to help the pot of cure.'

'Where can I find them?' asked Cud.

'In a hole in the floor under the post of my bed. You cannot get them without help.'

'It cannot be but I can do anything that has been done ever in your house,' said Cud.

With that he went to the bed, and whatever work he had in his life he never found a harder task than to move the post of the bed; but he found the sword of light, the pot of cure, and the rod of enchantment. He came to the Awus with the sword in one hand, and the two other things in the other hand.

'The head off you now if you don't take this hag and her family from under enchantment. Make men and women of her sons and daughters, a king of her husband, and a queen of herself in this kingdom, while water is running, and grass is growing, and you are to go to them with a gold apple every evening and morning as long as you live or any one lives who comes after you to the end of all ages.'

'I will do that,' said the Awus.

He gave the word, and the hag was as fine a queen as she was before. She and Cud went back to the castle. The twelve pigs were twelve young men, and the thirteenth without a head was the king. She opened the chamber of the twelve yellow hags, and they were as beautiful as ever. All were very grateful to Cud for the good turn he had done them.

'I had one son,' said the queen; 'while he was here he gave the old Awus enough to do.'

'Where is he now?' enquired Cud.

'In the Eastern World, in a field seven miles in length, and seven in width, and there isn't a yard of that field in which a spike is not standing taller than a man. There is not a spike, except one, without a king's son or a champion on it, impaled through his chin.'

'What name had your son?'

'Gold Boot.'

'I promise to bring Gold Boot here to you, or leave my own head on the spike.'

As early as the day rose Cud was ready, and away he went walking, and very little food had he with him. About midday he was at the enchanted field, in the Eastern World. He was walking till he came to Gold Boot. When he touched the body, the foot gave him a kick that sent him seven acres and seven ridges away, and put three bunches of the blood of his heart out of him.

'I believe what your mother said, that when you were living you were strong, and the strength you have now to be in you.'

'Don't think we are dead,' said Gold Boot; 'we are not. It is how we are enchanted and unable to rise out of this.'

'What put you in it?' asked Cud.

'A man will come out by and by with pipes, making music, and he'll bring so much sleep on you that he'll put you on that empty spike, and the field will be full. If you take my advice you will not wait for him.'

'My grief and my sorrow! I will never stir till I see all that is here,' replied Cud.

It wasn't long he was waiting when the piper came out, and the very first sound that he heard Cud ran and caught the pipes; whatever music the man was making, Cud played seven times better.

When Cud took the pipes, the piper ran crying into the castle where the wizard was.

'What is on you?' asked the wizard.

'A man caught my pipes, and he is a twice better player than what I am.'

'Never mind that, take these with you; these are the pipes that won't be long in putting sleep on him.'

When Cud heard the first note of these pipes, he struck the old ones against a stone, and ran and caught the new pipes. The piper rushed to the wizard; the old man went out, threw himself on his knees, and begged mercy.

'Never give him mercy,' said Gold Boot, 'till he burns the hill that is standing out opposite him.'

'You have no pardon to get till you set that hill there on fire,' answered Cud.

'That is as bad for me as to lose my head,' said the wizard.

'That same is not far from you unless you do what I bid,' replied Cud.

Sooner than lose his head he lighted the hill. When the hill began to burn, all the men except Gold Boot came from under enchantment as sound as ever, and rose off the spikes. Every one was making away, and no one asking who let him out. The hill was on fire except one spot in the middle of it. Gold Boot was not stirring. 'Why did you not make him set all the hill on fire?' asked he.

'Why did you not set the whole hill on fire?' demanded Cud of the wizard.

'Is it not all on fire?'

'Do you see the centre is not burning yet?'

'To see that bit on fire,' said the wizard, 'is as bad for me as to lose the head itself.'

'That same is not far from you,' said Cud.

'Sooner than lose the head I will light it.'

That moment he lighted the hill, and Cud saw the very woman he saw the first day sleeping in the little boat come toward him from the hill. He forgot that he had seen Gold Boot or the enchanted hag and her sons. The wizard, seeing this, stopped the centre fire, and Gold Boot was left on the spike. Cud and the woman embraced till they smothered each other with kisses and drowned each other with tears. After that they neither stopped nor stayed till they reached his little ship and sailed away on it; they never delayed till they came to where his two brothers and sister-in-law were under the boat. Cud took out the three bodies, put a drop of the cure on each one, and gave each a blow of the rod. They rose up in good health and sound vigour. All entered the ship and sailed toward Urhu.

They had only the sailing of one day before them, when Cud recollected his promise to bring Gold Boot to his mother.

'Take the wife to Fermalye,' said he to his brothers. 'I must go for Gold Boot; the king will give you food till I come. If you were to go to our own father he'd think that it is dead I am.'

Cud drew out his knife, cut a slip from a stick; this he threw into the sea. It became a ship, and away he sailed in that ship, and never stopped till he entered the harbour next the enchanted field. When he came to Gold Boot he gave him a drop of cure and a blow of the rod. He rose from the spike, well and strong. The two embraced then, went to the ship, and sailed away. They had not gone far when such a calm came that they cast anchor near shore, and Gold Boot began to get dinner. It wasn't long he was at it when they saw food at the foot of a tree on the shore.

'Who would be getting trouble with cooking, and such food as that on the shore?' said Gold Boot.

'Don't mind that food,' replied Cud.

'Whatever I think of I do,' said Gold Boot.

He went to shore with one jump, caught the food, sprang back, and laid it down for himself and Cud. When this was done there was food seven times better on the land again.

'Who would taste of this, and that table over there?' cried Gold Boot.

'Never mind it,' said Cud. 'If the man who owns this table was sleeping when you took it, he is not sleeping now.'

'Whatever I think of I must do,' replied Gold Boot.

'If you did that before, I will do it now,' said Cud, and he sprang to land. He looked up in the tree, and there he saw a man ready to take the life from him.

'Grief and sorrow!' said the man. 'I thought it was Gold Boot again. Take this table, with welcome, but I hope you'll invite me to dinner.'

'I will, indeed,' said Cud; 'and what name am I to give you?'

'The Wet Mantle Champion.'

Cud took one end of the table and the champion the other. Out they went to the ship with one bound. They sat down then together with Gold Boot at the table. When dinner was over, the wind rose, and they sailed on, never delaying till they came to the castle of Gold Boot's father, where there was a great welcome before them, and thanks beyond estimate.

'I will give you half my kingdom while I live and all of it when I die,' said the king, 'and the choice of my twelve daughters.'

'Many thanks to you,' replied Cud; 'the promise of marriage is on me already, but perhaps Wet Mantle is not married or promised.'

'I am not,' said Wet Mantle.

'You must have my chance,' said Cud.

Wet Mantle took Cud's place, and the king sent for a big dish priest, and a great wooden clerk. They came, and the couple were married. When the three days' wedding was over, Cud went away alone. While sailing near land he saw a castle by the sea, and as he drew near he wondered more and more. A raven was going in and out at the uppermost window, and each time bringing out something white. Cud landed, walked up from the strand, and went to the top of the castle. He saw a woman there, and the whole room full of white pigeons. She was throwing them one by one from a loft to the raven.

'Why do you throw those to the raven?' asked Cud of the woman.

'The raven is an enchanted brother of mine, who comes to this castle once in seven years. I can see him only while I am throwing him pigeons. I get as many pigeons as possible, to keep him with me while I can.'

'Keep him for a while yet,' said Cud.

He rushed to the ship, took his rod, and ran to the loft where the woman was. 'Entice him in further,' said Cud.

Cud struck the raven a blow, and he rose up as fine a champion as ever was seen.

'Your blow on me was good,' said the champion, 'and 'tis work you have now before you. Your two brothers are killed and under seven feet of earth in Fermalye. Your wife and her sister are to their knees in foul water and filth in the stable, and are getting two mouthfuls of water, and two of bread in the day till they die.'

Cud did not wait to hear more of the story. Away he went, and never stopped till he came to Fermalye. When he was coming to the castle all the children he met he was throwing at each other, he was so vexed. He took the wife and sister out of the stable, then dug up the brothers and brought them to life with the rod. The five made no delay after that, but went to the ship and sailed to Urhu. When near land he raised white flags on every mast.

'A ship is coming!' cried a messenger, running to the king. 'I am thinking it is Cud that is in it.'

'That's what I will never believe,' said the king, 'till he puts his hand into my hand.'

Since Cud left home, the father and mother had never risen from the fireside, but were sitting there always and crying. When the ship was three miles from land, Cud ran from the stern to the stem, sprang to land, ran into the castle, gave one hand to his mother, and the other to his father.

It wasn't one boat, but boats, that went out to the ship for the brothers and the women. When they came, all spent the night with great pleasure in the castle. Next day the king sent seven score of ships and one ship to sea to bring supplies for the wedding. When the ships came back laden from foreign parts, he sent messengers to invite all the people in the kingdom. They were coming till they blackened the hills and spotted the valleys. I was there myself, and we spent nine nights and nine days in great glee and pleasure.

CAHAL, SON OF KING CONOR, IN ERIN, AND BLOOM OF YOUTH, DAUGHTER OF THE KING OF HATHONY

There was a king in Hathony long ago who had an old castle by the sea. This king went out walking one day along the clean, smooth strand, and, while walking, the thought rose in him to take a sail near the shore. He stepped into his boat with attendants and men, and was sailing about in enjoyment and pleasure, when a wind came with a mist of enchantment, and drove the boat away through the sea with the king and his men.

They were going before the wind, without a sight of sky or sea; no man in the boat could see the man who sat next to him. They were that way moving in the mist without knowledge of where they were, or where they were going, and the boat never stopped till it sailed into a narrow harbour in a lonely place without house or habitation.

The king left the boat well fastened at the shore, and went his way, walking till he came to a castle, and what castle should it be but the castle of King Conor, in Erin.

King Conor received the King of Hathony with great hospitality and welcome.

When the two had spent some days in company, they became great friends, and made a match between their two children. The King of Hathony had a daughter called Bloom of Youth, who was nine years of age, and King Conor had a son ten years old, named Cahal.

When the King of Hathony wished to go back to his own land, King Conor of Erin gave a ship to him, and the king sailed away with good wishes and with supplies for a day and a year.

Bloom of Youth grew up in such beauty that she had not her equal in Hathony or in other lands, and Cahal, King Conor's son, became such a hero that no man knew was the like of him in any place.

On a day Cahal said to his father, 'Make up some treasure for me and stores for my ship. I must leave home now and be travelling through the world till I know is there a better man than myself in it.'

'It is, indeed, time for you to be going,' said King Conor, 'for in three years you are to marry Bloom of Youth, the daughter of the King of Hathony, and you should be making out the place now where her father lives.'

Next morning Cahal took what treasures his father gave him, and provisions, went to his ship and raised sails. Away he went on his voyage, sailing over the sea in one way and another, in this direction and that. He sailed one year and three-quarters of a second year, but found no man to give tale or tidings of the King of Hathony.

Once on a gloomy day he was sailing along through the waves, when a strong north wind rose, and blew with such force that he let his ship go with it.

Three days and nights the ship went before the north wind, and on the fourth day, in the morning, it was thrown in on a rocky coast.

Cahal saved his life and his sword, and went away walking through the country. On the evening of the fifth day he came to an old castle near the seashore, and said to himself, 'I will not go in here to ask for lodgings like any poor traveller.' With that he walked up and put a blow on the pole of combat that made the whole castle tremble.

Out rushed the messenger. 'What brought you here, and what do you want?' asked he of King Conor's son.

'I want men to meet me in combat, seven hundred champions on my right hand, seven hundred on my left, seven hundred behind me, and the same number in front of me.'

The man ran in and gave the message to the king.

'Oh,' said the King of Hathony, 'that is my son-in-law from Erin'; and out he went.

'Are you the son of King Conor?' asked the king.

'I am,' said Cahal.

'A hundred thousand welcomes to you,' said the king.

'Thankful am I for the welcomes, and glad to receive them,' said Cahal. 'I had great trouble in coming; it is not easy to find you.'

'It is not easy to find any man unless you know the road to his house,' said the king.

There was great feasting that night and entertainment for Cahal. Next day the king said, 'Your bride, my daughter, is gone these two months. Striker, son of the King of Tricks, came to my castle and stole her away from me.'

'My word for it, he will not keep her unless he is a better man than I am,' said Cahal.

'I am sure of that,' said the king, 'and I said so.'

'My own ship was wrecked on your coast, and now you must give me another in place of it,' said Cahal.

'I will,' said the king, 'and a good one; but you can do nothing on sea against Striker.'

'I am more used to the sea now than to land, I am so long on it,' answered Cahal.

'If you were born on the water and had lived every day of your life on it, you could do nothing at sea against Striker. There is not a man living who can face him at sea.'

Nothing would satisfy Cahal but to go against Striker by sea; so he took the ship which the king gave and sailed away, sailed week after week till he was within a day's journey of Striker's castle. Striker thrust his head up through the top of the castle then, and let a blast out through his mouth that sent Cahal's ship back twice the distance it had come.

King Conor's son sailed forward again, and again Striker blew him back as far as he had the first time.

Cahal sailed now to the castle of the King of Hathony.

'I said that you could do nothing against Striker on sea. If you wish to get the upper hand of him I will tell you what to do. Take this bridle and shake it behind the castle; whatever beast comes to you take that one, and ride away against Striker.'

When Cahal shook the bridle, out came the smallest and ugliest beast in the stables, a lean, shaggy mare.

'Oh, then, bad luck to you for coming,' said the king's son, 'and so many fine steeds in the stables.'

'That is the pony my daughter used to ride, that is the best horse in the stables; take her. She is not easy to ride though, for she is full of tricks and enchantment, but if you are the right man she'll not throw you. She goes on water as well as land, and you will be at your enemy's castle to-day.'

Cahal mounted, and away went the mare. She crossed one hill at the first leap, three at the second, then twelve hills and valleys at the third leap; went over land and sea, and never stopped till she was in front of Striker's castle, two hours before sunset.

Cahal sprang from the mare, and struck the pole of combat.

'What do you want?' asked the attendant, running out.

'I want seven hundred champions in combat at my right side, seven hundred at my left, seven hundred behind me, and seven hundred out before my face.'

The attendant went in, and out came the twenty-eight hundred against Cahal.

He went at the champions, and before sunset he had them in three heaps, a heap of their bodies, a heap of their heads, and a heap of their weapons.

Next morning Cahal struck the pole again.

'What do you want this time?' asked the attendant.

'Seven thousand champions against me for every hundred that I had yesterday.'

Out came the champions in thousands. As they were coming Cahal was going through them, and before the day was ended he had them in three heaps without leaving a man, a heap of their heads, a heap of their bodies, and a heap of their weapons.

He struck the pole on the third morning, and before the attendant had time to open his mouth, Cahal shouted, 'Send out every man in the place. I may as well spend one day on them all as to be calling for champions occasionally.'

The forces of Striker, son of the King of Tricks, were coming as fast as ever they could make their way through the gates. They were rushing at Cahal like showers of hail on a stormy day, but they could neither kill him nor get the upper hand. They could neither defend themselves nor hurt him, and Cahal never stopped till he had them all in a heap at one side.

Cahal struck the pole on the fourth day.

'What do you want now?' asked the attendant.

'Striker, son of the King of Tricks, in combat before me.'

Out came Striker, and fell upon Cahal. The two fought seven days and six nights without stopping or resting, then Striker called for a truce and got it. He went into his castle, healed himself in his cauldron of cure, ate enough, slept, and was as fresh as ever next morning. They spent three days and two nights in combat after that without rest.

Striker called for cessation a second time and got it. On the eleventh morning a goldfinch perched opposite Cahal and said, 'Bad luck to you for a foolish young man to be giving your enemy rest, time to eat, drink, and cure himself, and you lying outside at the foot of the wall in hunger and cold. Keep him working till he yields. Give him no rest till you snatch from his breast the pin which he has in the left side of it.'

They were struggling four days and nights without rest or cessation till the fifth morning, when Cahal snatched the pin from the bosom of Striker.

'Oh, spare my life!' cried Striker. 'I'll be your servant in every place, only spare me.'

'I want nothing of you,' said Cahal, 'but this: Send out my bride to me; you took her from her father, the King of Hathony, and she was to be my wife soon when you took her. Send her to me, and put no fog or enchantment on us while we are on the way home.'

'You ask more than I can give,' said Striker, 'for Wet Mantle, the hero, took that maiden from me two months ago. When going, she put him under bonds not to molest her for two days and two years.'

'Where can I find Wet Mantle?'

'That is more than I can tell; but put your nose before you and follow it.'

'That's a short answer, and I would take your life for three straws on account of it; but I'll let some other man have his chance to take the head off you.'

Cahal mounted his mare then, and was travelling over seas and dry land, – travelling a long time till he came at last to Wet Mantle's castle. He struck the pole of combat, and out came the messenger.

'Who are you, and what do you want?'

'Seven hundred at my right hand, seven hundred at my left, seven hundred behind me, and seven hundred before my face.'

'That's more men than you can find in this place,' said the messenger. 'Wet Mantle lives here in his own way, without forces or company; he keeps no man but me, and is very well satisfied.'

'Go then,' said Cahal, 'and tell him to come out himself to me.'

Wet Mantle came out, and the two fought seven days and six nights. Wet Mantle called for a truce then and got it. The hero went to his castle, cured himself, and was as fresh the eighth morning as the first. They began to fight, and the struggle continued three days and two nights. Wet Mantle called for a truce, and received it the second time. On the eleventh morning he was well again, and ready for the struggle.

'Oh, then, it is foolish and simple you are, and small good in your travelling the world,' cried a goldfinch to Cahal. 'Why are you out here in hunger and cold, and he cured and fresh in his castle? Give him no rest the next time, but fight till you tire him and take the mantle from him. He'll be as weak as a common man then, for it is in the mantle his strength is.'

On the eleventh morning they began for the third time and fought fiercely all day. In the evening Wet Mantle called for a rest.

'No,' said Cahal, 'you'll get no rest. There is no rest for either of us. You must fight till you or I yield.'

They fought on till the following evening. Wet Mantle called for rest a second time.

'No rest till this battle is ended,' cried Cahal.

They held on all that night venomously, and were fighting at noon of the following day. Then Cahal closed on his enemy, and tore the mantle from his body.

The hero without his mantle had no more strength than a common man.

'You are the best champion that ever I have met,' said he to Cahal. 'I will give you all that you ask, but don't kill me.'

'I have no wish to kill or to hurt you, though good treatment is not what you deserve from me. You caused me great trouble and hardship searching and travelling, not knowing where to find you. I want nothing of you but my bride, and your promise not to put fog or magic on us or harm us until we reach Erin in safety.'

'That is more than I can promise,' said Wet Mantle.

'Why so?' asked Cahal.

'The gruagach, Long Sweeper, took that maiden from me, and she put him under bonds not to molest her, or come near her for three days and three years.'

'Where can I find Long Sweeper?'

'That is more than I can tell,' said Wet Mantle. 'The world is wide, you have free passage through it, and you can be going this way and that till you find him; he lives in a very high castle, and he is a tall man himself; he has a very long broom, and when he likes he sweeps the sky with that broom three times in the morning, and the day that he sweeps, there is no man in the world that can contradict him or conquer him.'

Cahal went riding his pony from the north to the south, from the east to the west, and west to east, three years and two days. At daylight of the third day he saw a tall castle in the ocean before him. So tall was the castle that he could not tell the height of it, and a man on the summit twice as tall as the castle itself, and he with a broom sweeping the sky.

'Ah,' said Cahal to himself, 'I have you at last.'

He rode forward then to the castle, and struck the pole of combat.

'What do you want?' asked the messenger.

'I want men to meet me in combat.'

'Well, that is what you'll not get in this place. There is no man living on this island but Long Sweeper and myself. The Black Horseman came from the Western World three months ago, and killed every man, gave Long Sweeper great hardship and trouble, and after terrible fighting got the upper hand of him.'

'Well, if he has no men, let him come out himself, for I'll never leave the spot till I knock satisfaction out of Long Sweeper for the trouble he gave me before I could find him.'

Long Sweeper came out, and they began to fight; they fought for seven days and six nights. Toward evening of the seventh day Long Sweeper called for rest and got it. He went into his high castle, ate, drank, healed himself in his cauldron of cure, and slept well and soundly, while Cahal had to rest as best he was able on the ground beyond the wall. The eighth morning Long Sweeper went up on his castle and swept the sky back and forth three times, and got such strength that no man on earth could overcome him that day.

They fought three days and two nights, and fought all the time without rest. Long Sweeper called for rest then and got it, and was cured and refreshed as before. Next morning he mounted the castle, swept the sky three times with his broom, and was ready for combat.

Before Long Sweeper came, the goldfinch perched in front of Cahal and said, 'Misfortune to you, son of King Conor in Erin; 'tis to a bad place you came with your life to lose it, and isn't it foolish of you to give your enemy rest, while yourself has nothing to lie on but the earth, and nothing to put in your mouth but cold air? Give neither rest nor truce to your enemy. He will be losing strength till three days from now. If he gets no chance to sweep the sky, he'll be no better than a common man.'

That evening Long Sweeper called for rest.

'No,' said Cahal, 'you'll get no rest from me. We must fight till either one or the other yields.'

'That's not fair fighting.'

'It is not, indeed. I am ten days and nights without food, drink, or rest, while you have had them twice. We have not fought fairly so far, but we will hereafter. You must remain as you are now till one of us is conquered.'

They were fighting till noon, the thirteenth day. 'I am beaten,' said Long Sweeper. 'Whatever I have I am willing to give you, but spare my life, for if there is a good hero in the world you are he.'

'I want nothing of you,' said Cahal, 'but to send out to me my bride, Bloom of Youth, daughter of the King of Hathony, the maiden you took from Wet Mantle. You have caused me great hardship and trouble, but I'll let some one else take your life, or may you live as you are.'

'I cannot send out your bride,' said Long Sweeper, 'for she is not in my castle. The Black Horseman took her from me three months ago.'

'Where am I to find that man?'

'I might tell you to put your nose before you and walk after it, but I will not; I will give you a guide. Here is a rod; whichever way the rod turns, follow it till you come to the Western World, where the Black Horseman lives.'

Cahal mounted his mare, made off with the rod in his hand, and rode straight to the Black Horseman's castle. The messenger was in front of the castle before him.

'Tell your master to send out champions against me, or to come himself,' said Cahal.

That moment the Black Horseman himself was on the threshold. 'I am here all alone,' said he to Cahal. 'I have lost all my wealth, all my men, all my magic. I am now in a poor state, though I was living pleasantly and in greatness after the conflict in which I got the better of Long Sweeper. It's rich and strong I was after parting with that man, and I was waiting here to marry when White Beard from the Western World came, made war on me, and continued it for a day and a year; then he left me poor and lonely, as I am at this moment.'

'Well,' said Cahal, 'you have caused me great labour and hardship; but I ask nothing of you except to send out my bride, Bloom of Youth, to me, and not to bring fog or magic on her or on me till we reach home in safety.'

'White Beard took your bride from me, and he cannot marry her for four days and four years, for she put him under bond not to do so. I will tell you now how to find her. Do you see that broad river in front of us? It flows from the Northern to the Southern World, and there is no way to cross it unless a good hero does so by springing from one bank to the other. When White Beard took the maiden from me, they walked to the brink of the river; he placed the woman then on his shoulder and sprang over the river to the west. "Let me down, now," said the woman. "I will not," replied White Beard, "I have such regard for you that I will show you every place on the road." He did not let her down till he showed her everything between the river and the castle. "You may come down," said he, when they entered the castle (she could see everything from his shoulder, but nothing from the ground). When coming down she thrust a sleeping pin that she had in the head of the old man, and he fell fast asleep standing there. She has whatever she wishes to eat or to drink in the castle. All is in a mist of enchantment. She can see nothing outside the castle, but everything within. That was my home at one time. I was born and reared in that castle, and lived in it till White Beard drove me away with magic and violence. I came to this place and lived here a time without trouble, till I took Bloom of Youth from Long Sweeper. I was waiting to marry her, when White Beard came, destroyed all my forces, took away my enchantment, carried off Bloom of Youth, and left me here without strength or defence. But one thing is left me, and that I will give you. Here is a torch. When you cross the river, light it. You'll find the road, and no one has found it since I was there. When you light the torch follow the road to an old cottage, at one side from the castle. In this cottage is a henwife, who has lived there since my childhood. She will show the way to the castle and back to her cottage. From there you may journey homeward in safety, by lighting the torch a second time, and keeping it till you ride out of the castle's enchantment. This is all I have to tell you.'

Cahal rode briskly to the river, rode across, lighted his torch on the other side, saw a narrow bright road, but nothing on either side. The road was a long one, but he came to the end of it at the door of the henwife's old cottage. Cahal greeted the henwife.

'A hundred thousand welcomes,' said the old woman. 'You are here from my master, the Black Horseman, or you could not be in it. Can I help you in any way?'

'I want nothing of you but to show me the way to the castle of White Beard, where my bride is, and then bring me back to this place.'

'Follow me,' said the henwife, 'and leave your horse here.'

She took Cahal by the hand and went forward till she came to the castle and entered it. There Cahal saw the finest woman that ever he had met in the world. 'Well,' said he to himself, 'I am not sorry, after all my troubles and hardships, if you are the woman I am to marry.'

'A greeting to you, young hero,' said the woman. 'Who are you who have been able to come to this castle, and why are you here?'

'My name is Cahal, son of King Conor, in Erin. I am long travelling and fighting to find and to rescue my bride, Bloom of Youth, daughter of the King of Hathony. Who are you, fair lady?' asked Cahal.

'I am the daughter of the King of Hathony. The day before I was taken by Striker, son of the King of Tricks, my father told me that the son of King Conor, in Erin, was betrothed to me. You, I suppose, are that man?'

'I am,' said Cahal. 'Come with me now, I will free you; but what are we to do with White Beard?'

'Leave him as he is. There is no knowing what he would do should we rouse him.'

The two went with the henwife to her cottage. Cahal lighted the torch a second time, mounted the mare, put Bloom of Youth in front, rode first to Hathony, and then home to Erin.

King Conor made a great feast of welcome for Cahal and his bride. There were seven hundred guests at the short table, eight hundred at the long table, nine hundred at the round table, and a thousand in the grand hall. I was there and heard the whole story, but got no present except shoes of paper and stockings of buttermilk, and these a herder stole from me in crossing the mountains.

COLDFEET AND THE QUEEN OF LONESOME ISLAND

Once upon a time, and a long time ago it was, there lived an old woman in Erin. This old woman's house was at the northeast corner of Mount Brandon. Of all the friends and relatives that ever she had in the world there was but one left, her only son, Sean, nicknamed Fuarcosa (Coldfeet).

The reason that people called the boy Coldfeet was this: When a child he was growing always; what of him did not grow one hour grew another; what did not grow in the day grew in the night; what did not grow in the night grew in the day; and he grew that fast that when seven years old he could not find room enough in his mother's house. When night came and he was sleeping, whatever corner of the house his head was in, it was out of doors that his feet were, and, of course, they were cold, especially in winter.

It was not long till his legs as well as his feet were out of the house, first to the knees, and then to the body. When fifteen years old it was all that he could do to put his head in, and he lived outdoors entirely. What the mother could gather in a year would not support the son for a day, he was that large and had such an appetite.

Coldfeet had to find his own food, and he had no means of living but to bring home sheep and bullocks from whatever place he met them.

He was going on in this way, faring rather ill than well, when one day above another he said, 'I think I must go into the great world, mother. I am half starving in this place. I can do little good for myself as I am, and no good at all for you.'

He rose early next morning, washed his face and hands, asked assistance and protection of God, and if he did not, may we. He left good health with his mother at parting, and away he went, crossing high hills, passing low dales, and kept on his way without halt or rest, the clear day going and the dark night coming, taking lodgings each evening wherever he found them, till at last he came to a high roomy castle.

He entered the castle without delaying outside, and when he went in, the owner asked was he a servant in search of a master.

'I am in search of a master,' said Coldfeet.

He engaged to herd cows for small hire and his keeping, and the time of his service was a day and a year.

Next morning, when Coldfeet was driving the cattle to pasture, his master was outside in the field before him, and said, 'You must take good care of yourself, for of all the herders who took service with me never a man but was killed by one or another of four giants who live next to my pastures. One of these giants has four, the next six, the third eight, and the fourth twelve heads on him.'

'By my hand!' said Coldfeet, 'I did not come here to be killed by the like of them. They will not hurt me, never fear.'

Coldfeet went on with the cattle, and when he came to the boundary he put them on the land of the giants. The cows were not long grazing when one of the giants at his castle caught the odour of the strange herder and rushed out. When coming at a distance he shouted, 'I smell the blood of a man from Erin; his liver and lights for my supper tonight, his blood for my morning dram, his jawbones for stepping-stones, his shins for hurleys!'

When the giant came up he cried, 'Ah, that is you, Coldfeet, and wasn't it the impudence in you to come here from the butt of Brandon Mountain and put cattle on my land to annoy me?'

'It isn't to give satisfaction to you that I am here, but to knock satisfaction out of your bones,' said Coldfeet.

With that the giant faced the herder, and the two went at each other and fought till near evening. They broke old trees and bent young ones; they made hard places soft and soft places hard; they made high places low and low places high; they made spring wells dry, and brought water through hard, grey rocks till near sunset, when Coldfeet took the heads off the giant and put the four skulls in muddy gaps to make a dry, solid road for the cows.

Coldfeet drove out his master's cattle on a second, third, and fourth morning; each day he killed a giant, each day the battle was fiercer, but on the fourth evening the fourth giant was dead.

On the fifth day Coldfeet was not long on the land of the dead giants when a dreadful enchanted old hag came out against him, and she raging with anger. She had nails of steel on her fingers and toes, each nail of them weighing seven pounds.

'Oh, you insolent, bloodthirsty villain,' screamed she, 'to come all the way from Brandon Mountain to kill my young sons, and, poor boys, only that timber is dear in this country it's in their cradles they'd be to-day instead of being murdered by you.'

'It isn't to give satisfaction to you that I'm here, you old witch, but to knock it out of your wicked old bones,' said Coldfeet.

'Glad would I be to tear you to pieces,' said the hag; 'but 'tis better to get some good of you first. I put you under spells of heavy enchantment that you cannot escape, not to eat two meals off the one table nor to sleep two nights in the one house till you go to the Queen of Lonesome Island, and bring the sword of light that never fails, the loaf of bread that is never eaten, and the bottle of water that is never drained.'

'Where is Lonesome Island?' asked Coldfeet.

'Follow your nose, and make out the place with your own wit,' said the hag.

Coldfeet drove the cows home in the evening, and said to his master, 'The giants will never harm you again; all their heads are in the muddy gaps from this to the end of the pasture, and there are good roads now for your cattle. I have been with you only five days, but another would not do my work in a day and a year; pay me my wages. You'll never have trouble again in finding men to mind cattle.'

The man paid Coldfeet his wages, gave him a good suit of clothes for the journey, and his blessing.

Away went Coldfeet now on the long road, and by my word it was a strange road to him. He went across high hills and low dales, passing each night where he found it, till the evening of the third day, when he came to a house where a little old man was living. The old man had lived in that house without leaving it for seven hundred years, and had not seen a living soul in that time.

Coldfeet gave good health to the old man, and received a hundred thousand welcomes in return.

'Will you give me a night's lodging?' asked Coldfeet.

'I will indeed,' said the old man, 'and is it any harm to ask, where are you going?'

'What harm in a plain question? I am going to Lonesome Island if I can find it.'

'You will travel tomorrow, and if you are loose and lively on the road you'll come at night to a house, and inside in it an old man like myself, only older. He will give you lodgings, and tell where to go the day after.'

Coldfeet rose very early next morning, ate his breakfast, asked aid of God, and if he didn't he let it alone. He left good health with the old man, and received his blessing. Away with him then over high hills and low dales, and if any one wished to see a great walker Coldfeet was the man to look at. He overtook the hare in the wind that was before him, and the hare in the wind behind could not overtake him; he went at that gait without halt or rest till he came in the heel of the evening to a small house, and went in. Inside in the house was a little old man sitting by the fire.

Coldfeet gave good health to the old man, and got a hundred thousand welcomes with a night's lodging.

'Why did you come, and where are you going?' asked the old man. 'Fourteen hundred years am I in this house alone, and not a living soul came in to see me till yourself came this evening.'

'I am going to Lonesome Island, if I can find it.'

'I have no knowledge of that place, but if you are a swift walker you will come tomorrow evening to an old man like myself, only older; he will tell you all that you need, and show you the way to the island.'

Next morning early Coldfeet went away after breakfast, leaving good health behind him and taking good wishes for the road. He travelled this day as on the other two days, only more swiftly, and at nightfall gave a greeting to the third old man.

'A hundred thousand welcomes,' said the old man. 'I am living alone in this house twenty-one hundred years, and not a living soul walked the way in that time. You are the first man I see in this house. Is it to stay with me that you are here?'

'It is not,' said Coldfeet, 'for I must be moving. I cannot spend two nights in the one house till I go to Lonesome Island, and I have no knowledge of where that place is.'

'Oh, then, it's the long road between this and Lonesome Island, but I'll tell where the place is, and how you are to go, if you go there. The road lies straight from my door to the sea. From the shore to the island no man has gone unless the queen brought him, but you may go if the strength and the courage are in you. I will give you this staff; it may help you. When you reach the sea throw the staff in the water, and you'll have a boat that will take you without sail or oar straight to the island. When you touch shore pull up the boat on the strand; it will turn into a staff and be again what it now is. The queen's castle goes whirling around always. It has only one door, and that on the roof of it. If you lean on the staff you can rise with one spring to the roof, go in at the door, and to the queen's chamber.

'The queen sleeps but one day in each year, and she will be sleeping tomorrow. The sword of light will be hanging at the head of her bed, the loaf and the bottle of water on the table near by. Seize the sword with the loaf and the bottle, and away with you, for the journey must be made in a day, and you must be on this side of those hills before nightfall. Do you think you can do that?'

'I will do it, or die in the trial,' said Coldfeet.

'If you make that journey you will do what no man has done yet,' said the old man. 'Before I came to live in this house champions and hundreds of king's sons tried to go to Lonesome Island, but not a man of them had the strength and the swiftness to go as far as the seashore, and that is but one part of the journey. All perished, and if their skulls are not crumbled, you'll see them tomorrow. The country is open and safe in the daytime, but when night falls the Queen of Lonesome Island sends her wild beasts to destroy every man they can find until daybreak. You must be in Lonesome Island tomorrow before noon, leave the place very soon after midday, and be on this side of those hills before nightfall, or perish.'

Next morning Coldfeet rose early, ate his breakfast, and started at daybreak. Away he went swiftly over hills, dales, and level places, through a land where the wind never blows and the cock never crows, and though he went quickly the day before, he went five times more quickly that day, for the staff added speed to whatever man had it.

Coldfeet came to the sea, threw the staff into the water, and a boat was before him. Away he went in the boat, and before noon was in the chamber of the Queen of Lonesome Island. He found everything there as the old man had told him. Seizing the sword of light quickly and taking the bottle and loaf, he went toward the door; but there he halted, turned back, stopped a while with the queen. It was very near he was then to forgetting himself; but he sprang up, took one of the queen's golden garters, and away with him.

If Coldfeet strove to move swiftly when coming, he strove more in going back. On he raced over hills, dales, and flat places where the wind never blows and the cock never crows; he never stopped nor halted. When the sun was near setting he saw the last line of hills, and remembering that death was behind and not far from him, he used his last strength and was over the hilltops at nightfall.

The whole country behind him was filled with wild beasts.

'Oh,' said the old man, 'but you are the hero, and I was in dread that you'd lose your life on the journey, and by my hand you had no time to spare.'

'I had not, indeed,' answered Coldfeet. 'Here is your staff, and many thanks for it.'

The two spent a pleasant evening together. Next morning Coldfeet left his blessing with the old man and went on, spent a night with each of the other old men, and never stopped after that till he reached the hag's castle. She was outside before him with the steel nails on her toes and fingers.

'Have you the sword, the bottle, and the loaf?' asked she.

'I have,' said Coldfeet; 'here they are.'

'Give them to me,' said the hag.

'If I was bound to bring the three things,' said Coldfeet, 'I was not bound to give them to you; I will keep them.'

'Give them here!' screamed the hag, raising her nails to rush at him.

With that Coldfeet drew the sword of light, and sent her head spinning through the sky in the way that 'tis not known in what part of the world it fell or did it fall in any place. He burned her body then, scattered the ashes, and went his way farther.

'I will go to my mother first of all,' thought he, and he travelled till evening. When his feet struck small stones on the road, the stones never stopped till they knocked wool off the spinning-wheels of old hags in the Eastern World. In the evening he came to a house and asked lodgings.

'I will give you lodgings, and welcome,' said the man of the house; 'but I have no food for you.'

'I have enough for us both,' said Coldfeet, 'and for twenty more if they were in it'; and he put the loaf on the table.

The man called his whole family. All had their fill, and left the loaf as large as it was before supper. The woman of the house made a loaf in the night like the one they had eaten from, and while Coldfeet was sleeping took his bread and left her own in the place of it. Away went Coldfeet next morning with the wrong loaf, and if he travelled differently from the day before it was because he travelled faster. In the evening he came to a house, and asked would they give him a night's lodging.

'We will, indeed,' said the woman, 'but we have no water to cook supper for you; the water is far away entirely, and no one to go for it.'

'I have water here in plenty,' said Coldfeet, putting his bottle on the table.

The woman took the bottle, poured water from it, filled one pot and then another, filled every vessel in the kitchen, and not a drop less in the bottle. What wonder, when no man or woman ever born could drain the bottle in a lifetime.

Said the woman to her husband that night, 'If we had the bottle, we needn't be killing ourselves running for water.'

'We need not,' said the man.

What did the woman do in the night, when Coldfeet was asleep, but take a bottle, fill it with water from one of the pots, and put that false bottle in place of the true one. Away went Coldfeet next morning, without knowledge of the harm done, and that day he travelled in the way that when he fell in running he had not time to rise, but rolled on till the speed that was under him brought him to his feet again. At sunset he was in sight of a house, and at dusk he was in it.

Coldfeet found welcome in the house, with food and lodgings.

'It is great darkness we are in,' said the man to Coldfeet; 'we have neither oil nor rushes.'

'I can give you light,' said Coldfeet, and he unsheathed the sword from Lonesome Island; it was clear inside the house as on a hilltop in sunlight.

When the people had gone to bed Coldfeet put the sword into its sheath, and all was dark again.

'Oh,' said the woman to her husband that night, 'if we had the sword we'd have light in the house always. You have an old sword above on the loft. Rise out of the bed now and put it in the place of that bright one.'

The man rose, took the two swords out doors, put the old blade in Coldfeet's sheath, and hid away Coldfeet's sword in the loft. Next morning Coldfeet went away, and never stopped till he came to his mother's cabin at the foot of Mount Brandon. The poor old woman was crying and lamenting every day. She felt sure that it was killed her son was, for she had never got tale or tidings of him. Many is the welcome she had for him, but if she had welcomes she had little to eat.

'Oh, then, mother, you needn't be complaining,' said Coldfeet, 'we have as much bread now as will do us a lifetime'; with that he put the loaf on the table, cut a slice for the mother, and began to eat himself. He was hungry, and the next thing he knew the loaf was gone.

'There is a little meal in the house,' said the mother. 'I'll go for water and make stirabout.'

'I have water here in plenty,' said Coldfeet. 'Bring a pot.'

The bottle was empty in a breath, and they hadn't what water would make stirabout nor half of it.

'Oh, then,' said Coldfeet, 'the old hag enchanted the three things before I killed her and knocked the strength out of every one of them.' With that he drew the sword, and it had no more light than any rusty old blade.

The mother and son had to live in the old way again; but as Coldfeet was far stronger than the first time, he didn't go hungry himself, and the mother had plenty. There were cattle in the country, and all the men in it couldn't keep them from Coldfeet or stop him. The old woman and the son had beef and mutton, and lived on for themselves at the foot of Brandon Mountain.

In three quarters of a year the Queen of Lonesome Island had a son, the finest child that sun or moon could shine on, and he grew in the way that what of him didn't grow in the day grew in the night following, and what didn't grow that night grew the next day, and when he was two years old he was very large entirely.

The queen was grieving always for the loaf and the bottle, and there was no light in her chamber from the day the sword was gone. All at once she thought, 'The father of the boy took the three things. I will never sleep two nights in the one house till I find him.'

Away she went then with the boy – went over the sea, went through the land where wind never blows and where cock never crows, came to the house of the oldest old man, stopped one night there, then stopped with the middle and the youngest old man. Where should she go next night but to the woman who stole the loaf from Coldfeet. When the queen sat down to supper the woman brought the loaf, cut slice after slice; the loaf was no smaller.

'Where did you get that loaf?' asked the queen.

'I baked it myself.'

'That is my loaf,' thought the queen.

The following evening she came to a house and found lodgings. At supper the woman poured water from a bottle, but the bottle was full always.

'Where did you get that bottle?'

'It was left to us,' said the woman; 'my grandfather had it.'

'That is my bottle,' thought the queen.

The next night she stopped at a house where a sword filled the whole place with light.

'Where did you find that beautiful sword?' asked the queen.

'My grandfather left it to me,' said the man. 'We have it hanging here always.'

'That is my sword,' said the queen to herself.

Next day the queen set out early, travelled quickly, and never stopped till she came near Brandon Mountain. At a distance she saw a man coming down hill with a fat bullock under each arm. He was carrying the beasts as easily as another would carry two geese. The man put the bullocks in a pen near a house at the foot of the mountain, came out toward the queen, and never stopped till he saluted her. When the man stopped, the boy broke away from the mother and ran to the stranger.

'How is this?' asked the queen; 'the child knows you.' She tried to take the boy, but he would not go to her.

'Have you lived always in this place?' asked the queen.

'I was born in that house beyond, and reared at the foot of that mountain before you. I went away from home once and killed four giants, the first with four, the second with six, the third with eight, and the fourth with twelve heads on him. When I had the giants killed, their mother came out against me, and she raging with vengeance. She wanted to kill me at first, but she did not. She put me under bonds of enchantment to go to the castle of the Queen of Lonesome Island, and bring the sword of light that can never fail to cut or give light, the loaf of bread that can never be eaten, and the bottle of water that can never be drained.'

'Did you go?' asked the queen.

'I did.'

'How could you go to Lonesome Island?'

'I journeyed and travelled, enquiring for the island, stopping one night at one place, and the next night at another, till I came to the house of a little man seven hundred years old. He sent me to a second man twice as old as himself, and the second to a third three times as old as the first man.

'The third old man showed me the road to Lonesome Island, and gave me a staff to assist me. When I reached the sea I made a boat of the staff, and it took me to the island. On the island the boat was a staff again.

'I sprang to the top of the queen's turning castle, went down and entered the chamber where she was sleeping, took the sword of light, with the loaf and the bottle, and was coming away again. I looked at the queen. The heart softened within me at sight of her beauty. I turned back and came near forgetting my life with her. I brought her gold garter with me, took the three things, sprang down from the castle, ran to the water, made a boat of the staff again, came quickly to mainland, and from that hour till darkness I ran with what strength I could draw from each bit of my body. Hardly had I crossed the hilltop and was before the door of the oldest old man when the country behind me was covered with wild beasts. I escaped death by one moment. I brought the three things to the hag who had sent me, but I did not give them. I struck the head from her, but before dying she destroyed them, for when I came home they were useless.'

'Have you the golden garter?'

'Here it is,' said the young man.

'What is your name?' asked the queen.

'Coldfeet,' said the stranger.

'You are the man,' said the queen. 'Long ago it was prophesied that a hero named Coldfeet would come to Lonesome Island without my request or assistance, and that our son would cover the whole world with his power. Come with me now to Lonesome Island.'

The queen gave Coldfeet's old mother good clothing, and said, 'You will live in my castle.'

They all left Brandon Mountain and journeyed on toward Lonesome Island till they reached the house where the sword of light was. It was night when they came and dark outside, but bright as day in the house from the sword, which was hanging on the wall.

'Where did you find this blade?' asked Coldfeet, catching the hilt of the sword.

'My grandfather had it,' said the woman.

'He had not,' said Coldfeet, 'and I ought to take the head off your husband for stealing it when I was here last.'

Coldfeet put the sword in his scabbard and kept it. Next day they reached the house where the bottle was, and Coldfeet took that. The following night he found the loaf and recovered it. All the old men were glad to see Coldfeet, especially the oldest, who loved him.

The queen with her son and Coldfeet with his mother arrived safely in Lonesome Island. They lived on in happiness; there is no account of their death, and they may be in it yet for ought we know.

LAWN DYARRIG, SON OF THE KING OF ERIN, AND THE KNIGHT OF TERRIBLE VALLEY

There was a king in his own time in Erin, and he went hunting one day. The king met a man whose head was out through his cap, whose elbows and knees were out through his clothing, and whose toes were out through his shoes. The man went up to the king, gave him a blow on the face, and drove three teeth from his mouth. The same blow put the king's head in the dirt. When he rose from the earth the king went back to his castle, and lay down sick and sorrowful.

The king had three sons, and their names were Ur, Arthur, and Lawn Dyarrig. The three were at school that day and came home in the evening. The father sighed when the sons were coming in.

'What is wrong with our father?' asked the eldest.

'Your father is sick on his bed,' said the mother.

The three sons went to their father and asked what was on him.

'A strong man that I met to-day gave me a blow in the face, put my head in the dirt, and knocked three teeth from my mouth. What would you do to him if you met him?' asked the father of the eldest son.

'If I met that man,' replied Ur, 'I would make four parts of him between four horses.'

'You are my son,' said the king. 'What would you do if you met him?' asked he then, as he turned to the second son.

'If I had a grip on that man I would burn him between four fires.'

179

'You, too, are my son. What would you do?' asked the king of Lawn Dyarrig.

'If I met that man I would do my best against him, and he might not stand long before me.'

'You are not my son. I would not lose lands or property on you,' said the father. 'You must go from me, and leave this tomorrow.'

On the following morning the three brothers rose with the dawn; the order was given Lawn Dyarrig to leave the castle, and make his own way for himself. The other two brothers were going to travel the world to know could they find the man who had injured their father. Lawn Dyarrig lingered outside till he saw the two, and they going off by themselves.

'It is a strange thing,' said he, 'for two men of high degree to go travelling without a servant.'

'We need no one,' said Ur.

'Company wouldn't harm us,' said Arthur.

The two let Lawn Dyarrig go with them then as a serving-boy, and set out to find the man who had struck down their father. They spent all that day walking, and came late to a house where one woman was living. She shook hands with Ur and Arthur, and greeted them. Lawn Dyarrig she kissed and welcomed, called him son of the King of Erin.

''Tis a strange thing to shake hands with the elder and kiss the younger,' said Ur.

'This is a story to tell,' said the woman; 'the same as if your death were in it.'

They made three parts of that night. The first part they spent in conversation, the second in telling tales, the third in eating and drinking, with sound sleep and sweet slumber. As early as the day dawned next morning, the old woman was up and had food for the young men. When the three had eaten she spoke to Ur, and this is what she asked of him, 'What was it that drove you from home, and what brought you to this place?'

'A champion met my father, took three teeth from him, and put his head in the dirt. I am looking for that man to find him alive or dead.'

'That was the Green Knight from Terrible Valley. He is the man who took the three teeth from your father. I am three hundred years living in this place, and there is not a year of the three hundred in which three hundred heroes fresh, young, and noble have not passed on the way to Terrible Valley, and never have I seen one coming back, and each of them had the look of a man better than you. And now, where are you going, Arthur?'

'I am on the same journey with my brother.'

'Where are you going, Lawn Dyarrig?'

'I am going with these as a servant,' said Lawn Dyarrig.

'God's help to you, it's bad clothing that's on your body,' said the woman; 'and now I will speak to Ur. A day and a year since a champion passed this way; he wore a suit as good as was ever above ground. I had a daughter sewing there in the open window. He came outside, put a finger under her girdle, and took her with him. Her father followed straightway to save her, but I have never seen daughter or father from that day to this. That man was the Green Knight of Terrible Valley. He is better than all the men that could stand on a field a mile in length and a mile in breadth. If you take my advice you'll turn back and go home to your father.'

'Tis how she vexed Ur with this talk, and he made a vow to himself to go on. When Ur did not agree to turn home, the woman said to Lawn Dyarrig, 'Go back to my chamber, you'll find in it the apparel of a hero.'

He went back, and there was not a bit of the apparel that he did not go into with a spring.

'You may be able to do something now,' said the woman, when Lawn Dyarrig came to the front. 'Go back to my chamber and search through all the old swords. You will find one at the bottom; take that.'

He found the old sword, and at the first shake that he gave he knocked seven barrels of rust out of it; after the second shake, it was as bright as when made.

'You may be able to do well with that,' said the woman. 'Go out now to that stable abroad, and take the slim white steed that is in it. That one will never stop nor halt in any place till he brings you to the Eastern World. If you like, take these two men behind you; if not, let them walk. But I think it is useless for you to have them at all with you.'

Lawn Dyarrig went out to the stable, took the slim white steed, mounted, rode to the front, and catching the two brothers, planted them on the horse behind him.

'Now, Lawn Dyarrig,' said the woman, 'this horse will never stop till he stands on the little white meadow in the Eastern World. When he stops, you'll come down and cut the turf under his beautiful right front foot.'

The horse started from the door, and at every leap he crossed seven hills and valleys, seven castles with villages, acres, roods, and odd perches. He could overtake the whirlwind before him seven hundred times before the whirlwind behind could overtake him once. Early in the afternoon of the next day he was in the Eastern World. When he dismounted, Lawn Dyarrig cut the sod from under the foot of the slim white steed in the name of the Father, Son, and Holy Ghost, and Terrible Valley was down under him there. What he did next was to tighten the reins on the neck of the steed and let him go home.

'Now,' said Lawn Dyarrig to the brothers, 'which would ye rather be doing, making a basket or twisting gads (withes)?'

'We would rather be making a basket; our help is among ourselves,' answered they.

Ur and Arthur went at the basket and Lawn Dyarrig at twisting the gads. When Lawn Dyarrig came to the opening with the gads, all twisted and made into one, they hadn't the ribs of the basket in the ground yet.

'Oh, then, haven't ye anything done but that?'

'Stop your mouth,' said Ur, 'or we'll make a mortar of your head on the next stone.'

'To be kind to one another is the best for us,' said Lawn Dyarrig. 'I'll make the basket.'

While they'd be putting one rod in the basket he had the basket finished.

'Oh, brother,' said they, 'you are a quick workman.'

They had not called him brother since they left home till that moment.

'Who will go in the basket now?' asked Lawn Dyarrig, when it was finished, and the gad tied to it.

'Who but me?' said Ur. 'I am sure, brothers, if I see anything to frighten me ye'll draw me up.'

'We will,' said the other two.

He went in, but had not gone far when he cried to pull him up again.

'By my father and the tooth of my father, and by all that is in Erin dead or alive, I would not give one other sight on Terrible Valley!' cried he, when he stepped out of the basket.

'Who will go now?' asked Lawn Dyarrig.

'Who will go but me?' answered Arthur.

Whatever length Ur went, Arthur didn't go the half of it.

'By my father and the tooth of my father, I wouldn't give another look at Terrible Valley for all that's in Erin dead or alive!'

'I will go now,' said Lawn Dyarrig, 'and as I put no foul play on you, I hope ye'll not put foul play on me.'

'We will not, indeed,' said they.

Whatever length the other two went, Lawn Dyarrig didn't go the half of it till he stepped out of the basket and went down on his own feet. It was not far he had travelled in Terrible Valley when he met seven hundred heroes guarding the country.

'In what place here has the Green Knight his castle?' asked he of the seven hundred.

'What sort of a sprisawn goat or sheep from Erin are you?' asked they.

'If we had a hold of you, that's a question you would not put the second time; but if we haven't you, we'll not be so long.'

They faced Lawn Dyarrig then and attacked him; but he went through them like a hawk or a raven through small birds. He made a heap of their feet, a heap of their heads, and a castle of their arms.

After that he went his way walking, and had not gone far when he came to a spring. 'I'll have a drink before I go farther,' thought he. With that he stooped down and took a drink of the water. When he had drunk he lay on the ground and fell asleep.

Now there wasn't a morning that the lady in the Green Knight's castle didn't wash in the water of that spring, and she sent a maid for the water each time. Whatever part of the day it was when Lawn Dyarrig fell asleep, he was sleeping in the morning when the girl came. She thought it was dead the man was, and she was so in dread of him that she would not come near the spring for a long time. At last she saw he was asleep, and then she took the water. Her mistress was complaining of her for being so long.

'Do not blame me,' said the maid. 'I am sure that if it was yourself that was in my place you'd not come back so soon.'

'How so?' asked the lady.

'The finest hero that a woman ever laid eyes on is sleeping at the spring.'

'That's a thing that cannot be till Lawn Dyarrig comes to the age of a hero. When that time comes he'll be sleeping at the spring.'

'He is in it now,' said the girl.

The lady did not stay to get any drop of the water on herself, but ran quickly from the castle. When she came to the spring she roused Lawn Dyarrig. If she found him lying, she left him standing. She smothered him with kisses, drowned him with tears, dried him with garments of fine silk, and with her own hair. Herself and himself locked arms and walked into the castle of the Green Knight. After that they were inviting each other with the best food and entertainment till the middle of the following day. Then the lady said –

'When the Green Knight bore me away from my father and mother, he brought me straight to this castle, but I put him under bonds not to marry me for seven years and a day, and he cannot; still I must serve him. When he goes fowling he spends three days away, and the next three days at home. This is the day for him to come back, and for me to prepare his dinner. There is no stir that you or I have made here to-day but that brass head beyond there will tell of it.'

'It is equal to you what it tells,' said Lawn Dyarrig, 'only make ready a clean, long chamber for me.'

She did so, and he went back into it. Herself rose up then to prepare dinner for the Green Knight. When he came she welcomed him as every day. She left down his food before him, and he sat to take his dinner. He was sitting with knife and fork in hand when the brass head spoke. 'I thought when I saw you taking food and drink with your wife that you had the blood of a man in you. If you could see that sprisawn of a goat or sheep out of Erin taking meat and drink with her all day, what would you do?'

'Oh, my suffering and sorrow!' cried the knight. 'I'll never take another bite or sup till I eat some of his liver and heart. Let three hundred heroes fresh and young go back and bring his heart to me, with the liver and lights, till I eat them.'

The three hundred heroes went, and hardly were they behind in the chamber when Lawn Dyarrig had them all dead in one heap.

'He must have some exercise to delay my men, they are so long away,' said the knight. 'Let three hundred more heroes go for his heart, with the liver and lights, and bring them here to me.'

The second three hundred went, and as they were entering the chamber, Lawn Dyarrig was making a heap of them, till the last one was inside, where there were two heaps.

'He has some way of coaxing my men to delay,' said the knight. 'Do you go now, three hundred of my savage hirelings, and bring him.'

The three hundred savage hirelings went, and Lawn Dyarrig let every man of them enter before he raised a hand, then he caught the bulkiest of them all by the two ankles and began to wallop the others with him, and he walloped them till he drove the life out of the two hundred and ninety-nine. The bulkiest one was worn to the shin bones that Lawn Dyarrig held in his two hands. The Green Knight, who thought Lawn Dyarrig was coaxing the men, called out then, 'Come down, my men, and take dinner!'

'I'll be with you,' said Lawn Dyarrig, 'and have the best food in the house, and I'll have the best bed in the house. God not be good to you for it, either.'

He went down to the Green Knight and took the food from before him and put it before himself. Then he took the lady, set her on his own knee, and he and she went on eating. After dinner he put his finger under her girdle, took her to the best chamber in the castle, and remained there till morning. Before dawn the lady said to Lawn Dyarrig –

'If the Green Knight strikes the pole of combat first, he'll win the day; if you strike first, you'll win, if you do what I tell you. The Green Knight has so much enchantment that if he sees it is going against him the battle is, he'll rise like a fog in the air, come down in the same form, strike you, and make a green stone of you. When yourself and himself are going out to fight in the morning, cut a sod a perch long in the name of the Father, Son, and Holy Ghost; you'll leave the sod on the next little hillock you meet. When the Green Knight is coming down and is ready to strike, give him a blow with the sod; you'll make a green stone of him.'

As early as the dawn Lawn Dyarrig rose and struck the pole of combat. The blow that he gave did not leave calf, foal, lamb, kid, or child waiting for birth, without turning them five times to the left and five times to the right.

'What do you want?' asked the knight.

'All that's in your kingdom to be against me the first quarter of the day, and yourself the second quarter.'

'You have not left in the kingdom now but myself, and it is early enough for you that I'll be at you.'

The knight faced him, and they went at each other and fought till late in the day. The battle was strong against Lawn Dyarrig when the lady stood in the door of the castle.

'Increase on your blows and increase on your courage,' cried she. 'There is no woman here but myself to wail over you, or to stretch you before burial.'

When the knight heard the voice, he rose in the air like a lump of fog. As he was coming down, Lawn Dyarrig struck him with the sod on the right side of his breast, and made a green stone of him.

The lady rushed out then, and whatever welcome she had for Lawn Dyarrig the first time, she had twice as much now. Herself and himself went into the castle and spent that night very comfortably. In the morning they rose early, and collected all the gold, utensils, and treasures. Lawn Dyarrig found the three teeth of his father in a pocket of the Green Knight, and took them. He and the lady brought all the riches to where the basket was. 'If I send up this beautiful lady,' thought Lawn Dyarrig, 'she may be taken from me by my brothers; if I remain below with her, she may be taken from me by people here.' He put her in the basket, and she gave him a ring so that they might know each other if they met. He shook the gad, and she rose in the basket.

When Ur saw the basket he thought, 'What's above let it be above, and what's below let it stay where it is.'

'I'll have you as wife forever for myself,' said he to the lady.

'I put you under bonds,' said she, 'not to lay a hand on me for a day and three years.'

'That itself would not be long even if twice the time,' said Ur.

The two brothers started home with the lady; on the way Ur found the head of an old horse with teeth in it and took them, saying, 'These will be my father's three teeth.'

They travelled on, and reached home at last. Ur would not have left a tooth in his father's mouth, trying to put in the three that he had brought; but the father stopped him.

Lawn Dyarrig, left in Terrible Valley, began to walk around for himself. He had been walking but one day when whom should he meet but the lad Shortclothes, and he saluted him. 'By what way can I leave Terrible Valley?' asked Lawn Dyarrig.

'If I had a grip on you that's what you wouldn't ask of me a second time,' said Shortclothes.

'If you have not touched me you will before you are much older.'

'If I do, you will not treat me as you did all my people and my master.'

'I'll do worse to you than I did to them,' said Lawn Dyarrig.

They caught each other then, one grip under the arm and one grip on the shoulder. 'Tis not long they were wrestling when Lawn Dyarrig had Shortclothes on the earth, and he gave him the five thin tyings dear and tight.

'You are the best hero I have ever met,' said Shortclothes; 'give me quarter for my soul – spare me. When I did not tell you of my own will, I must tell in spite of myself.'

'It is as easy for me to loosen you as to tie you,' said Lawn Dyarrig, and he freed him. The moment he was free, Shortclothes said –

'I put you under bonds, and the misfortune of the year to be walking and going always till you go to the northeast point of the world, and get the heart and liver of the serpent which is seven years asleep and seven years awake.'

Lawn Dyarrig went away then, and never stopped till he was in the northeast of the world, where he found the serpent asleep.

'I will not go unawares on you while you are asleep,' said Lawn Dyarrig, and he turned to go. When he was going, the serpent drew him down her throat with one breath.

Inside he found three men playing cards in her belly. Each laughed when he looked at Lawn Dyarrig.

'What reason have you for laughing?' asked he.

'We are laughing with glee to have another partner to fill out our number.'

Lawn Dyarrig did not sit down to play. He drew his sword, and was searching and looking till he found the heart and liver of the serpent. He took a part of each, and cut out a way for himself between two ribs. The three card-players followed when they saw the chance of escape.

Lawn Dyarrig, free of the serpent, never stopped till he came to Shortclothes, and he was a day and three years on the journey, and doing the work.

'Since you are not dead now,' said Shortclothes, 'there is no death allotted to you. I'll find a way for you to leave Terrible Valley. Go and take that old bridle hanging there beyond and shake it; whatever beast comes and puts its head into the bridle will carry you.'

Lawn Dyarrig shook the bridle, and a dirty, shaggy little foal came and put head in the bridle. Lawn Dyarrig mounted, dropped the reins on the foal's neck, and let him take his own choice of roads. The foal brought Lawn Dyarrig out by another way to the upper world, and took him to Erin. Lawn Dyarrig stopped some distance from his father's castle, and knocked at the house of an old weaver.

'Who are you?' asked the old man.

'I am a weaver,' said Lawn Dyarrig.

'What can you do?'

'I can spin for twelve and twist for twelve.'

'This is a very good man,' said the old weaver to his sons. 'Let us try him.'

The work they would be doing for a year he had done in one hour.

When dinner was over the old man began to wash and shave, and his two sons began to do the same.

'Why is this?' asked Lawn Dyarrig.

'Haven't you heard that Ur, son of the king, is to marry tonight the woman that he took from the Green Knight of Terrible Valley?'

'I have not,' said Lawn Dyarrig; 'but as all are going to the wedding, I suppose I may go without offence.'

'Oh, you may,' said the weaver. 'There will be a hundred thousand welcomes before you.'

'Are there any linen sheets within?'

'There are,' said the weaver.

'It is well to have bags ready for yourself and two sons.'

The weaver made bags for the three very quickly. They went to the wedding. Lawn Dyarrig put what dinner was on the first table into the weaver's bag, and sent the old man home with it. The food of the second table he put in the eldest son's bag, filled the second son's bag from the third table, and sent the two home.

The complaint went to Ur that an impudent stranger was taking all the food.

'It is not right to turn any man away,' said the bridegroom; 'but if that stranger does not mind he will be thrown out of the castle.'

'Let me look at the face of the disturber,' said the bride.

'Go and bring the fellow who is troubling the guests,' said Ur, to the servants.

Lawn Dyarrig was brought right away, and stood before the bride, who filled a glass with wine and gave it to him. Lawn Dyarrig drank half the wine, and dropped in the ring which the lady had given him in Terrible Valley.

When the bride took the glass again the ring went of itself with one leap to her finger. She knew then who was standing before her.

'This is the man who conquered the Green Knight, and saved me from Terrible Valley,' said she to the King of Erin; 'this is Lawn

Dyarrig, your son.'

Lawn Dyarrig took out the three teeth, and put them in his father's mouth. They fitted there perfectly, and grew into their old place. The king was satisfied; and as the lady would marry no man but Lawn Dyarrig he was the bridegroom.

'I must give you a present,' said the bride to the queen. 'Here is a beautiful scarf which you are to wear as a girdle this evening.'

The queen put the scarf around her waist.

'Tell me now,' said the bride to the queen, 'who was Ur's father?'

'What father could he have but his own father, the King of Erin?'

'Tighten, scarf,' said the bride.

That moment the queen thought that her head was in the sky, and the lower half of her body down deep in the earth.

'Oh, my grief and my woe!' cried the queen.

'Answer my question in truth, and the scarf will stop squeezing you. Who was Ur's father?'

'The gardener,' said the queen.

'Whose son is Arthur?'

'The king's son.'

'Tighten, scarf,' said the bride.

If the queen suffered before, she suffered twice as much this time, and screamed for help.

'Answer me truly, and you'll be without pain; if not, death will be on you this minute. Whose son is Arthur?'

'The swine-herd's.'

'Who is the king's son?'

'The king has no son but Lawn Dyarrig.'

'Tighten, scarf.'

The scarf did not tighten, and if the bride had been commanding it for a day and a year it would not have tightened, for the queen told the truth that time. When the wedding was over, the king gave Lawn Dyarrig half his kingdom, and made Ur and Arthur his servants.

ART, THE KING'S SON, AND BALOR BEIMENACH, TWO SONS-IN-LAW OF KING UNDER THE WAVE

The King of Leinster was at war for twenty years, and conquered all before him. He had a son named Art; and, when the wars were over, this son was troubled because he could find no right bride for himself. No princess could suit him or his father; for they wanted an only daughter. In this trouble they went to the old druid.

'Wait,' said the druid, 'till I read my book of enchantment; and then I will tell you where to find such a woman.'

He read his book, but could find no account of an only daughter of the right age and station. At last the druid said to the king, 'Proclaim over all Erin that if any man knows of such a princess he is to come to this castle and tell you.'

The king did as the druid advised. At long last a sailor walked the way, and went to the king. 'I know,' said he, 'of the woman you wish.'

'Who is she?' asked the king.

'The only daughter of the King of Greece, and she is beautiful. But it is better to keep your son at home than to send him abroad; for there is no man who could not find a good wife in Erin.'

Art would not listen to this advice, but said, 'I will go and get that one.'

Next morning he made ready, took farewell of his father, and away he went on his journey. He rode a fine steed to the seashore; there he took a ship, and nothing more is told of him till he touched land in Greece. The King of Greece received Art with great welcome, gave a feast of seven days in his honour, and sent heralds through the city declaring that any man who would fall asleep till the end of the seven days would have the head swept off his body.

Silk and satin were spread under Art's feet, and respect of every kind shown him. He was entertained seven days, and at last, when the king didn't ask him what journey he was on, he said, 'It is a wonder to me that you do not ask what brought me, and why I am travelling.'

'I am not surprised at all,' said the king. 'A good father's son like you, and a man of such beauty, ought to travel all nations, and see every people.'

'I am not travelling to show myself nor to see people. Men told me that you have an only daughter. I want her in marriage, and 'tis for her sake that I am here.'

'I have never heard news I liked better,' said the king; 'and if my daughter is willing, and her mother is satisfied, you have my blessing.'

Art went to the queen and told her the cause of his coming.

'If the king and my daughter are satisfied,' replied she, 'that is the best tale that man could bring me.'

Art went to the princess, and she said, 'If my father and mother are willing, your words are most welcome to me; but there is one obstacle between us – I can marry no man but the man who will bring me the head of the Gruagach of Bungling Leaps.'

'Where is he to be found?' asked Art.

'If 'twas in the east he was, I would direct you to the west; and if 'twas in the west he was, I would send you to the east: but not to harm you would I do this, for thousands of men have gone toward that gruagach, and not a man of them has ever come back.'

'Your opinion of me is not very high. I must follow my nose and find the road.'

Next morning Art took farewell of the king, and went his way travelling to know could he find the gruagach. At that time gruagachs and heroes lived in old castles. Art enquired and enquired till he heard where the gruagach lived.

At last he came to the castle, and shouted outside; but if he did it was no use for him, he got no answer. Art walked in, found the gruagach on the flat of his back, fast asleep and snoring. The gruagach had a sword in his hand. Art caught the sword, but could not stir it from the grasp of the gruagach.

''Tis hard to say,' thought he, 'that I could master you awake, if I can do nothing to you in your slumber; but it would be a shame to strike a sleeping man.'

He hit the gruagach with the flat of his sword below the knee, and woke him. The gruagach opened his eyes, sat up, and said, 'It would be fitter for you to be herding cows and horses than to be coming to this place to vex me.'

'I am not here to give excuse or satisfaction to you,' said Art, 'but to knock satisfaction out of your flesh, bones, and legs, and I'll take the head off you if I can.'

'It seems, young man, that it is a princess you want; and she will not marry you without my head.'

'That is the truth.'

'What is your name?' asked the gruagach; 'and from what country do you come?'

'My name is Art, and I am son of the King of Leinster, in Erin.'

'Your name is great, and there is loud talk of you, but your size is not much; and if the princess were in question between us, I would think as little of putting that small hill there on the top of the big one beyond it as of killing you. For your father's sake, I would not harm you; your father is as good a man for a stranger to walk to as there is in the world; and for that reason go home and don't mind me or the princess, for your father and mother waited long for you, and would be sorry to lose you.'

'Very thankful am I,' said Art, 'for your kind speech; but as I came so far from home, and want the princess, I'll knock a trial out of you before I leave this place.'

Next morning the two faced each other, and fought like wild bulls, wild geese, or wolves, fought all day with spears and swords. Art was growing weak, and was not injuring the gruagach till evening, when he thought, 'Far away am I from father, mother, home, and country.' With that he got the strength of a hundred men, gave one blow to the gruagach under the chin, and sent his head spinning through the air. That moment the body went down through the earth.

When the body disappeared, Art thought the head would come down like any other thing; but the earth opened, and the head flew into the earth and vanished.

'I will go back to the castle of the King of Greece,' thought Art, 'and tell him the whole story.'

On the way to the castle, and while passing a cabin, a big old man came out of the cabin, and cried, 'Welcome, Art, son of the King of Leinster. It is too far you are going tonight. Stay with me, if you like my entertainment.'

'Very thankful am I,' said Art, 'and glad to stay with you. It is weak and tired I am.'

When he went in, the old man stripped him, put him first into a cauldron of venom, and then into a cauldron of cure, and he was as well as ever.

'Would go against the gruagach tomorrow?' asked the old man.

'I would if I knew where to find him.'

'You will find him where he was to-day; but he will be twice as strong tomorrow, since you vexed him to-day.'

After breakfast Art went to the castle, and found the gruagach asleep, as the first time, struck him with the flat of his sword, but so hard that he saw stars.

'Art, son of the King of Leinster, you are not satisfied yet; but you will suffer.'

'I am not satisfied,' said Art. 'I'll have your head or you will have mine.'

'Go home to your father and mother; don't trouble me: that is my advice.'

'I am thankful to you,' said Art, jestingly; 'but I'll take a trial of you.'

They fought as before. The gruagach had twice the strength of the first day; and Art was knocking no quarters out of him, but suffering from every blow, his flesh falling and his blood flowing.

'I am not to last long,' thought Art, 'unless I can do something.' He remembered his father and mother then, and how far he was from home; that moment the strength of two hundred men came to him. With one blow he swept off the gruagach's head and sent it twice as far into the sky as on the first day; the body sank through the earth. Art stood at the place where the body had vanished.

When the head was coming down, and was near, he caught it and held it firmly by the hair; then, cutting a withe, he thrust it through the ears and, throwing the head over his shoulder, started for the castle of the King of Greece; but before reaching the old man's cabin, he met three men and with them a headless body.

'Where are ye going?' asked Art.

'This body lost its head in the Eastern World, and we are travelling the earth to know can we find a head to match it.'

'Do you think this one would do?' asked Art of one of the men.

'I don't know,' said he; 'it is only for us to try.'

The moment the head was put on the body, men, head, and body went down through the earth.

Art went to the old man, and told him of all that had happened.

'You were very foolish,' said the old man, 'to do what you did. Why did you not keep the head and bring it to me? I would tell you what to do.' The old man cured Art's wounds, and after supper he asked, 'Will you fight the gruagach again?'

'I will.'

'Well, if you have the luck to knock the head off him a third time, never part with it till you come to me.'

Art went a third time to the gruagach, struck him with the flat of his sword, and knocked ferns out of his eyes.

'Oh, ho! Art, son of the King of Leinster, you are not satisfied yet, it seems. To-day will tell all. You'll fall here.'

They went at each other with venom; and each sought the head of the other so fiercely that each hair on him would hold an iron apple. The gruagach had the upper hand till evening. Art thought of home then, of the young princess, and of the mean opinion that she had of him, and gave such a blow that the gruagach's head vanished in the sky. The body went through the earth, and Art stood as before at the place where it sank till he saw the head coming; he seized it, cut two withes, passed them through the ears, threw the head over his shoulder, and went toward the old man's cabin. He was within one mile of the house, when he saw, flying from the southeast, three ravens, and each bird seemed the size of a horse. At that time a terrible thirst came on him; he put the gruagach's head on the ground, and stooped to drink from a spring near the wayside; that moment one of the ravens swept down and carried off the head.

'I am in a worse state now than ever,' said Art, lamenting.

He went to the cabin of the old man, who received him well, and cured him, and said, 'You may go home now, since you did not keep the head when you had it; or you may go into a forest where there is a boar, and that boar is far stronger and fiercer than the gruagach: but if you can kill the boar, you will win yet, if you do what I tell you. When the boar is dead, open the body and hide in it. The three ravens will come after a while to eat; you can catch one of them, and hold it till the others bring the head.'

Art went away to the forest. He was not long in it when the boar caught the scent of him, and ran at him, snapped at his body, and took pieces out of it. Art defended himself till evening, and was more losing than gaining, when he remembered home and that princess who thought so little of his valour. He got the strength of four hundred men then, and made two even halves of the boar. When Art tried to draw his sword, it was broken at the hilt: and he let three screeches out of him that were heard all over the kingdom. He could not prepare the carcass, so he went to the old man with the sword hilt.

'A hundred thousand welcomes to you,' said the old man; 'and you deserve them. You are the best man I have seen in life.'

'I do not deserve the welcomes,' said Art; ''Tis badly the day has gone with me: my sword is broken.'

'I will give you a better one,' said the old man, taking him to a room where there was nothing but swords. 'Here are swords in plenty; take your choice of them.'

Art tried many, but broke one after another. At last he caught an old rusty blade, and shook it. The sword screeched so fiercely that it was heard in seven kingdoms, and his father and mother heard it in Erin.

'This blade will do,' said Art.

'Come, now, and we'll prepare the boar,' said the old man.

The two went and dressed the boar in the way to give Art room within the body, and a place to seize the raven. The old man went to a hilltop, at a distance, and sat there till he heard the three ravens coming, and they cawing as before. 'Oh, it is ye that are coming!' thought he. The birds came to the ground, and walked about, till at last one of them began to peck at the carcass. Art caught that one quickly by the neck; the bird struggled and struggled.

'You might as well stop,' said Art; 'you'll not go from me. This fellow's head, or the head ye took yesterday,' said Art to the other two.

'Kill not our brother,' cried they; 'we'll bring the head quickly.'

'He has but two hours to live, unless ye bring here the head ye took from me.'

The ravens were not gone one hour when the gruagach's head was in Art's hands, and the raven was free.

'Come home with me now,' said the old man. Art went with him. 'Show this head to the princess,' said the old man; 'but do not give it to her; bring it back here to me.'

Art went to the king's castle, and, showing the head to the princess, said, 'Here is the head which you wanted; but I will not marry you.' He turned away then, went to the old man, and gave him the head. The old man threw the head on a body which was lying in the cabin; the head and the body became one, and just like the old man.

'Now, Art, king's son from Erin, the gruagach was my brother, and for the last three hundred years he was under the enchantment of that princess, the only daughter of the King of Greece. The princess is old, although young in appearance; my brother would have killed me as quickly as he would you; and he was to be enchanted till you should come and cut the head off him, and show it to the princess, and not marry her, and I should do as I have done. My brother and I will stay here, take care of our forests, and be friends to you. Go you back to Erin: a man can find a good wife near home, and need not look after foreign women.'

Art went to Erin, and lived with his father and mother. One morning he saw a ship coming in, and only one man on board, the Red Gruagach, and he having a golden apple on the end of a silver spindle, and throwing the apple up in the air and catching it on the spindle.

The Red Gruagach came to Art, and asked, 'Will you play a game with me?'

'I have never refused to play,' said Art; 'but I have no dice.'

The gruagach took out dice; they played. Art won. 'What is your wish?' asked the gruagach.

'Get for me in one moment the finest woman on earth, with twelve attendant maidens and thirteen horses.'

The Red Gruagach ran to his ship, and brought the woman with her maidens; the horses came bridled and saddled. When Art saw the woman, he fell in love, took her by the hand, and went to the castle.

They were married that day. The Red Gruagach would not sail away; he stayed near the castle and watched. Art's young wife knew this, and would not let her husband leave the castle without her.

Two or three months later she fell ill, and sent for the old king. 'You must guard Art, and keep him safe,' said she, 'till I recover.'

Next morning the king was called aside for some reason, and Art went out of the castle that moment. At the gate he met the gruagach, who asked him to play. They played with the gruagach's dice, and Art lost.

'Give your sentence,' said he to the gruagach.

'You will hear it too soon for your comfort. You are to bring me the sword of light, and the story of the man who has it.'

Art's wife saw the king coming back. 'Where is Art?' asked she.

'Outside at the gate.'

She sprang through the door, though sick, but too late.

'You are not a husband for me now, you must go from me,' said she to Art. 'The man who has the sword of light is my sister's husband; he has the strength of thousands in him, and can run with the speed of wild beasts. You did not know me, did not know that I was not that gruagach's daughter; you did not ask me who I was. Now you are in trouble, you must go. Sit on the horse that I rode, and that the gruagach gave you, take the bridle in your right hand, and let the horse go where he pleases; he will face the ocean, but a road will open before him, and he will never stop till he comes to my father's castle. My father is King Under the Wave. The horse will stop at steps in front of the castle; you will dismount then. My father will ask where you got that steed, and you will say you got him when you won him and the daughter of King Under the Wave from the Red Gruagach.'

Next morning Art took farewell of his wife and his father and mother, started, and never stopped nor dismounted till he came to the steps outside the castle-yard where horsemen used to mount and dismount. He came down then.

'Where did you get that horse?' asked King Under the Wave; 'and where is the rider who left my castle on his back?'

'I won him and the daughter of King Under the Wave from the Red Gruagach.'

'Ah, 'tis easily known to me that it was the Foxy Gruagach who stole my child. Now, who are you, and where are you going?'

'I am Art, son of the King of Leinster, in Erin.'

King Under the Wave gave a hundred thousand welcomes to Art then, and said, 'You are the best king's son that has ever lived; and if my daughter was to go from me, I am glad that it is to you she went. It is for the fortune that you are here, I suppose?'

'I am not here for a fortune; but I am in heavy trouble. I am in search of the sword of light.'

'If you are going for that sword, I fear that you will not be a son-in-law of mine long. It is the husband of another daughter of mine who has the sword of light now; and while he has it, he could kill the whole world. But I like you better, and will send servants to the stable to get you the worst horse for tonight; you will need the best afterward. Balor Beimenach, this son-in-law of mine, will grow stronger each time you go to his castle. One of my men will ride with you, and show you where Balor lives, and show you the window of the room where he sleeps. You will turn your horse's back to the window, and call out, 'Are you asleep, Balor Beimenach?' He will reply, and call out, 'What do you want?' You will answer, 'The sword of light and the story of Balor Beimenach.' Put spurs to your horse that instant, and ride away, with what breath the horse has. I will have the twelve gates of this castle open before you, to know will you bring the life with you. Balor is bound not to cross a gate or a wall of this castle without my request, or to follow any man through a gate or over a wall of mine. He must stop outside.'

On the following day, Art and a serving-man rode away; the man pointed out Balor's castle, and the window of his bedchamber. In the evening, Art rode up to the window, and shouted, 'Are you asleep, Balor Beimenach?'

'Not very soundly. What do you want?'

'The sword of light and the story of Balor Beimenach.'

'Wait, and you will get them!'

Art put spurs to his horse, and shot away. Balor Beimenach was after him in a flash. Art's horse was the worst in the stables of King Under the Wave, though better than the best horse in another kingdom. Still Balor was gaining on him, and when he came near the castle, he had not time to reach the gate. He spurred over the wall; but if he did, Balor cut his horse in two behind the saddle, and Art fell in over the wall with the front half.

Balor was raging; he went to his castle, but slept not a wink – walked his chamber till morning to know would Art come again.

Next evening, Art rode to the window on a better horse, and called out, 'Balor Beimenach, are you asleep?' and raced away. Balor followed, and followed faster. Art could not reach the gate before him, so he spurred his horse over the wall. Balor cut this one in two just at the saddle. Art tumbled down from the wall with his life.

This enraged Balor more than the first escape; he slept not a wink that night, but was walking around the whole castle and cursing till morning.

King Under the Wave gave Art the best horse in his stable, for the third night, and said, 'This is your last chance with horses. I hope you will escape; but I'm greatly in dread that Balor will catch you. Now put this horse to full speed before you shout, and you will have some chance if your horse runs with what speed there is in him.'

Art obeyed the king. But Balor killed that horse as he had the other two, and came nearer killing Art; for he cut a piece of the saddle behind him, and Art came very near falling outside the wall; but he fell in, and escaped with his life.

'Well,' said King Under the Wave, on the fourth day, 'no horse that ever lived could escape him the fourth time. Every vein in his body is wide open from thirst for blood; he would use every power that is in him before he would let you escape. But here is where your chance is. Balor has not slept for three nights; he will be sound asleep this time; the sword of light will be hanging above his head near his grasp. Do you slip into the room, and walk without noise; if you can touch the sword, you will have all Balor's strength, and then he will give you the story.'

Art did as the king directed. He slipped into the room, saw the sword of light hanging just above Balor's head. He went up without noise till he caught the hilt of the sword; and that moment it let out a screech that was heard throughout the dominions of King Under the Wave, and through all Erin.

Balor woke, and was very weak when he saw Art. The moment Art touched the hilt of the sword, he had all the strength that Balor had before. The screech that the sword gave put Balor in such fear that he fell to the floor, struck his face against the bed-post, and got a great lump on his forehead.

'Be quiet,' said Art; 'the sword is mine, and now I want the story.'

'Who are you?' asked Balor, 'and what land are you from? It seems that you are a friend of my father-in-law; for he is shielding and aiding you these four nights.'

'I am a friend of his, and also his son-in-law. I wish to be your friend as well.'

'What is your name?' asked Balor.

'Art, son of the King of Leinster, in Erin.'

'I would rather you had the sword than any other man save myself.'

Balor rose, and went to his wife, and said, 'Come with me to your father's castle.'

King Under the Wave gave a great feast, and when the feast was over Balor Beimenach took Art aside, and told him this story: 'I was married to my wife but a short time, and living in that castle beyond, when I wanted to go to a fair. When not far from the castle, I found I had left my whip behind, and went back for it. For years there had lived in my castle a cripple. On returning I found that my wife had disappeared with this cripple. I went after them in a rage. When I reached her, she struck me with a rod of enchantment, and made a white horse of me. She gave me then to a servant, who was to take grain to a mill with me. I had no saddle on my back, only a chain to cut and gall me. Though a horse, I had my own knowledge. I wanted freedom. The boy who drove me misused me, and beat me. I broke his leg with a kick, and ran away among wild hills to pasture. I had the best grass, and lived for a time at my ease; but my wife heard of me, and had me brought home. She struck me again with her rod of enchantment, made a wolf of me. I ran away to rocky places. The wolves of the mountains bit and tore me; but at last they grew friendly. I took twelve of these with me, and we killed my wife's cattle, day and night. She collected hunters and hounds, who killed six of the wolves. The other six and I were more harmful than ever. A second party killed the other six, and I was alone. They surrounded me; there was no escape then. I saw among the hunters my own father-in law. I ran to King Under the Wave, fell down before him, looked into his face; he pitied and saved me, took me home with him.

'My wife was at her father's that day, and knew me. She begged the king to kill me; but he would not; he kept me. I served him well, and he loved me. I slept in the castle. One night a great serpent came down the chimney, and began to crawl toward the king's little son, sleeping there in the cradle. I saw the serpent, and killed it. My wife was at her father's castle that night, and rose first on the following morning. She saw the child sleeping, and the serpent lying dead. She took the child to her own chamber, rubbed me with blood from the serpent, and told the king that I had eaten the child. "I begged you long ago to kill that wolf," said she to her father; "if you had followed my advice you would not be without your son now." She turned and went out.

'Right there on a table was the rod of enchantment, which my wife had forgotten. I sprang toward the king; he was startled, and struck me with the rod, without knowing its power. I became a man, was myself again, and told the king my whole story. We went to my wife's chamber; there the king found his son living and well. King Under the Wave gave command then to bring seven loads of turf with seven barrels of pitch, make one pile of them, and burn his daughter and the cripple on the top of the pile.

'"Grant me one favor," cried I. "I will," said the king. "Spare your daughter; she may live better now." "I will," said the king; "but they will burn the cripple."

'That is my story for you. Go now, and tell it to the Red Gruagach; keep the sword in your hand while telling the story; and when you have finished, throw the sword into the air, and say, 'Go to Balor Beimenach!' It will come to me. When you need the sword, send me word; I will throw it to you; and we'll have the strength of thousands between us.'

Art gave a blessing to all, and mounted his wife's steed; the road through the sea opened before him. The wife received him with a hundred thousand welcomes. After that he went to the Red Gruagach, and, holding the sword of light in his hand, told the story. When the story was finished, he threw the sword in the air, and said, 'Go to Balor Beimenach.'

'Why did you not give me the sword?' cried the Red Gruagach, in a rage.

'If I was bound to bring the sword, I was not bound to give it to you,' answered Art. 'And now leave this place forever.'

Art lived happily with his wife, and succeeded his father.

SHAWN MACBREOGAN AND THE KING OF THE WHITE NATION

There was a very rich man once who lived near Brandon Bay, and his name was Breogan.

This Breogan had a deal of fine land, and was well liked by all people who knew him. One morning as he was walking on the strand for himself, he found, above the highest tide, a little colt, barely the size of a goat; and a very nice colt he was.

'Oh, what a beautiful little beast!' said Breogan; 'he doesn't belong to any one in this country. He is not mine; but still and all I'll take him. If an owner comes the way, sure he can prove his claim, if he is able.'

Breogan carried the colt to the stable, and fed him as well as any beast that he had. The colt was thriving well; and when twelve months were passed, it was a pleasure to look at him. Breogan put him in a stable by himself after that, and kept him three years. At the end of the third year, it isn't a little colt he was, but a grand, fiery steed. Breogan invited all his friends and neighbours to a feast and a great merrymaking. 'This will be a good time,' thought he, 'to find a man to ride the strange colt.'

There was a splendid race-course on the seashore. The appointed day came, and all the people were assembled. The horse was brought out, bridled and saddled, and led to the strand. The place was so crowded that a pin falling from the sky would not fall on any place but the head of some person old or young, some man, woman, or child that was there at the festival.

For three days the women of the village were cooking food for all that would come; there was enough ready, and to spare. Breogan strove to come at a man who would ride the horse; but not a man could he find. The horse was so fiery that all were in dread of him.

Not to spoil sport for the people, Breogan made up his mind to ride himself. As soon as the man mounted, and was firm in the saddle, the horse stood on his hind-legs, rose with a leap in the air, and away with him faster than any wind, first over the land, and then over the sea. The horse never stopped till he came down on his fore-feet in Breasil, which is a part of Tir nan Og (the Land of the Young).

Breogan found himself now in the finest country man could set eyes on. He rode forward, looking on all sides with delight and pleasure, till out before him he saw a grand castle, and a beautiful gate in front of it, and the gate partly open.

'Well,' thought he, 'I'll go in here for a bit, to know are there people living inside.' With that he tied the bridle to one of the bars of the gate, and left the horse, thinking to come back in a short time. He went to the door of the castle, and knocked on it. A woman came and opened the door to him.

'Oh, then, a hundred thousand welcomes to you, Breogan from Brandon,' said she.

He thanked her, and was greatly surprised when he heard her calling him by name. She brought him then to a parlour; and, though he had fine rooms in his own house, he hardly knew at first how to sit in this parlour, it was that grand and splendid. He wasn't long sitting, when who should come in but a young woman, a beauty; the like of her he had never seen before in his life. She was first in every way, in good looks as well as in manners. She sat down at his side, and welcomed him.

Breogan remained in the castle a few hours, eating, drinking, talking, and enjoying himself. At long last he thought, 'I must be going'; and then he said so.

The first woman laughed. 'Well, now, my good friend,' said she, 'of all the men that ever came to this place – and it's many a man that came here in my time – there never was a worse man to care for his horse than what you are. Your poor beast is tied to a bar of the gate outside since you came, and you have never as much as thought that he was dry or hungry; and if I had not thought of him, it's in a bad state he'd be now. How long do you think you are in this castle?'

'Oh, then, I am about seven hours in it.'

'You are in this country just seven years,' said the woman. 'The beauty and comfort of this Land of the Young is so great that the life of twelve months seems the length of one hour in another place.'

'If I am here that long, I must be going this minute,' said Breogan.

'Well,' said the woman, 'if you are going, I must ask you one question. There will be a child in this castle; and as you are the father, 'tis you that should name it. Now what will the name be?'

'If 'tis a son, you'll call him Shawn, the son of Breogan, from Brandon in Erin. You'll rear him for seven years. At the end of that time give him your blessing and the means of making a journey to Erin. Tell him who I am; and if he is anything of a hero, he'll not fail to make me out.'

Breogan left his blessing with the women, went to the gate, and found his horse standing there, tied in the same way that he left him. He untied the beast, mounted, and away through the air with him, leaving Breasil behind, and never stopped nor halted till he came down about a mile from his own house, near Brandon, exactly seven years from the day that he left it. Seeing on the strand a great number of people, he wondered why they were in it, and what brought them together. A large, fine-looking man was passing the way, and Breogan called out to him: 'What are these people all doing that I see on the strand?' asked he.

'You must be a stranger,' said the man, 'not to know what these people are here for.'

'I am no stranger,' said Breogan; 'but I went out of the country a few years before this, and while I was gone there were changes.'

'If a man leaves his own country for a short time itself,' said the other, 'he will find things changed when he comes again to it. I will tell you why these people are here. We had in this place a fine master, and it's good and kind he was to us. He went out to the strand one day, walking, and found a little colt above the high tide. He took the colt home, reared and fed him three years. Then this man gathered the people to give them a feast, and to know could he find some one to ride the horse. When no one would venture, he mounted himself; and all saw how the horse rose in the air, made a leap over the harbour, and then away out of sight. We think that he fell, and was drowned in the sea; for neither Breogan nor the horse was seen ever after. We are sorry for the man, because he was kind to us; but 'tis equal what became of the horse. After waiting seven years, Breogan's wife is to be married this evening to some great man from the North. We don't know what kind is he. He may destroy us, or drive us out of our houses.'

Breogan thanked the man for his words, and hurried on toward his own house. The servants saw him coming, knew him, and cried, 'Here comes the master!' and there was a great stir up and down in the house. Next minute the wife heard the news; and out she ran to meet her husband. Any man would think she was glad to see Breogan. 'Why are all the people here to-day?' asked he of the wife.

'And was not it this day seven years that you put the country behind you, wherever you went? You left dinner here ready; and the dinner is in the same state it was the day you went away from me. I thought it better to send for the people again, and eat the dinner in memory of you that prepared it.'

The husband said nothing. The people ate the dinner; and every man, woman, and child went home satisfied.

At the end of another seven years, Breogan made a great dinner again. All was ready; a great crowd of people were present. The day being fine, you could see far in every direction.

'Look, now,' said Breogan, to one of his men who had very good eyesight. 'Look out toward the water, to know can you see any one coming. Seven years ago to-day, I came home from Breasil, in the Land of the Young; and my son, if I have one, is to be here to-day. He ought to be coming by this time.'

The man looked out as well as he could. 'I see a boat with one mast coming toward us,' said he; 'and it's sailing faster than any boat I have ever set eyes on. In the boat I can see only one young man; and very young he is too.'

'Oh, that is he,' said Breogan.

The boat came in at full sail; and it wasn't long till the youth was standing before his father. 'Who are you?' asked Breogan.

'My name is Shawn MacBreogan.'

'If that is your name, sit down here at dinner; for you are my son.'

When the feast was over, the people went home. When Breogan's wife found out who the boy was, she wouldn't give the breadth of a ha'penny piece of his body for a fortune, she was that fond of him.

Things went on well till one day when Breogan and his son were out hunting. The day being warm, they sat down to rest; and the son said to the father, 'Since I came to you in Erin, you seem vexed in yourself. I have not asked what trouble is on you, or is there anything amiss with you.'

'All things are well with me but one thing,' said Breogan. 'There is some understanding between my wife and a man in the north of Erin. I'm in dread of my life; for while I was in Breasil she saw this man, and the day I came home they were going to be married. Since then I have not slept soundly in bed; for messages are passing between them.'

'Very well, father, I'll put an end to that soon,' said Shawn. He rose on the following morning, caught his hurley in his right hand, and his ball in the left. He threw up the ball, then struck it with the hurley, and was driving it that way before him till he reached the north of Erin, and never let his ball touch the ground even one time. He enquired for his father's opponent. When he found out the house, he knocked at the door. 'Is your master inside?' asked he.

'He is,' said the servant.

'Go,' said Shawn, 'and tell him that I want him, and not to delay, as I must be at dinner in Brandon this evening.'

The master of the house came out, and, seeing a boy there before him, thought it strange that he should speak rudely to a man like himself. 'If you don't beg my pardon this minute, I'll take the head off you,' said the man.

'Well,' said Shawn, 'I am not here to beg pardon of you nor of any man; but I came to have satisfaction for the trouble you put on my father, and I far away from him.'

'Who is your father?'

'My father is Breogan of Brandon.'

Out the man went; and the two stood on a fine green plain, and began to fight with swords, cutting each other's flesh. They were not long at the swords when Shawn said, 'It is getting late, and I must be at home before dinner to-day, as I promised; there is no use in delaying.' With that he rose out of his body, and gave the man a blow between the head and shoulders that put the head a mile from the body. Shawn caught the head before it touched earth; then, grasping it by the hair, he left the body where it fell, took his hurley in his right hand, threw his ball in the air, and drove it far to the south with the hurley; and he drove it across Erin in that way, the ball never touching ground from the far north of Erin to Brandon. Holding the ball and hurley in his hand, he went into the house, and laid the head at his father's feet.

'Now, my dear father,' said he, 'here is the head of your enemy; he'll trouble you no more from this out.'

When Breogan's wife saw the head, she was cut to the heart and troubled; though she would not let any man know it. One day when the father and son came home from killing ducks, she was groaning, and said she was ready to die.

'Is there any cure for you here or there in the world?' asked Shawn.

'There is no getting the cure that would heal me; there is no cure but three apples from the white orchard in the White Nation.'

'Well,' said the boy, 'I promise you not to eat the third meal at the one table, nor sleep the second night in the one bed, till I get three apples from the White Nation.'

The father was very angry when they came out of the bed-room. 'Sure,' said he, 'it would be enough for you to risk your life for your own mother.'

'Well, I must go now,' said Shawn; 'the promise is given; I'll not break my word.' So away with him on the following morning; and on that day's journey he came to a glen, and in it a house. In the house there was no living creature but a white mare with nine eyes.

'A hundred thousand welcomes to you, Shawn MacBreogan from Brandon. You must be tired and hungry after the day's journey,' cried the mare. 'Go in now to the next room, and take supper, and strengthen yourself.'

He went to the next room, and inside in it was a table, and on the table was everything that the best king could wish for. He ate, drank, and went then and gave a hundred thousand thanks for the supper. He stood near the fire for a while; then the mare said, 'Come here, and lie under my head; wonder at nothing you see, and let no word out of you.'

He did as the mare said. About dusk three seals came in, and went to the supper-room. They threw off their sealskins, and became three as fine young men as one could look at.

'I wish Shawn MacBreogan from Brandon were here tonight. I'd be glad to see him, and give him a present, and have his good company,' said one of the three.

'I'd be glad to see him, too,' said the second; 'and I'd give him a present.'

'So would I,' said the third.

'Go to them now,' said the mare; 'enjoy their company. In the morning you'll ask for the presents.'

He went out among them.

'A hundred thousand welcomes to you, Shawn MacBreogan,' cried the young men; 'and 'tis glad we are to see you.'

They drank wine then, sang songs, and told tales, and never slept a wink all the night. Before sunrise they went as seals; and when going Shawn said, 'I hope you will not forget the presents you promised last evening.'

'We will not,' said the eldest. 'Here is a cloak for you. While it is on you, you'll be the finest man in the world to look at.'

'Here is a ball,' said the second. 'If you throw it in the air, and wish for anything you like, you will have it before the ball comes to the ground.'

The third gave a whistle: 'When you blow this,' said he, 'every enemy that hears it will lie down asleep, and be powerless; and, besides, you're to have the white mare to ride.'

He took the gifts.

'Give me a feed of grain before we start,' said the mare. 'No man has sat on me without being turned into froth and blown away, or else thrown and killed. This will not happen to you; still I must throw you three times: but I'll take you to a soft place where you'll not be killed.'

Shawn mounted her then, and she tossed him. She threw him very far the first time. He was badly shocked, but recovered. The second and third times it was easier. The fourth time he mounted for the journey. It was not long till he came to the seashore. On the third day he was in sight of land in the White Nation. The mare ran over the water and swiftly, without trouble; no bird ever went with such speed.

When Shawn came near the castle, he stopped before a house at the edge of the town, and asked a lodging of the owner, an old man.

'I'll give you that,' said the old man, 'and welcome, and a place for your horse.' After supper Shawn told his errand.

'I pity you,' said the man. 'I am in dread you'll lose your life; but I'll do what I can for you. No man has ever been able to get one of those apples; and if a stranger is caught making up to them, the king takes his head without mercy or pardon. There is no kind of savage beast in the world but is guarding the apples; and there is not a minute in the night or the day when some of the beasts are not watching.'

'Do you know what virtue is in the apples?' asked Shawn.

'I do well,' said the old man; 'and it's I that would like to have one of them. If a man is sick, and eats even one bite of an apple, he'll be well; if old, he'll grow young again, and never know grief from that out; he will always be happy and healthy. I'll give you a pigeon to let loose in the orchard; she will go flying from one tree to another till she goes to the last one. All the beasts will follow her; and while they are hunting the pigeon, you will take what you can of the apples: but I hope you will not think it too much to give one to me.'

'Never fear,' said Shawn, 'if I get one apple, you'll have the half of it; if two, you'll have one of them.'

The old man was glad. Next morning at daybreak Shawn took the pigeon, mounted the mare, and away with him then to the orchard. When the pigeon flew in, and was going from tree to tree with a flutter, the beasts started after her. Shawn sprang in on the back of the mare, left her, and went to climb the first tree that he met for the apples; but the king's men were at him before he could touch a single apple, or go back to the mare. They caught him, and took him to the king. The mare sprang over the wall, and ran to the house of the old man. Shawn told the king his whole story, said that his father was Breogan of Brandon, and his mother the Princess of Breasil in the Land of the Young.

'Oh,' said the king, 'you are the hero that I am waiting for this long time. A fine part of my kingdom is that island beyond; but 'tis taken by a giant who holds it with an army of hirelings. Clear that island of the giant and his men, bring me his head, and you'll have the apples.'

Shawn went to the old man, then to the mare, and told her.

'You can do that without trouble,' said she; 'you have the power needed to do it.'

Shawn took his breakfast, then sat on the mare, and rode toward the island. Just before the mare touched the land, Shawn sounded the whistle; and every one who heard it was asleep the next instant. Shawn took his sword then, swept the head off the giant, and before evening there wasn't a man alive on the island except Shawn himself. He tied the giant's head to the saddle-bow, mounted the mare, and was ready to start, when she spoke to him: 'Be careful not to look back toward the island till you come down from my back.' With that she swept on, and soon they were nearing the castle. While crossing the yard, Shawn thought, 'I have the island cleared; the head is safe on me; and the apples are mine.' With that he forgot the mare's words, and turned to look back at the island; but as he did, he fell from the saddle, and where should he fall but down on a dust-heap. A son of the comb woman, a youth who fed dogs and small animals, was lying there at the time, and he sickly and full of sores. Shawn's cloak slipped from his shoulders, and fell on this dirty, foul fellow; that moment he sprang up the finest-looking man in the kingdom. He fastened the cloak on his shoulders, mounted the white mare, and rode to the castle. The king was that glad when he looked at the head of the giant that he didn't know where to put the counterfeit hero who brought it.

'How did you clear the island?' asked the king; 'and was it a hard task to take the head off the giant?'

'Oh, then,' said the dog-feeder, 'there was never such a battle in the world as the battle to-day on that island between myself and the giant with his forces; and 'tis well I earned what will come to me.'

'You'll get good pay,' said the king; 'I promised you apples from my white orchard; but I'll give you more, I'll give you my youngest daughter in marriage, and that island for her portion. My daughter will not be of age to marry for a year and a day. Till that time is out, you'll live with me here in the castle.'

Believe me, the dog-feeder was a great man in his own mind that evening.

There was one woman in the yard who saw the deception, and that was the henwife. She knew well what the dog-feeder was, and 'tis often she said, 'He's the greatest liar on earth, and kind mother for him.' She drew Shawn into her own house, and he sick and full of sores, just like the dog-feeder, not a man in the world would have known him. She nursed and tended Shawn. On the sixth day he was able to speak; but he lay in great weakness, and covered with sores.

'How am I to be cured?' asked he of the henwife.

'I know,' answered she; 'I spoke to a wise woman to-day, and got the right cure for you.' With that the henwife went down to a spring that belonged to the king's youngest daughter, and pulled up nine rushes growing near it. Three of these she threw away, and kept six of them. She cut the white from the green parts, crushed them in water, gave Shawn some of the water to drink, and rubbed the rest on his body. A week was not gone, when he was as sound and well as ever.

Shawn heard now the whole story of the dog-feeder's lies and prosperity. He took service himself in the castle; and a few days after that the king gave a hunt, and invited all the guests in the castle to go with him. Shawn had to go as a basket-boy, and carry provisions like any servant. Toward evening, when the company were on a wild moor twenty miles from the castle, a thick mist fell, and all were afraid that their lives would be gone from them.

'I can take you to a castle,' said Shawn.

'Take us,' said the king.

'I will if you will give me your daughter to marry.'

'She is promised to another,' said the king.

'I have the best right to her,' said Shawn. 'It was I cleared the island.'

'I don't believe you,' said the king.

'We'll be lost, every man of us,' said the chief hunter; 'give him the promise, he may be dead before the day of the wedding.'

The king gave his promise. The basket-boy stepped behind a great rock, threw up the ball, and wished for the finest castle on earth. Before the ball touched the ground the king, the guests, and attendants were in a castle far finer than any they had looked on in daylight or seen in a dream. The best food and drink of all kinds were in it, shining chambers and beds of silk and gold. When all had eaten and drunk their fill, they fell asleep to sweet music, and slept soundly till morning. At daybreak each man woke up, and found himself lying on the wild moor, a tuft of rushes under his head, and the grey sky above him. Glad to see light, they rose and went home.

Now the henwife told the king's daughter the story of Shawn, who had cleared out the island, and the comb-woman's son, the deceiver. When the year was ended, and the day came for the marriage, the king's daughter said she would marry no man but the man who would ride the white mare with nine eyes (the mare could either kill or make froth of a man). The comb-woman's son was the first man to mount; but the cloak fell from him, and he vanished in froth blown away by the wind, and no one saw sight of him from that day to this. Sixteen king's sons tried to ride the white mare, and were killed every man of them; but their bodies were found. Shawn, who had taken the cloak, sat on the mare, and rode three times past the castle. At the door the mare knelt for him to come down.

The king's daughter would have jumped through her window, and killed herself, if her maids had not held her. She rushed down the stairs, kissed Shawn, and embraced him. The wedding began then. It lasted for a day and a year, and the last was the best day of all.

When the wedding was over, Shawn remembered the mare, and went to the stable. She had not been fed, and a white skin was all that was left of her. When Shawn came to the mare's place, three young men and two women were playing chess in it.

'Oh, I forgot the mare from the first day of the wedding till this moment,' said Shawn; and he began to cry.

'Why are you crying?' asked the elder of the two women.

He told the reason.

'You needn't cry,' said the woman; 'I can revive her.' With that she took the skin, put it on herself; and that minute she was the white mare. 'Would you rather see me a white mare as I am now, or the woman that I was a minute ago?'

'The woman,' said Shawn.

She took off the skin, and was a woman again. She told him then how the king, her father, made three seals of her brothers and a white mare of herself, to be in those forms till a hero should come who could clear out the island. 'You cleared the island,' said she; 'and we are all free again.'

The king gave the island to his son-in-law, and as many apples from the orchard as he wished. The first thing that Shawn did was to take an apple to the old man who gave him lodgings when he came to the White Nation. At the first bite he swallowed, the old man was twenty-one years of age, young and hearty, and so happy that it would do any man good to have one look at him.

Shawn and his young wife lived another day and a year with her father, and then they went to visit his father in Brandon. From pretending to be sick, Breogan's wife became sick in earnest, and died. Breogan himself was now old and dissatisfied.

'The least I can do,' thought Shawn, 'is to give him an apple.' He gave him the apple. Breogan ate it, was twenty-one years of age; and if ever a man was glad in Erin, 'twas he was.

Shawn left the father young and happy at Brandon, and went back himself with his wife to the island.

THE COTTER'S SON AND THE HALF SLIM CHAMPION

Once upon a time there was a poor cotter in Erin, and he had three sons. Whether it was well or ill that he reared them, he reared them, and then died. When their father was dead and buried, the three sons lived with their mother for a day and a year; and at the end of that time the eldest brother said, 'I will go to seek my fortune in the world.'

He took his mother's blessing with him, and went away on the following morning.

The two sons and the mother lived on together for another day and a year, when the second son said, 'I will go out to seek my fortune.'

He went away like the first brother.

The mother and the youngest son lived on together for a day and a year, and then the mother died. When she was buried, the youngest of the three brothers, whose name was Arthur, went out in the world to seek his fortune. He travelled, and was walking always for a day and a year without finding a master, till on the afternoon of the last day of the year he took service with a hill.

On the last day of Arthur's service with the hill, the Half Slim Champion came in the afternoon, and asked would he play a game of cards.

'If you win,' said the champion, 'you will have a castle with lands and cattle of all kinds; if you lose, you will do me a service.'

'I will play,' answered Arthur.

With that they sat down to play; and Arthur won. Now, Arthur had lands and a castle, cattle of all kinds, and wealth in abundance.

The Half Slim Champion went his way; and Arthur lived for a day and a year on his lands. On the last day of the year, the champion came in the afternoon, and with him was the most beautiful lady that man could set eyes on. 'Will you play a second game?' asked the champion. 'If you lose, you will do me a service; if you win, I give you this lady as wife.'

'I will play with you,' said Arthur.

They played, and Arthur won.

Arthur lived with his wife in the castle for a day and a year; and on the last afternoon, the champion came the way leading a hound.

They played the third time, and Arthur won the hound. The champion went his way; and again Arthur lived for a day and a year with his wife in the castle in ease, in plenty, and in great delight.

On the afternoon of the last day, the champion came the fourth time. Arthur's wife saw him at a distance, and said to her husband, 'My advice is to play no more with that champion. Remain as you are, and keep out of harm's way.'

But Arthur would not listen to the wife, nor be said by her. He went out to play with the champion, and lost.

'I put you under bonds,' said the champion, 'not to sleep two nights in the same bed, nor eat two meals off the same table; but to be walking through the world, and searching always till you find the birth that has never been born, and that never will be.'

The champion turned, walked away, and disappeared. Arthur went home in grief; and when he sat down the chair that was under him broke into pieces.

'I told you,' said the wife, 'not to play with him. What has he put on you?'

'To be walking and searching, ever and always, through the world till I find the birth that has never been born, and never will be.'

'Take the hound with you,' said the wife, 'and go first to the castle of the son of the King of Lochlin. Take service with him; you may learn something there.'

Away went Arthur next morning, and the hound with him. They were long on the road, lodging one time at a house, and another time where the night found them, till at last a great castle was in sight. When the hound saw the castle, he grew so wild with delight that he broke his chain, and rushed away. But if he did, Arthur followed; and when the hound sprang into the castle, Arthur was at his side.

'It was lucky for you,' cried the son of the King of Lochlin, 'to come in with the hound. Without that you'd have been done for. Who are you, and where are you going?'

'I am a man in search of a master.'

'I am seeking a man,' said the king's son. 'Will you take service with me?'

'I will,' answered Arthur.

He hired for a day and a year, and wages according to service.

Arthur went to work on the following morning, and his first task was to bring fagots from the forest. When he went to the forest, he found half of it green, and the other half dry. Nothing was growing in the dry part; all was withered and dead. Arthur collected dry fagots, and brought them to the castle. In the evening he spoke to the king's son, and this is what he asked of him, 'Why is half of your forest green, and the other half withered and dry?'

'A day and seven years ago,' said the king's son, 'a terrible serpent came the way, and took half of my forest for herself. In that part she is living till this time – that is the green part. She knocked the life out of my half – that is the dry part.'

'Why do you not take wood from the green part?' asked Arthur.

'Neither you nor all who ever came before you could do that,' said the son of the king. Next morning Arthur went out for fagots the second time. He stopped before the largest green tree to be found in the forest, and was cutting away at it. The moment the serpent saw this, she came out, and called, 'Why are you cutting my timber?'

'I am cutting it because I am sorry to see you as you are,' said

Arthur, 'without a roof over you or a shelter of any kind. I wish to build a house to protect you.'

When the serpent heard this, she was glad and thankful to Arthur. When he had two wedges in the tree, and it partly cut, he said, 'If yourself would only come over now, and put your tail in the cut and help me, we could throw down this tree.'

She went to him then, and put her tail in the cut. Arthur knocked out the wedges, and left her tail in the tree. She begged and cried, screaming, 'The tree is killing me; the tree is killing me! Let me free! Let me out of this!'

'It wasn't to let you out that I put you in,' replied Arthur.

What he did then was to jump behind her, and vex her until he got her in the way that, out of rage and great strength, she tore up the tree with its roots, and seven acres and seven ridges of land with it. Arthur was vexing the serpent until she rushed into the dry part of the forest, and was fastened among the trees; then he cut down dry trees, and piled them on the serpent and on the green tree till they were the size of a hill. In the evening he drove her to the castle before him, with all the hill of dry wood on her. When a maid was going from the castle for water, and saw this, she ran in with the story that Arthur was coming home with the serpent, and all the dry wood of the forest above on her back.

When the people inside heard this, they were in dread that she'd kill them all, and they rushed out to run away. There was one girl in the castle who heard the tidings too late, or was slow in preparing, for when she was ready, the serpent was at the door.

'Where are the people of the castle?' asked Arthur.

'All made away, and took their lives with them,' said she.

'Run now and call them back,' said Arthur.

'I'm in dread to go out. I will not go unless you take the head off the serpent.'

Arthur swept the head off the serpent. The girl ran after the people, and brought them back. Arthur piled all the wood near the castle. The king's son was delighted to have so much fuel, and was so glad that he took Arthur to his bed to sleep that night with him.

'It's a wonder,' said Arthur, 'such a good king's son as you to be without a wife.'

'I had a wife,' said the king's son; 'but the giant with five heads, five necks, and five lumps on his heads, came and took her to the Eastern World.'

'Why did you not take her from him?'

'Neither I, nor you, nor all that ever came before us could do that.'

On the following morning Arthur rose, washed his face, rubbed his eyes, and said to the king's son, 'I am going to the Eastern World to bring back your wife.' Away he went; but the king's son would not believe that any man living could bring back the wife.

When Arthur came to the castle of the giant in the Eastern World, the giant himself was not in it, only the wife of the King of Lochlin's son, who said, 'There is no use in your delaying in this place; you'll be killed, if you stay till the giant comes home.'

'I'll never leave this castle till I see the giant; and when I go home you'll go with me.'

It wasn't long till Arthur heard the great voice of the giant. As he came toward the castle the bottom of the forest was rising to the top, and the top of the forest was going to the bottom. In front of the giant went a shaggy goat, and another behind him. In his hand was a club with a yellow flea on the end of it; on one shoulder he carried a dead hag, and on the other a great hog of a wild boar.

'Fu fa my beard!' cried the giant. 'I catch the smell of a lying rogue from Erin, too big for one bite and too small for two. I don't know whether to blow him away through the air, or put him under my feet.'

'You filthy giant, 'tis not to give satisfaction to you, or the like of you, that I came, but to knock satisfaction out of you.'

'I want only time till morning to give you what you came for,' said the giant.

It was daybreak when Arthur was up and struck the pole of combat. There wasn't a calf, kid, lamb, foal, or child awaiting birth that didn't turn five times to the right and five times to the left from the strength of the blow.

'What do you want?' asked the answering man.

'Seven hundred against me, and then seven hundred to every hundred of these, till I find the man who can put me down.'

'You fool of the world, it would be better for you to hide under a leaf than to stand before the giant.'

The giant came out to Arthur; and the two went at each other like two lions of the desert or two bulls of great growth, and fought with rage. They made the softest places hardest, and the hardest places softest; they brought spring wells up through dry slate rocks, and great tufts of green rushes through their own shoe-strings. The wounds that they made on each other were so great that little birds flew through them, and men of small growth could crawl through on their hands and knees.

It was dark and the end of the day, when Arthur cried out, 'It is a bad thing for me, filthy giant, to have a fine day spent on you!'

With that he gave him one blow on the five necks, and sent the five heads flying through the air. After a while the heads were coming down, croning (singing the coronach), Arthur caught them, and struck the giant's breast with them; the body and heads fell dead on the ground. The wife of the son of the King of Lochlin ran out now, smothered Arthur with kisses, washed him with tears, and dried him with a cloak of fine silk; she put her hand under his arm, and they went to the castle of the giant. The two had good entertainment, plenty to eat, and no bit dry. They made three parts of that night – one part for conversation, one for tales, and one for soft sleep.

When they rose in the morning, the woman said, 'It is a poor thing for us to go and leave here behind all the gold the giant had.'

'Let us not be in so great a hurry; we'll find a cure for that,' said Arthur.

They went out, found three ships belonging to the giant, and filled them with gold. When the three ships were laden, Arthur took hawsers and lashed the first ship to the second, the second to the third, raised the anchors, and sailed away. When he was in sight of Lochlin, a messenger was walking toward the water, and saw the ships coming. He ran to the castle, and cried to the king's son, 'The servant-boy is coming, and bringing your wife with him.'

'That I will never believe,' said the king's son, 'till she puts her hand in my hand.'

The king's son had kept his head by the fire, without rising from the hearth, all the time that Arthur was away. When the wife came in, and put her hand on his hand, he rose up, and shook seven tons of ashes from himself, with seven barrels of rust.

There was great gladness in the castle; and the king's son was ready to do anything for Arthur, he was so thankful to him. Arthur's time was out on the following day. The king's son spoke to him, and asked, 'What am I to give you now for the service? What wages do you expect?'

'No more than is just. I hope that you will find out for me who is the birth that has never been born, and that never will be.'

'That is no great thing for me to discover,' said the king's son.

There was a hollow place in the wall of the castle near the fireplace, and in that hollow the king's son kept his own father, and gave him food. He opened a secret door, and brought out the old king.

'Now tell me, father,' said he, 'who is it that has never been born, and never will be?'

'That's a thing of which no tidings have been given, or ever will be,' replied the king.

When the father wasn't giving him the answer he wanted, the son put the old king, standing, on a red-hot iron griddle.

'It's fried and roasted you'll be till you answer my question, and tell who is the birth that has never been born, and that never will be,' said the son.

The old king stood on the griddle till the marrow was melting in the bones of his feet. They took him off then; and the son asked him a second time.

'That's a question not to be answered by me,' said the king.

He was put, standing, again on the red-hot griddle, and kept on it, till the marrow was melting in the bones to his knees.

'Release me out of this now,' cried the king; 'and I will tell where that birth is.'

They took him from the griddle. He sat down then, and told this story to his son, in presence of Arthur: –

'I was walking out beyond there in the garden one day, when I came on a beautiful rod, which I cut and took with me. I discovered soon after that that was a rod of enchantment, and never let it go from me. When I went walking or riding in the day, I took the rod with me. In the night, I slept with it under my pillow. Misfortune came on me at last; for I left the rod in my chamber one time that I started away to go fowling. After I had gone a good piece of road, I remembered the rod, and hurried home then to get it.

'When I came to the castle I found a dark tall man inside in my chamber with the queen. They saw me, and I turned from the door to let them slip out, and think that I had not seen them. I went to the door not long after, and opened it. Your mother was standing inside, not two feet from the threshold. She struck me right there with the rod, and made a wild deer of me.

'When she had me a deer, she let out a great pack of hounds; for every hand's breadth of my body there was a savage dog to tear me, and hunt me to death. The hounds chased me, and followed till I ran to the far away mountains. There I escaped. So great was my swiftness and strength that I brought my life with me.

'After that I went back to injure the queen; and I did every harm in my power to her grain, and her crops, and her gardens.

'One day she sprang up from behind a stone wall, when I thought no one near, struck me with the rod, and made a wolf of me. She called a hunt then. Hounds and men chased me fiercely till evening. At nightfall I escaped to an island in a lake where no man was living. Next day I went around each perch of that island. I searched every place, and found only a she-wolf.

'But the wolf was a woman enchanted years before – enchanted when she was within one week of her time to give birth to a hero. There she was; but the hero could not be born unless she received her own form again.

'There was little to eat on the island for the she-wolf, and still less after I came. What I suffered from hunger in that place no man can know; for I had a wolf's craving, and only scant food to stop it. One day above another, I was lying half asleep, half famished, and dreaming. I thought that a kid was there near me. I snapped at it, and awoke. I had torn open the side of the she-wolf. Before me was an infant, which grew to the size of a man in one moment. That man is the birth that has never been born, and never will be; that man is the Half Slim Champion.

'When I snapped at the she-wolf, I bit her so deeply that I took a piece from behind the ear of the child, and killed the mother. When you go back to the Half Slim Champion, and he asks who is the man that has never been born, and never will be, you will say: "Try behind your own ear, you will find the mark on him."

'The infant, grown to a man before my eyes, attacked me, to kill me. I ran, and he followed. He hunted me through every part of that island. At last I had no escape but to swim to the country-side opposite. I sprang to the water, though I had not the strength of the time when I went from the hunters; but on the way were two rocks. On these I drew breath, and then came to land. I could not have swum five perches farther.

'I lived after that in close hiding, and met with no danger till I was going through a small lane one evening, and, looking behind, saw the hero whose mother I killed on the island. I started; he rushed along after me. I came to a turn, and was thinking to go over the wall, and escape by the fields, when I met my false queen. She struck me with the rod in her fright, and I got back my own form again. I snatched the rod quickly, and struck her. "You'll be a wolf now," said I; "you'll have your own share of misfortune." With that she sprang over the wall, a grey wolf, and ran off through the pastures.

'The dark tall man was a little behind and saw everything. He turned to escape; but I struck him with the rod, and made a sheep of the traitor, in hopes that the grey wolf might eat him. The hero saw all, saw the wolf that I was, turned into a man. I entered the castle; he followed me. I took you at once with me, showed you this hollow place near the chimney, and hid in it. The hero searched every foot of the castle, but found no trace of me. He had no knowledge of who I was; and when you denied that I was here, he waited one day, a second day, and then went away, taking your sister and the best hound at the castle.

'That hero of the island, whose mother I killed, is the Half Slim Champion. There is nothing he wishes so much as my death; and when he hears who it was that has never been born, and never will be, he will know that I am alive yet, and he'll kill half the people in Lochlin, unless he kills me first of all, or this champion kills him.'

When Arthur heard this story, he went away quickly from the castle of the King of Lochlin, and never stopped till he came to the hill where he played cards the first time. The Half Slim Champion was before him there, standing.

'Have you found the answer, and can you tell who has never been born, and never will be?'

'Try behind your own ear, and you'll find the mark on him.'

'That's true,' said the champion, 'and the man who killed my mother is alive yet; but if he is, he will not be so long, and you'll not leave this till you and I have a trial.'

The two went at each other then; and it was early enough in the day when Arthur had the head off the champion. He put a gad through his ears, took the head on his shoulder, hurried back to the King of Lochlin, and threw it on the floor, saying, 'Here is the head of the Half Slim Champion.'

When the old king heard these words in his place of concealment, he burst out the wall, and went through the end of the castle, so great was his joy. As soon as he was in the open air, free from confinement and dread, he became the best man in Lochlin.

They made three parts of that night, which they passed in great enjoyment, and discovered that Arthur's wife was the sister of the son of the King of Lochlin, the lady who was carried away by the Half Slim Champion, and lost in a game of cards.

When the old king got the head of the Half Slim Champion, he gave the three ships full of gold to Arthur, and would have given six ships, if he had had them, he was so glad to be free. Arthur took farewell of the old king and his son, and sailed away with his three ships full of gold to Erin, where his wife was.

BLAIMAN, SON OF APPLE, IN THE KINGDOM OF THE WHITE STRAND

There was a king in Erin long ago who had two sons and one daughter. On a day of days, the daughter walked into her father's garden, in which she saw an apple-tree with only one apple on it; she took the apple, and ate it.

There was an old druid in the castle, who saw the king's daughter going out, and met her coming in.

'Well,' said he, 'you had the look of a maiden when you were going out, and you have the look of a married woman coming in.'

Those who were near heard the saying of the druid, and it was going the rounds till it came to the king. The king went at once to the druid, and asked, 'What is this that you say about my daughter?'

'I say nothing,' answered the druid.

'You must tell me your words,' said the king, 'and prove them, or lose your head.'

'Oh, as you are going that far you must give me time, and if a few months do not prove my words true, you may cut the head off me.'

The princess was then taken to the top of the king's castle, where no one could see her but her maid. There she remained till she gave birth to a son with a golden spot on his poll, and a silver spot on his forehead. He was so beautiful that if sunshine and breeze ever rested on a child, they would rest on him; and what of him did not grow in the day grew at night. He grew so quickly that soon he was as large as the king's sons, his uncles, and rose out to be a great champion.

One day when the two sons of the king were hunting, there was snow on the ground, and they killed a hare. Some of the hare's blood fell on the snow, and they said that that was a beautiful meeting of colours. They were wondering could any woman be found with such colours on her face, white shining through the red. When they came home in the evening, they asked the old druid could a woman of that sort be found. He answered that if she could itself, little good would it do them; they could find wives good enough for them near home. They said that that was no matter, but to tell them where was the woman they had asked for.

'That woman,' said the druid, 'is the daughter of the King of the kingdom of the White Strand. Hundreds of champions have lost their heads for her; and if you go, you will lose your heads too.'

The elder son said, 'We do not mind that; we will go.'

The brothers had no vessel to take them to the kingdom of the White Strand; and the elder said he would build one. He took tools one morning, and started for the seashore. When just outside the castle, he heard a voice, asking, 'Where are you going, king's son?'

'I am going to make a turkey-pen,' answered the young man. 'May you prosper in justice and truth,' said the voice.

The king's son began to build the ship that day; and in the evening what had he built but a turkey-pen. When he came home, they asked what had he made.

'Nothing; I made only a turkey-pen.'

'Oh,' said the second son, 'you are a fool. I knew that you could do nothing good.'

On the following morning, the second son started for the seashore; and the voice spoke to him, and asked, 'Where are you going, king's son?'

'To build a pig-sty,' answered he. 'May you prosper in justice and truth,' said the voice.

He worked all day; and in the evening it was a pig-sty that he had. He came home; and now the brothers were doleful because they had not a ship in which to sail to the princess.

The following morning, the king's grandson said, 'Give me the tools, to see can I myself do anything.'

'What can you do, you fool?' asked the uncles.

'That matters not,' replied he. He left the castle; and at the place where the voice spoke to his uncles, it spoke to him also, and asked, 'What are you going to do, Blaiman, son of Apple?' (He did not know his origin till then.)

'I am going to build a ship,' said Blaiman.

'That it may thrive with you in justice and truth,' said the voice.

He went off to the edge of a wood that was growing at the seashore, gave one blow to a tree, and it went to its own proper place in the vessel. In the evening Blaiman had the nicest ship that ever moved on the deep sea. When finished, the ship was at the edge of the shore; he gave it one blow of a sledge, and sent it out to deep water. Blaiman went home full of gladness.

'What have you made?' asked the uncles.

'Go out and see for yourselves,' answered Blaiman.

The two went, and saw the ship in the harbour. They were delighted to see the fine vessel, as they themselves could not build it. The voice had built it with Blaiman in return for his truth.

Next morning provisions for a day and a year were placed in the vessel. The two sons of the king went on board, raised the sails, and were moving out toward the great ocean. Blaiman saw the ship leaving, and began to cry; he was sorry that, after building the ship, it was not he who had the first trial of his own work. When his mother heard him, she grew sorry too, and asked what trouble was on him; and he told her that after he had built the ship, he wanted to have the first trial of it.

'You are foolish,' said she. 'You are only a boy yet; your bones are not hard. You must not think of going to strange countries.'

He answered, that nothing would do him but to go. The old king, the grandfather, wanted Blaiman to stay; but he would not.

'Well,' said the king, 'what I have not done for another I will do now for you. I will give you my sword; and you will never be put back by any man while you keep that blade.'

Blaiman left the house then; the vessel was outside the harbour already. He ran to the mouth of the harbour, and, placing the point of his sword on the brink of the shore, gave one leap out on board. The two uncles were amazed when they saw what their nephew had done, and were full of joy at having him with them. They turned the ship's prow to the sea, and the stern to land. They raised to the tops of the hard, tough, stained masts the great sweeping sails, and took their capacious, smoothly-polished vessel past harbours with gently sloping shores, and there the ship left behind it pale-green wavelets. Then, with a mighty wind, they went through great flashing, stern-dashing waves with such force that not a nail in the ship was unheated, or a finger on a man inactive; and so did the ship hurry forward that its stern rubbed its prow, and it raised before it, by dint of sailing, a proud, haughty ridge through the middle of the fair, red sea.

When the wind failed, they sat down with the oars of fragrant beech or white ash, and with every stroke they sent the ship forward three leagues on the sea, where fishes, seals, and monsters rose around them, making music and sport, and giving courage to the men; and the three never stopped nor cooled until they sailed into the kingdom of the White Strand. Then they drew their vessel to a place where no wave was striking, nor wind rocking it, nor the sun splitting it, nor even a crow of the air dropping upon it; but a clean strand before it, and coarse sand on which wavelets were breaking. They cast two anchors toward the sea, and one toward land, and gave the vessel the fixing of a day and a full year, though they might not be absent more than one hour.

On the following day they saw one wide forest as far as the eye could reach; they knew not what manner of land was it.

'Would you go and enquire,' said Blaiman to the elder uncle, 'what sort of a country that is inside?' The uncle went in, very slowly, among the trees, and at last, seeing flashes of light through the forest, rushed back in terror, the eyes starting out of his head.

'What news have you?' asked Blaiman.

'I saw flashes of fire, and could not go farther,' said the elder king's son.

'Go you,' said Blaiman to the other, 'and bring some account of the country.'

He did not go much farther than the elder brother, then came back, and said, 'We may as well sail home again.'

'Well,' said Blaiman, 'ye have provisions for a day and a year in this vessel. I will go now, and do ye remain here; if I am not back before the end of the day and the year, wait no longer.' He gave them good by, then went on, and entered the forest. It was not long till he met with the flashes. He did not mind them, but went forward; and when he had gone a good distance, he found the trees farther apart and scattered. Leaving the trees, he came out on a broad, open plain; in the middle of the plain was a castle; in front of the castle twelve champions practising at feats of arms; and it was the flashes from the blows of their swords that he and his uncles had seen in the forest. So skilled were the champions that not one of them could draw a drop of blood from another.

Blaiman was making toward them. By the side of the path there was a small hut, and as he was passing the door, an old woman came out, and hailed him. He turned, and she said, 'A hundred thousand welcomes to you, Blaiman, son of Apple, from Erin.'

'Well, good woman,' said Blaiman, 'you have the advantage. You know me; but I have no knowledge of you.'

'I know you well,' said she; 'and it's sorry I am that you are here. Do you see those twelve men out there opposite? You are going to make for them now; but rest on your legs, and let the beginning of another day come to you.'

'Your advice may be good,' said Blaiman, and he went in. The old woman prepared his supper as well as it was ever prepared at his grandfather's house at home, and prepared a bed for him as good as ever he had. He slept enough, and he wanted it. When day overtook him on the morrow, he rose, and washed his face and hands, and asked mercy and help from God, and if he did not he let it alone; and the old woman prepared breakfast in the best way she could, and it was not the wrong way. He went off then in good courage to the castle of the king; and there was a pole of combat in front of the castle which a man wanting combat would strike with his sword. He struck the pole a blow that was heard throughout the whole kingdom.

'Good, good!' said the king; 'the like of that blow was not struck while I am in this castle.'

He put his head through a window above, and saw Blaiman outside.

Around the rear of the castle was a high wall set with iron spikes. Few were the spikes without heads on them; some heads were fresh, some with part of the flesh on them, and some were only bare skulls. It was a dreadful sight to see; and strong was the man that it would not put fright on.

'What do you want?' asked the king of Blaiman.

'Your daughter to marry, or combat.'

''Tis combat you will get,' said the king; and the twelve champions of valour were let out at him together. It was pitiful to see him; each one of the twelve aiming a blow at him, he trying to defend himself, and he all wounded and hacked by them. When the day was growing late, he began to be angry; the noble blood swelled in his breast to be uppermost; and he rose, with the activity of his limbs, out of the joints of his bones over them, and with three sweeping blows took the twelve heads off the champions. He left the place then, deeply wounded, and went back to the old woman's cabin; and if he did, it was a pleasure for the old woman to see him. She put him into a cauldron of venom, and then into a cauldron of cure. When he came out, he was perfectly healed; and the old woman said –

'Victory and prosperity to you, my boy. I think you will do something good; for the twelve were the strongest and ablest of all the king's forces. You have done more than any man that ever walked this way before.'

They made three parts of the night: the first part, they spent in eating and drinking; the second, in telling tales and singing ballads; the third, in rest and sound sleep.

He had a good sleep, and he needed it. Being anxious, he rose early; and as early as he rose, breakfast was ready before him, prepared by the old woman. He ate his breakfast, went to the king's castle, and struck the pole.

'What do you want?' asked the king, thrusting his head through the window.

'Seven hundred men at my right hand, seven hundred at my left, seven hundred behind me, and as many as on the three sides out before me.'

They were sent to him four deep through four gates. He went through them as a hawk through a flock of small birds on a March day, or as a blackbird or a small boy from Iraghti Conor between two thickets. He made lanes and roads through them, and slew them all. He made then a heap of their heads, a heap of their bodies, and a heap of their weapons. Trembling fear came on the king, and Blaiman went to the old woman's cabin.

'Victory and prosperity to you, my boy; you have all his forces stretched now, unless he comes out against you himself; and I'm full sure that he will not. He'll give you the daughter.'

She had a good dinner before him. He had fought so well that there was neither spot nor scar on his skin; for he had not let a man of the forty-two hundred come within sword's length of his body. He passed the night as the previous night.

Next morning after breakfast, he went to the castle, and with one blow made wood lice of the king's pole of combat. The king went down to Blaiman, took him under the arm, and, leading him up to the high chamber where the daughter was, put her hand in his.

The king's daughter kissed Blaiman, and embraced him, and gave him a ring with her name and surname written inside on it. This was their marriage.

Next day Blaiman, thinking that his uncles had waited long enough, and might go back to Erin, said to the king, 'I will visit my uncles, and then return hither.'

His wife, an only child, was heir to the kingdom, and he was to reign with her.

'Oh,' said the king, 'something else is troubling me now. There are three giants, neighbours of mine, and they are great robbers. All my forces are killed; and before one day passes the giants will be at me, and throw me out of the kingdom.'

'Well,' said Blaiman, 'I will not leave you till I settle the giants; but now tell where they are to be found.'

'I will,' said the king; and he gave him all needful instruction. Blaiman went first to the house of the youngest giant, where he struck the pole of combat, and the sound was heard over all that giant's kingdom.

'Good, good!' said the giant; 'the like of that blow has never been struck on that pole of combat before,' and out he came.

'A nerve burning of the heart to you, you miserable wretch!' said the giant to Blaiman; 'and great was your impudence to come to my castle at all.'

'It is not caring to give you pleasure that I am,' said Blaiman, 'but to knock a tormenting satisfaction out of your ribs.'

'Is it hard, thorny wrestling that you want, or fighting with sharp grey swords in the lower and upper ribs?' asked the giant.

'I will fight with sharp grey swords,' said Blaiman.

The giant went in, and fitted on his wide, roomy vest, his strong, unbreakable helmet, his cross-worked coat-of-mail; then he took his bossy, pale-red shield and his spear. Every hair on his head and in his beard was so stiffly erect from anger and rage that a small apple or a sloe, an iron apple or a smith's anvil, might stand on each hair of them.

Blaiman fitted on his smooth, flowery stockings, and his two dry warm boots of the hide of a small cow, that was the first calf of another cow that never lay on any one of her sides. He fitted on his single-threaded silken girdle which three craftsmen had made, underneath his broad-pointed, sharp sword that would not leave a remnant uncut, or, if it did, what it left at the first blow it took at the second. This sword was to be unsheathed with the right hand, and sheathed with the left. He gave the first blood of battle as a terrible oath that he himself was, the choice champion of the Fenians, the feather of greatness, the slayer of a champion of bravery; a man to compel justice and right, but not give either justice or right; a man who had earned what he owned in the gap of every danger, in the path of every hardship, who was sure to get what belonged to him, or to know who detained it.

They rushed at each then like two bulls of the wilderness, or two wild echoes of the cliff; they made soft ground of the hard, and hard ground of the soft; they made low ground of high, and high ground of low. They made whirling circles of the earth, and mill-wheels of the sky; and if any one were to come from the lower to the upper world, it was to see those two that he should come. They were this way at each other to the height of the evening. Blaiman was growing hungry; and through dint of anger he rose with the activity of his limbs, and with one stroke of his sword cut off the giant's head. There was a tree growing near. Blaiman knocked off a tough, slender branch, put one end of it in through the left ear and out through the right, then putting the head on the sword, and the sword on his shoulder, went home to the king. Coming near the castle with the giant's head, he met a man tied in a tree whose name was Hung Up Naked.

'Victory and prosperity to you, young champion,' said the man; 'you have done well hitherto; now loose me from this.'

'Are you long there?' asked Blaiman.

'I am seven years here,' answered the other.

'Many a man passed this way during that time. As no man of them loosed you, I will not loose you.'

He went home then, and threw down the head by the side of the castle. The head was so weighty that the castle shook to its deepest foundations. The king came to the hall-door, shook Blaiman's hand, and kissed him. They spent that night as the previous night; and on the next day he went to meet the second giant, came to his house, and struck the pole of combat. The giant put out his head, and said, 'You rascal, I lay a wager it was you who killed my young brother yesterday; you'll pay for it now, for I think it is a sufficient length of life to get a glimpse of you, and I know not what manner of death I should give you.'

'It is not to offer satisfaction that I am here,' said Blaiman, 'but to give you the same as your brother.'

'Is it any courage you have to fight me?' asked the giant.

'It is indeed,' said Blaiman; ''tis for that I am here.'

'What will you have?' asked the giant; 'hard, thorny wrestling, or fighting with sharp grey swords?'

'I prefer hard, thorny wrestling,' said Blaiman; 'as I have practised it on the lawns with noble children.'

They seized each other, and made soft places hard, and hard places soft; they drew wells of spring water through the hard, stony ground in such fashion that the place under them was a soft quagmire, in which the giant, who was weighty, was sinking. He sank to his knees. Blaiman then caught hold of him firmly, and forced him down to his hips.

'Am I to cut off your head now?' asked Blaiman.

'Do not do that,' said the giant. 'Spare me, and I will give you my treasure-room, and all that I have of gold and silver.'

'I will give you your own award,' said Blaiman. 'If I were in your place, and you in mine, would you let me go free?'

'I would not,' said the giant.

Blaiman drew his broad, shadowy sword made in Erin. It had edge, temper, and endurance; and with one blow he took the two heads off the giant, and carried the heads to the castle. He passed by Hung Up Naked, who asked him to loose him; but he refused. When Blaiman threw the heads down, much as the castle shook the first day, it shook more the second.

The king and his daughter were greatly rejoiced. They stifled him with kisses, drowned him with tears, and dried him with stuffs of silk and satin; they gave him the taste of every food and the odour of every drink – Greek honey and Lochlin beer in dry, warm cups, and the taste of honey in every drop of the beer. I bailing it out, it would be a wonder if I myself was not thirsty.

They passed that night as the night before. Next morning Blaiman was very tired and weary after his two days' fight, and the third giant's land was far distant.

'Have you a horse of any kind for me to ride?' asked he of the king.

'Be not troubled,' said the king. 'There is a stallion in my stable that has not been out for seven years, but fed on red wheat and pure spring water; if you think you can ride that horse, you may take him.'

Blaiman went to the stable. When the horse saw the stranger, he bared his teeth back to the ears, and made a drive at him to tear him asunder; but Blaiman struck the horse with his fist on the ear, and stretched him. The horse rose, but was quiet. Blaiman bridled and saddled him, then drove out that slender, low-sided, bare-shouldered, long-flanked, tame, meek-mannered steed, in which were twelve qualities combined: three of a bull, three of a woman, three of a fox, and three of a hare. Three of a bull – a full eye, a thick neck, and a bold forehead; three of a woman – full hips, slender waist, and a mind for a burden; three of a hare – a swift run against a hill, a sharp turn about, and a high leap; three of a fox – a light, treacherous, proud gait, to take in the two sides of the road by dint of study and acuteness, and to look only ahead. He now went on, and could overtake the wind that was before him; and the wind that was behind, carrying rough hailstones, could not overtake him.

Blaiman never stopped nor stayed till he arrived at the giant's castle; and this giant had three heads. He dismounted, and struck the pole a blow that was heard throughout the kingdom. The giant looked out, and said, 'Oh, you villain! I'll wager it was you that killed my two brothers. I think it sufficient life to see you; and I don't know yet what manner of death will I put on you.'

'It is not to give satisfaction to you that I am here, you vile worm!' said Blaiman. 'Ugly is the smile of your laugh; and it must be that your crying will be uglier still.'

'Is it hard, thorny wrestling that you want, or fighting with sharp grey swords?' asked the giant.

'I will fight with sharp grey swords,' said Blaiman.

They rushed at each other then like two bulls of the wilderness. Toward the end of the afternoon, the heavier blows were falling on Blaiman. Just then a robin came on a bush in front of him, and said, 'Oh, Blaiman, son of Apple, from Erin, far away are you from the women who would lay you out and weep over you! There would be no one to care for you unless I were to put two green leaves on your eyes to protect them from the crows of the air. Stand between the sun and the giant, and remember where men draw blood from sheep in Erin.'

Blaiman followed the advice of the robin. The two combatants kept at each other; but the giant was blinded by the sun, for he had to bend himself often to look at his foe. One time, when he stretched forward, his helmet was lifted a little, Blaiman got a glimpse of his neck, near the ear. That instant he stabbed him. The giant was bleeding till he lost the last of his blood. Then Blaiman cut the three heads off him, and carried them home on the pommel of his saddle. When he was passing, Hung Up Naked begged for release; but Blaiman refused and went on. Hung Up Naked praised him for his deeds, and continued to praise. On second thought, Blaiman turned back, and began to release Hung Up Naked; but if he did, as fast as he loosened one bond, two squeezed on himself, in such fashion that when he had Hung Up Naked unbound, he was himself doubly bound; he had the binding of five men hard and tough on his body. Hung Up Naked was free now; he mounted Blaiman's steed, and rode to the king's castle. He threw down the giant's heads, and never stopped nor stayed till he went to where the king's daughter was, put a finger under her girdle, bore her out of the castle, and rode away swiftly.

Blaiman remained bound for two days to the tree. The king's swine-herd came the way, and saw Blaiman bound in the tree. 'Ah, my boy,' said he, 'you are bound there, and Hung Up Naked is freed by you; and if you had passed him as you did twice before, you need not be where you are now.'

'It cannot be helped,' said Blaiman; 'I must suffer.'

'Oh, then,' said the swine-herd, 'it is a pity to have you there and me here; I will never leave you till I free you.'

Up went the swine-herd, and began to loosen Blaiman; and it happened to him as to Blaiman himself: the bonds that had been on Blaiman were now on the swine-herd.

'I have heard always that strength is more powerful than magic,' said Blaiman. He went at the tree, and pulled it up by the roots; then, taking his sword, he made small pieces of the tree, and freed the swine-herd.

Blaiman and the swine-herd then went to the castle. They found the king sitting by the table, with his head on his hand, and a stream of tears flowing from his eyes to the table, and from the table to the floor.

'What is your trouble?' asked Blaiman.

'Hung Up Naked came, and said that it was himself who killed the giant; and he took my daughter.'

When he found that his wife was taken, and that he knew not where to look for her, Blaiman was raging.

'Stay here tonight,' said the king.

Next morning the king brought a table-cloth, and said, 'You may often need food, and not know where to find it. Wherever you spread this, what food you require will be on it.'

Although Blaiman, because of his troubles, had no care for anything, he took the cloth with him. He was travelling all day, and at nightfall came to a break in the mountain, a sheltered spot, and he saw remains of a fire.

'I will go no farther tonight,' said he. After a time he pulled out the table-cloth, and food for a king or a champion appeared on it quickly. He was not long eating, when a little hound from the break in the mountain came toward him, and stood at some distance, being afraid to come near.

'Oh,' said the hound, 'have you crumbs or burned bread-crusts that you would give me to take to my children, now dying of hunger? For three days I have not been able to hunt food for them.'

'I have, of course,' said Blaiman. 'Come, eat enough of what you like best, and carry away what you can.'

'You have my dear love forever,' said the hound. 'You are not like the thief that was here three nights ago. When I asked him for help, he threw a log of wood at me, and broke my shoulder-blade; and I have not been able to find food for my little children since that night. Doleful and sad was the lady who was with him; she ate no bite and drank no sup the whole night, but was shedding tears. If ever you are in hardship, and need my assistance, call for the Little Hound of Tranamee, and you will have me to help you.'

'Stay with me,' said Blaiman, 'a part of the night; I am lonely, and you may take with you what food you can carry.'

The hound remained till he thought it time to go home; Blaiman gave him what he could carry, and he was thankful.

Blaiman stayed there till daybreak, spread his cloth again, and ate what he wanted. He was in very good courage from the tidings concerning his wife. He journeyed swiftly all day, thinking he would reach the castle of Hung Up Naked in the evening; but it was still far away.

He came in the evening to a place like that in which he had been the night previous, and thought to himself, I will stay here tonight. He spread his cloth, and had food for a king or a champion. He was not long eating, when there came opposite him out a hawk, and asked, 'Have you crumbs or burned crusts to give me for my little children?'

'Oh,' said Blaiman, 'come and eat your fill, and take away what you are able to carry.'

The hawk ate his fill. 'My love to you forever,' said the hawk; 'this is not how I was treated by the thief who was here three nights ago. When I asked him for food, he flung a log of wood at me, and almost broke my wing.'

'Give me your company a part of the night; I am lonely,' said Blaiman.

The hawk remained with him, and later on added, 'The lady who went with the thief was doleful and careworn; she ate nothing, but shed tears all the time.' When going, and Blaiman had given him all the food he could carry, the hawk said, 'If ever you need my assistance, you have only to call for the Hawk of Cold Cliff, and I will be with you.'

The hawk went away, very thankful; and Blaiman was glad that he had tidings again of his wife. Not much of next day overtook him asleep. He rose, ate his breakfast, and hastened forward. He was in such courage that he passed a mountain at a leap, a valley at a step, and a broad untilled field at a hop. He journeyed all day till he came to a break in the mountain; there he stopped, and was not long eating from his cloth, when an otter came down through the glen, stood before him, and asked, 'Will you give me crumbs or burned crusts for my little children?'

Blaiman gave him plenty to eat, and all he could carry home. 'My love to you forever,' said the otter. 'When you need aid, call on the Otter of Frothy Pool, and I will be with you. You are not like the thief who was here three nights ago, having your wife with him. She was melting all night with tears, and neither ate nor drank. You will reach the castle of Hung Up Naked tomorrow at midday. It whirls around like a millstone, continually, and no one can enter but himself; for the castle is enchanted.'

The otter went home. Blaiman reached the castle at midday, and knew the place well, from the words of the otter. He stood looking at the castle; and when the window at which his wife was sitting came before him, she saw him, and, opening the window, made a sign with her hand, and told him to go. She thought that no one could get the upper hand of Hung Up Naked; for the report had gone through the world that no man could kill him.

'I will not go,' said Blaiman. 'I will not leave you where you are; and now keep the window open.'

He stepped back some paces, and went in with one bound through the window, when it came around the second time.

While Hung Up Naked was tied to the tree, the tributes of his kingdom remained uncollected; and when he had the woman he wanted safe in his castle, he went to collect the tributes. She had laid an injunction on him to leave her in freedom for a day and a year. She knew when he would be returning; and when that time was near she hid Blaiman.

'Good, good!' cried Hung Up Naked, when he came. 'I smell on this little sod of truth that a man from Erin is here.'

'How could a man from Erin be here?' asked Blaiman's wife. 'The only person from Erin in this place is a robin. I threw a fork at him. There is a drop of blood on the fork now; that is what you smell on the little sod.'

'That may be,' said Hung Up Naked.

Blaiman and the wife were planning to destroy Hung Up Naked; but no one had knowledge how to kill him. At last they made a plan to come at the knowledge.

'It is a wonder,' said the woman to Hung Up Naked, 'that a great man like yourself should go travelling alone; my father always takes guards with him.'

'I need no guards; no one can kill me.'

'How is that?'

'Oh, my life is in that block of wood there.'

'If it is there, 'tis in a strange place; and it is little trouble you take for it. You should put it in some secure spot in the castle.'

'The place is good enough,' said he.

When Hung Up Naked went off next day, the wife told Blaiman all she had heard.

'His life is not there,' answered Blaiman; 'try him again tonight.'

She searched the whole castle, and what silk or satin or jewels she found, she dressed with them the block of wood. When Hung Up Naked came home in the evening, and saw the block so richly decked, he laughed heartily.

'Why do you laugh?' asked the woman.

'Out of pity for you. It is not there that my life is at all.'

On hearing these words, she fainted, was stiff and cold for some time, till he began to fear she was dead.

'What is the matter?' asked Hung Up Naked.

'I did not think you would make sport of me. You know that I love you, and why did you deceive me?'

Hung Up Naked was wonderfully glad. He took her to the window, and, pointing to a large tree growing opposite, asked, 'Do you see that tree?'

'I do.'

'Do you see that axe under my bed-post?' He showed the axe. 'I cannot be killed till a champion with one blow of that axe splits the tree from the top to the roots of it. Out of the tree a ram will rush forth, and nothing on earth can come up with the ram but the Hound of Tranamee. If the ram is caught, he will drop a duck; the duck will fly out on the sea, and nothing on earth can catch that duck but the Hawk of Cold Cliff. If the duck is caught, she will drop an egg into the sea, and nothing on earth can find that egg but the Otter of Frothy Pool. If the egg is found, the champion must strike with one cast of it this dark spot here under my left breast, and strike me through the heart. If the tree were touched, I should feel it, wherever I might be.'

He went away next morning. Blaiman took the axe, and with one blow split the tree from top to roots; out rushed the ram. Blaiman rushed after him through the fields. Blaiman hunted the ram till he was dropping from weariness. Only then did he think of the hound, and cry, 'Where are you now, Little Hound of Tranamee?'

'I am here,' said the hound; 'but I could not come till you called me.'

The hound seized the ram in one moment; but, if he did, out sprang a duck, and away she flew over the sea. Blaiman called for the Hawk of Cold Cliff. The hawk caught the duck; the duck dropped an egg. He called the Otter of Frothy Pool; the otter brought the egg in his mouth. Blaiman took the egg, and ran to the castle, which was whirling no longer; the enchantment left the place when the tree was split. He opened the door, and stood inside, but was not long there when he saw Hung Up Naked coming in haste. When the tree was split, he felt it, and hurried home. When nearing the castle, his breast open and bare, and he sweating and sweltering, Blaiman aimed at the black spot, and killed Hung Up Naked.

They were all very glad then. The hawk, hound, and otter were delighted; they were three sons of the king of that kingdom which Hung Up Naked had seized; they received their own forms again, and all rejoiced.

Blaiman did not stay long. He left the three brothers in their own castle and kingdom. 'If ever you need my assistance,' said Blaiman to the brothers, 'send for me at my father-in-law's.' On his return, he spent a night at each place where he had stopped in going.

When the king saw his daughter and Blaiman, he almost dropped dead from joy. They all spent some days very happily. Blaiman now thought of his uncles; and for three days servants were drawing every choice thing to his vessel. His wife went also to the ship. When all was ready, Blaiman remembered a present that he had set aside for his mother, and hurried back to the castle, leaving his wife on the ship with his uncles. The uncles sailed at once for Erin. When Blaiman came back with the present, he found neither wife, ship, nor uncles before him. He ran away like one mad, would not return to his father-in-law, but went wild in the woods, and began to live like the beasts of the wilderness. One time he came out on an edge of the forest, which was on a headland running into the sea, and saw a vessel near land; he was coming that time to his senses, and signalled. The captain saw him, and said, 'That must be a wild beast of some kind; hair is growing all over his body. Will some of you go to see what is there? If a man, bring him on board.'

Five men rowed to land, and hailed Blaiman. He answered, 'I am from Erin, and I am perishing here from hunger and cold.' They took him on board. The captain treated him kindly, had his hair cut, and gave him good clothing. Where should the captain be sailing to but the very same port of his grandfather's kingdom from which Blaiman had sailed. There was a high tide when the ship neared, and they never stopped till she was in at the quay. Blaiman went on shore, walked to the chief street, and stood with his back to a house. Soon he saw men and horses carrying and drawing many kinds of provisions, and all going one way.

'Why are these people all going one way?' enquired Blaiman of a man in the crowd.

'You must be a stranger,' answered the man, 'since you do not know that they are going to the castle. The king's elder son will be married this evening. The bride is the only daughter of the King of the kingdom of the White Strand; they brought her to this place twelve months ago.'

'I am a stranger,' said Blaiman, 'and have only come now from sea.'

'All are invited to the wedding, high and low, rich and poor.'

'I will go as well as another,' said Blaiman; and he went toward the castle. He met a sturdy old beggar in a long grey coat. 'Will you sell me the coat?' enquired Blaiman.

'Take your joke to some other man,' answered the beggar.

'I am not joking,' said Blaiman. 'I'll buy your coat.'

The beggar asked more for the coat than he thought would be given by any one.

'Here is your money,' said Blaiman.

The beggar gave up the coat, and started to go in another direction.

'Come back here,' said Blaiman. 'I will do you more good, and I need your company.'

They went toward the castle together. There was a broad space in front of the kitchen filled with poor people, for the greater part beggars, and these were all fighting for places. When Blaiman came, he commanded the crowd to be quiet, and threatened. He soon controlled all, and was himself neither eating nor drinking, but seeing justice done those who were eating and drinking. The servants, astonished that the great, threatening beggar was neither eating nor drinking, gave a great cup of wine to him. He took a good draught of the wine, but left still a fair share in the cup. In this he dropped the ring that he got from his wife in her own father's castle, and said to a servant, 'Put this cup in the hand of the bride, and say, "'Tis the big beggar that sends back this much of his wine, and asks you to drink to your own health."'

She was astonished, and, taking the cup to the window, saw a ring at the bottom. She took the ring, knew it, and ran out wild with delight through the people. All thought 'twas enchantment the beggar had used; but she embraced him and kissed him. The servants surrounded the beggar to seize him. The king's daughter ordered them off, and brought him into the castle; and Blaiman locked the doors. The bride then put a girdle around the queen's waist, and this was a girdle of truth. If any one having it on did not tell the truth, the girdle would shrink and tighten, and squeeze the life out of that person.

'Tell me now,' said the bride, 'who your elder son's father is.'

'Who is he,' said the queen, 'but the king?'

The girdle grew tighter and tighter till the queen screamed, 'The coachman.'

'Who is the second son's father?'

'The butler.'

'Who is your daughter's father?'

'The king.'

'I knew,' said the bride, 'that there was no kingly blood in the veins of the two, from the way that they treated my husband.' She told them all present how the two had taken her away, and left her husband behind. When Blaiman's mother saw her son, she dropped almost dead from delight.

The king now commanded his subjects to bring poles and branches and all dry wood, and put down a great fire. The heads and heels of the queen's two sons were tied together, and they were flung in and burned to ashes.

Blaiman remained a while with his grandfather, and then took his wife back to her father's kingdom, where they lived many years.